MW01196402

The Apostate's Woman

by

Lois Meier

authorHOUSE™

1663 LIBERTY DRIVE, SUITE 200
BLOOMINGTON, INDIANA 47403
(800) 839-8640
WWW.AUTHORHOUSE.COM

First published by AuthorHouse 06/15/05

ISBN: 1-4208-4437-7 (sc)

Library of Congress Control Number: 2005905253

Printed in the United States of America
Bloomington, Indiana

This book is printed on acid-free paper.

Table of Contents

This intimate story about Euphemie, wife of apostate Chiniquy, takes place in Illinois and Canada before and after the U.S. Civil War.

By Lois Meier with a grant from The Illinois Arts Council

Chapter 1
The Angry Bishop

"He's coming! He's coming!" shouted excited young John Mason, the lookout, riding his horse at a fast pace toward the crowd gathered on the lawn of the village Catholic Church. "There's a whole bunch of fancy carriages."

Bishop Duggan, completing the last leg of his journey from Chicago, hastened past acre after acre of crops strangely deserted under the hot August sun. He found the lack of industry on the part of the French Canadian settlers in his diocese neither surprising nor displeasing. He knew why they were not in the fields. He had sent out a bulletin ordering their presence at two o'clock on August 3, 1858, in the village church of Ste. Anne to hear his indictment against their priest, Father Chiniquy.

The target of the irate bishop's wrath, the fiery Chiniquy, was brought to this land in 1851 as a colonizer for the Church of Rome. For six years, he had been nothing but a thorn in the side of Bishop Duggan's predecessor, Bishop O'Regan. Not only had that stormy petrel distributed Bibles and encouraged his followers to read and interpret the scriptures themselves, he had thrown scorn on the precious practices of the church he professed to represent—on the prayers to Sainte Mary, confession, masses, scapulars, indulgences, penances—labeling them superstitions and foolish practices

O'Regan had Chiniquy transferred to a tiny outpost called Cahokia in the Quincy diocese, but Chiniquy refused to go as ordered even though threatened with excommunication if he disobeyed. He then ignored an

1

arrest of excommunication tacked on his door in 1856 by O'Regan's deputies. Chiniquy contended the document was not signed by the bishop's hand or by the vicar and was therefore a complete nullity according to the laws of the church.

To add injury to insult, he assaulted the bishop himself by sending to Pope Pius IX public accusations that had been published against the bishop with copies of the numerous suits the bishop had sustained before the civil courts including the sentences of the judges who had condemned him. There were over 200 pages of documents in all. Chiniquy begged the Pope, "Please take away from our midst this unworthy bishop." He also sent copies of the documents to Emperor Napoleon III of France, who was then all-powerful in Rome. He was the very guardian and protector of the Pope. Chiniquy reported to the Emperor that Bishop O'Regan had taken the church from the Chicago French Canadians and given it to the Irish, and he expressed his fear that the same thing would happen to his French church.

As a result, O'Regan was called to Rome, where the Pope reviewed his behavior. He was removed from the Chicago bishopric and sent to a remote bishopric called "Dora" while Chiniquy was allowed to remain the pastor of the French Canadian churches in Ste. Anne and Kankakee. Much to the chagrin of Bishop Duggan, who was O'Regan's replacement, Father Chiniquy continued his reformation activities.

Duggan, with his Irish temper roused, resolved to go to the Chiniquy colony himself to excommunicate the apostate and rescue his followers. Fluent in French, he had no doubt his appeal in their own language would win the wayward French Canadians back to the folds of the Church of Rome.

There was excitement in the air on the church lawn. By one o'clock hundreds of men, women and children had arrived in buggies and on foot. Father Chiniquy encouraged all to come—men, women, children and even the sick and disabled—so all could hear the accusations brought against their priest and his answers to the charges. The waxing and waning drones of insects called cicadas, ordinarily so lazy and dreamy in early August, filled the air that day with a strident sound, which reached a higher pitch with each repetition.

Euphemie Allard, considered by some an old maid at 23, albeit a very attractive old maid, sat with her parents on the grass near the right edge of the outdoor platform. On a small blanket beside her were Mina Morais, age four, and her baby brother, Stephen, the children of Euphemie's invalid cousin, Marie.

"So Evaloe isn't coming?" her mother asked.

"No, Marie is worse today. She seems to sense all the excitement."

"No wonder," commented Euphemie's father. "No one can talk of anything else."

Euphemie nodded. "Evaloe was going to bring her, but just getting ready made her terribly restless. He was afraid to come with her and afraid to leave her alone. I offered to stay with her, but he sent me on with Mina and Stephen because the children make her nervous, too."

"What a shame!" said her mother sadly. "To think that birthing a dear baby like Stephen could cause such havoc on Marie's nerves." She bent down and patted Stephen, who smiled at her happily. "I brought a jug of grape juice and some sugar cookies if you and the children are hungry."

"I am sure the children would like some, but I am too excited to eat anything." Turning to her father, she asked in a low voice, "Papa, I never did understand just what they are accusing Father Chiniquy of. What did he do?"

It's a long involved story and not something for a pretty girl like you to fret about. The gist of it is his thinking is not in line with the church authorities on many things."

"Such as?"

"Well, you know some of them. He openly questions the church's interpretation of its authority. He believes we can go straight to Jesus with our prayers and need not appeal to His mother, Mary."

"And he also feels," added her mother, "that it is all right for us Catholics to eat meat on Friday, and he wants to do away with the confessional box."

"Oh," said Euphemie thoughtfully. "I know if Father Chiniquy says these things are all right, they must be, but..."

"Hush, Child," her father said in a quiet, firm voice. "I have given the matter much thought. We are doing the right thing to follow Father Chiniquy."

Euphemie knew better than persist in her questioning. Although her father was more liberal than his friends on the question of formal education for the girls in the family, he held tight to the right and duty of the father to make decisions, as the head of the household, on church matters. It would never have been imagined by him, and certainly not by Euphemie, that someday she would be privy to the whole story which she would help Father Chiniquy prepare for the entire world to read, both in her time and in the century to follow.

She asked, "What do you suppose will happen today, Papa?"

Her father shrugged his shoulders. "Who knows? Father Chiniquy said Bishop Duggan will try to persuade us to burn our Bibles and convince us to return to the Church of Rome and submit ourselves to the Pope and to the bishops."

Euphemie almost hoped that would happen. Her parents' attitude throughout the controversy continued to amaze her. Although she was a dutiful daughter and had always respected their opinions and decisions, she found it difficult to go along with their unquestioning belief in whatever Father Chiniquy said. Having been schooled in the Catholic Academy in Montreal to fear and respect the authority of the church, she felt extremely uncomfortable in the schism. Whenever she listened to Father Chiniquy speak, she could believe anything he said; but once away from his dominating personality, she was overwhelmed with serious doubts. She ardently hoped he would retract his controversial statements. Then perhaps life in the colony could go on with everyone comfortably conforming to the rules laid down by the Reverend Fathers.

As if reading her thoughts, her father said, "The bishop claims he is going to unmask Father Chiniquy and show us what kind of man he is. I don't think there is any intention to coax him back to the Church of Rome. Bishop Duggan sent word he is going to speak to us in French so we can thoroughly understand what we are getting ourselves in for if we continue to follow Father Chiniquy."

Euphemie was alarmed to learn there was little hope that Father Chiniquy would be forgiven even if he wanted to be. She wondered with apprehension what indeed were they getting themselves in for. Her father seemed to be looking forward to the contest of wills; and, strangely enough, her mother, aware of his attitude, approved of it.

More and more families arrived as the time for the meeting drew nigh.

'It's a good thing we built the platform outside. What a crowd!" commented Pierre Arseneau standing nearby.

With Mina and Stephen content to sit quietly on the blanket, Euphemie had time to observe the tall platform. Its hewn plank floor was covered with carpets. A sofa and a dozen or so chairs were awaiting the arrival of the bishop and his following of priests. There was a large table covered with books placed on the south end of the platform. The August sun shone brightly, and a warm breeze fluttered the yellowing leaves of the large maple trees. Euphemie was grateful for the shade. The big maples had been carefully preserved by the workmen six years earlier when they cleared the ground to erect the chapel.

She saw Father Chiniquy moving through the crowd, stopping to talk to people along the way. Several small boys followed along, stopping when he stopped. He chatted easily as if unaware his fate was soon to be decided. He wore a simple long black cassock. On a heavy gold chain around his neck hung a large pendant. He was proud of that pendant and often spoke of how excited he was when the Pope sent it to him for his successful temperance crusade in Canada.

Euphemie knew he must be in his late forties, but he had so much vitality, he seemed much younger. He was short, measuring as he described himself five feet, five thumbs high. In the pulpit, he appeared much taller. It always surprised Euphemie to observe how short he was in a crowd. She had heard that as a young man he was slender as well as short and was often referred to by his colleagues as "Petit Chiniquy." He said one time his critics sometimes called him the small-sized reformer and his enemies said, "He is hardly bigger than a tobacco box," or "I think I can put him in my vest pocket." The comment that made him chuckle just to repeat it was, "Has he not the appearance of a salted sardine?" He had gained weight since the days on the trail. In the past six years his body thickened and hardened. The physical effort of building a new colony agreed with him.

He approached the platform. He said something to the children and they obediently hurried off to join their parents as he mounted the steps and turned toward the crowd. It took a few minutes for everyone to quiet down.

"I am glad," he addressed the crowd, "that so many of you have come today to hear Bishop Duggan. He is due here any moment. In his letter he said he plans to explain to you the folly of reading and interpreting the scriptures yourselves. He will try to convince you that there is no salvation save in the Church of Rome."

A rumble of comments ran through the crowd.

Father Chiniquy quieted them with a wave of his hand. "I want you to promise me you will not interrupt, that you will listen politely and intently to all the bishop has to say."

Many protested. Euphemie shivered with apprehension.

He continued, "I am sincere. Give him your most reverent attention. If he fulfills his promise to show you that I am a depraved man, a wicked man, you must turn me out."

"No! No! Never!"

Euphemie was incredulous. Surely the bishop would not say Father Chiniquy was wicked and depraved.

"If he proves to you that you have neither the right to read nor the intelligence to understand the scriptures, if he convinces you that out of the Church of Rome there is no salvation, you must, without an hour's delay, return to the church and submit yourselves to the Pope's bishops."

He raised his voice and thundered the challenge. " But if he fails, you know what you have to do. A great and decisive debate will be fought here. I have only one word more to say, dearly beloved, from this moment and through the solemn hour of conflict, let us humbly but fervently ask our great God, through His beloved and eternal Son, to look down on us in His mercy, enlighten us, and strengthen us, that we may be true to Him, to ourselves and to His Gospel. Let us all kneel in prayer."

Chapter II
The Confrontation

Bishop Duggan surveyed the crowd as he pulled up to the church in his shiny ebony carriage emblazoned with his golden crest and drawn by a matched pair of Arabian horses. He was followed by a retinue of priests in a half dozen assorted carriages. He bristled when he saw Father Chiniquy mingling and laughing with the crowd. Euphemie thought he looked very distinguished in his white surplice and his official white *bonnet quarre*. As soon as the carriages neared the church, Father Chiniquy gave the signal and Philip Gladu, who was standing at the base of the steeple, tugged on a rope that hoisted the American Flag above the cross on the steeple

Euphemie's father whispered loudly, "Father Chiniquy said he was going to do that to warn the ambassador of the Pope that he is treading the Land of Freedom and Liberty."

Euphemie could see the bishop pale as he looked up at the stars and stripes waving above the cross. Trembling at the audacity of her beloved Father Chiniquy, she was startled to hear the crowd shout, "Hurrah for the flag of the free and the brave!"

Several priests in the other carriages jumped down and started to hurry away.

"Look at that!" exclaimed Euphemie's mother. "Where are they going?"

"They act scared," observed her husband in disbelief.

The crowd snickered and Father Chiniquy called out, "Please don't run away. You are safe here." The priests sheepishly returned and huddled near the bishop's carriage.

Father Chiniquy approached the bishop with hand outstretched. Bishop Dugan brushed aside his helping hand and descended unaided from his carriage. Instead of striking out immediately for the platform, he hesitated nervously near the carriage until his grand vicar, the Rev. Mailloux, alighted from the second carriage. Euphemie remembered the Rev. Mailloux from her school days in Canada.

Bishop Duggan whispered a few words in the vicar's ear. The Rev. Mailloux turned to the crowd and announced in French, "My dear French Canadian countrymen. Here is your Holy Bishop. Kneel down and he will give you his benediction."

Euphemie started to rise from her chair to kneel when she felt her father's restraining hand on her arm.

"Wait, my dear," he cautioned.

To her surprise, no one knelt.

The Rev. Mailloux raised his voice to its highest pitch and cried, "My dear fellow countrymen: this is your Holy Bishop. He comes to visit you. Kneel down that he will give you his benediction."

Once more, Euphemie prepared to rise, but she first looked around and saw that nobody knelt.

A voice from the crowd called out, "Do you not know, Sir, we do no longer bend the knee before any man? It is only before God we kneel."

"Amen! Amen!," cried the crowd. Euphemie found herself joining in on the second amen. Stephen loved the noise and excitement. Mina put her hands over her ears and fell over on the blanket.

Father Chiniquy stepped forward and motioned politely for Bishop Duggan to mount the platform. The bishop, lifting his white robes with his left arm, brushed past Father Chiniquy's helping hand and fumbled his way up the stairs. On the fourth step, he turned and saw Father Chiniquy following him. In a clear, commanding French he said, "I don't want you on this platform. Go down and let my priests alone accompany me."

Euphemie was aghast at such rudeness.

The bishop put out his right hand to prevent Father Chiniquy from climbing any farther and almost fell backwards into his arms. Bishop

Duggan, a tall, heavy-set fair-haired Irishman, made quite a contrast to short, swarthy Father Chiniquy, who pushed the big bishop firmly up the last two steps as he said distinctly, "It may be that you do not want me here, but I want to be at your side to answer you." In a low firm voice, he added, "Remember, you are not on your ground here, but on mine!"

When they approached the chairs, Father Chiniquy offered the bishop the most comfortable one which he refused, preferring to choose another. His priests gathered around him, not to protect him, it seemed to Euphemie, but rather to be protected by him

There was no need to quiet the crowd. They were listening and watching with close attention. Father Chiniquy said, "My Lord, the people and pastor of Ste. Anne are exceedingly pleased to see you in our midst. We promise to listen attentively to what you say." He hesitated and then added, "on condition that we have the privilege of answering you." .

The bishop answered angrily, "I don't want you to say a word here."

Euphemie's early training kept her from hissing as some of the others did, but she began to develop a distinct dislike for the arrogant bishop.

In accordance with Father Chiniquy's request, the waiting crowd listened respectfully as the bishop began his address in quite good French. His voice was loud and accusing. He tried to prove that out of the Church of Rome there is no salvation. He contended that the people have neither the right to read nor the ability to understand the scriptures. He ended his argument for their return to the Roman Catholic Church by turning to Father Chiniquy and shouting, "You are a wicked rebel. You forget that when you were ordained a priest, you swore you would never interpret the Holy Scriptures according to your own fallible private judgment; you solemnly promised that you would take them only according to the unanimous consent of the Holy Fathers speaking to you through your superiors. Have not the Holy Fathers been approved by the Popes, by all the bishops of the Church? We have then, here, the true doctrine that must guide us. But instead of submitting yourself with humility, you boldly appeal to the Scriptures, against the decisions of the Popes and bishops, against the voice of all your superiors speaking to you through the Holy Fathers. Where will this boldness end? Ah! I tremble for you. You are on the high road to heresy. Go from here into a monastery to do penance for your sins. You say that you have never been excommunicated in a legal way?   Well, you will not say that any longer for I EXCOMMUNICATE YOU BEFORE THIS WHOLE ASSEMBLY."

Euphemie gasped.   Cries of anger exploded from the crowd.   Bishop Duggan stepped backwards and for support gripped the edge of the table filled with Father Chiniquy's reference books.   His *bonnet¹quarre* was askew.   Father Chiniquy went to the front of the platform, raised his hand to silence the crowd and began to speak.

"I must confess, to my shame, that the…"

Bishop Duggan smiled smugly.   Euphemie sighed with relief.   He was not going to continue to rebel.

To her horror, Father Chiniquy continued, "that the degrading principles of absolute submission of the inferior to the superiors, which flattens everything to the ground in the Church of Rome, had so completely wrought their deadly work on me that it was my wish to attain to the supreme perfection of the priest of Rome, to become like a stick in the hands of my superiors—like a corpse in their presence."

Before the bishop could grasp the direction his confession was taking, Father Chiniquy went on, "But my God was stronger than his unfaithful and blind servant and he never allowed me to go down to the bottom of that abyss of folly and impiety.   In spite of myself, I had left in me sufficient manhood to express my doubts about the doctrine of my Church."

The bishop stepped forward and pulled forcibly on the priest's arm. Shrugging him off, Father Chiniquy announced, "I do not want to revolt against my superiors.   I have spent many a sleepless night, weeping and praying through the long dark hours.   I feel I have probably compromised myself forever in the eyes of my superiors, who were the absolute masters of my destiny.   At first, I condemned myself for that inopportune appeal to the Holy Scriptures against the direction of my superiors.   I asked God to destroy in me that irresistible tendency to constantly go to the Word of God to know the truth instead of remaining at the feet of my superiors with the rest of the clergy.   But thank God that blasphemous prayer was never granted."

Euphemie clenched her knees tightly together to still their shaking. Where was all this leading?   Surely Father Chiniquy was unwise to be so boldly outspoken.

The bishop tried to interrupt, but Father Chiniquy was determined to go on.

"Yes, when you ordain a priest, you make him swear that he will never interpret the Holy Scriptures, except according to the unanimous consent of the Holy Fathers, but how can we know their unanimous consent without studying them?"

He pushed the bishop aside and walked to the table where he picked up several volumes.

"Is it not strange that not only the priests do not study the Holy Fathers, but the only one who is trying to study them is ridiculed and suspected of heresy?" he asked as he thumbed through the volumes stopping to make brief references.

"Is it my fault if Origen never believed in the eternal punishment of the damned, if St. Cyprien denied the supreme authority of the Bishop of Rome, if St. Augustine positively said that nobody was obliged to believe in purgatory, if St. John Chrysostom publicly denied the obligations of auricular confession?" He held high the volumes.

Euphemie felt as if a great blow had been delivered to the pit of her empty stomach. Surely Father Chiniquy would be severely punished for talking that way about the Holy Fathers.

The bishop was furious. Rather than give Father Chiniquy the satisfaction of debating the very issues he had come to condemn, he ignored him completely. He stepped to the edge of the platform to plead with a tense but gentle and sincere voice for the French Canadians to abandon this apostate. He urged them to think of their friends and relatives, their very dear mothers and fathers in Canada, weeping over their inclinations to apostasy. He spoke with great earnestness of the desolation felt by their loved ones at the news of their defection from the mother church.

Euphemie thought of her two grandmothers in Montreal and some of her favorite teachers at the academy. Tears rolled down her cheeks.

The bishop resumed, "My dear friends, please tell me what will be your guide in the ways of God after you have left the holy church of your fathers, the church of your country? Who will lead you in the ways of God?"

He stood surveying the crowd made up for the most part of young families who had indeed left devout Catholic relatives in Canada. A profound silence, solemn and complete except for the cry of a small baby here and there and the drone of the cicadas, hung in the air a few seconds. Euphemie looked to Father Chiniquy to speak up and say he would lead them, but he stood silently watching the reaction of his people.

The bishop, assuming that the long strange silence was proof he had successfully touched the sensitive hearts and he was to win the day, exclaimed a second time with still more power and pleading, "My dear French Canadian friends: I ask you in the name of Jesus Christ, your Savior and mine, in the name of your desolated mothers, fathers and friends who are weeping along the banks of your beautiful St. Lawrence River, I ask you in the name of your beloved Canada! Answer me! Now that you refuse to obey the Holy Church of Rome, who will guide you in the ways of salvation?"

Another silence.

Then old Leon LeVeque raised a Bible over his head with his two hands and shouted, "The Bible is all we want to guide us. As for you, Sir, you had better go away and come here no more."

"Amen!" cried the crowd. "The Bible. *The Holy Bible.* Go away, Sir, and never come again."

Mina began to cry and Euphemie moved quickly to the blanket to comfort her. Stephen, worn out by the excitement, had fallen asleep. When Father Chiniquy went to the front of the platform and started to speak again, the bishop clutched his shoulder. He cautioned in a furious voice, "No, no, no. Not another word from you."

The people saw the bishop's restraint on their priest and were angry. About 30 men surged toward the platform. In indignation, they cried, "He denies us the right of free speech. He refuses to hear what our pastor has to say. Down with him."

Euphemie could not believe it was really happening. Gaston Bourgeois and Ed Delibec tried to scale the platform but were pushed off the steps by the priests. The height of the platform prevented the men from jumping up to confront the bishop. In vain, Father Chiniquy raised his voice to calm his people. No voice could be heard in the confusion.

A group of men lifted the new schoolteacher, Francis Bechard, to the platform. He spoke in Father Chiniquy's ear for a moment and then turned to the surging crowd. Although he was young, he was highly respected by everyone. His presence and a wave from his hand acted like magic. The crowd quieted.

"Let us hear what Bechard has to say," they cried.

In his powerful, melodious voice he begged the people to cease being angry and to thank God their eyes were opened. He cautioned that they must not commit violence; they must let the bishop and his priests depart in peace.

Euphemie sighed with relief. "God bless you, Francis Bechard," she whispered.

"Will you do that?" Francis begged.

"Yes! Yes!" replied the people.

Ed Delibec added, "But on one condition….that they never come again."

Francis Bechard closed by shouting as he raised both arms over his head, "People of Ste. Anne. You have just gained a most glorious victory. Hurrah for the Village of Ste. Anne."

"Hurrah for the Village of Ste. Anne!" echoed the crowd.

What nerve it took for Francis to do that! He was only a year or two older than Euphemie, she knew, but he dared to confront an angry bishop and an even angrier crowd and succeeded in bringing them to their senses.

Father Chiniquy moved toward the priests huddled about their bishop and said something to them as he motioned toward their carriages. He beckoned his brother, Achille, and pointed to a group of young men. Apparently he was arranging a safe passageway for the bishop's exit. Euphemie was glad to see Achille Chiniquy in charge. He was a husky, adventuresome type, rugged and tough, and much admired by all the colonists. He gathered a half dozen young men, and they pushed back the crowd to make a space through which Father Chiniquy and Achille led the bishop and the priests to their carriages. Their drivers sat with the reins in their hands. The bishop had lost the scrimmage that day, but the set of his shoulders and his angry stride made it quite clear the war was not over

Euphemie, emotionally drained from the drama and almost too weak to stand, was amazed at the vigor and boldness of some of the women who made their way to the carriages. Her friend, Emilie Soucie, broke through the ranks of the cordon and ran toward the departing bishop. As he climbed into his carriage, she gave him a poke in the back with her parasol and shouted, "Away with you! And never come here again!"

Euphemie trembled to see the bishop so angry. What would become of all of them when in his wrath he exerted all his power against Father Chiniquy and his followers?

Chapter III
Marie's Problems

Euphemie gathered up the sleeping Stephen and laid him gently in the baby buggy. She took Mina by the hand. "Come, Cherie, let's go home and see your papa." To her mother, she said, "Mama, I must hurry. Evaloe will be eager to hear about the meeting."

Her mother nodded with understanding. "I'll help your father take these chairs back home, and I'll walk over to see Marie. She might be glad to have some company."

"Don't worry about the chairs, Bernice. I can manage them by myself. First, I want to talk to Father Chiniquy and Achille. You walk along with Euphemie and the children."

The two women and the little girl walked down the sloping churchyard. Euphemie had to pull back on the handles to keep the buggy from rolling down the hill to the street. "Come along, Mina," she urged. "We must hurry."

The little girl broke into a trot and raced on ahead.

"Not that fast, Mina. Come back," Euphemie called. Then she saw that Mina was running toward Evaloe, who was hurrying up the hill, his face pinched with anxiety.

"He's heard the shouting," Euphemie said. "He's probably worried that something might have happened to Mina and Stephen."

Evaloe picked up Mina and kissed her on both cheeks as he hurried toward Euphemie. When he was close enough to speak without being heard by other departing villagers, he said urgently, "Euphemie, see if you can find Dr. Legris. Hurry!"

"What's the matter? What happened?" Euphemie asked.

"It's Marie." He put Mina down, and she started toward home. "She tried to slash her wrist with my razor. I got it away from her in time, but she's still bleeding. I've got to get back there. Mina, come back. Wait for me."

Euphemie's mother immediately took charge. "I'll take the children to our house. Don't worry about them. Euphemie, run back to the platform. I saw Dr. Legris talking with Achille there as we left."

Euphemie thought she was going to faint. Her mother's matter-of-fact response to the emergency brought her to her senses. She gathered up her skirt and sprinted with unladylike strides to seek the doctor. The drama of the bishop's confrontation seemed almost ridiculous compared with the immediacy of dealing with Marie's frantic efforts to end her problems.

Dr. Legris was still standing by the platform. Euphemie, torn between the need to save time and the desire to save Marie's reputation, suppressed her impulse to shout to him. He suspected there was some medical emergency, excused himself from Achille and hastened toward her. He picked up his medical bag, which he had brought along in the event there was any emergency. Together they quickly returned to the house. The doctor commended Evaloe on his emergency measures to stop the flow of blood before great damage was done. He gave Marie a sedative and massaged her shoulders and neck until she relaxed and went to sleep.

He sat down for a talk with Evaloe. He said gently but very firmly that Evaloe must have Marie admitted to the insane asylum where she could be treated and cared for. He said he would arrange for Evaloe to visit her at any time. Evaloe shook his head stubbornly. Euphemie knew he would never consent to putting Marie away.

"If you continue to ignore my advice," the doctor warned, "I will have to recommend that the children be taken away. This is not a safe place for them."

The threat was said in all kindness, but it fell on Evaloe and Euphemie like a thunderbolt. She knew Evaloe would not risk the lives of his children nor could he bear to part with them. She suspected, on the other hand, that he dreaded the wrath of Marie's parents if he followed the doctor's advice. She physically ached for him in his dilemma.

Evaloe said he would have to consult Marie's family in Three Rivers, Canada. Dr. Legris offered to send a letter explaining the extreme need of institutional care. In spite of all the good doctor could say, Evaloe was not to be comforted. He was consumed with guilt and condemned himself for Marie's condition brought on by bearing his baby. Euphemie wished Father Chiniquy would come. He always knew what to say. As if in answer to her prayers, he stepped up on the porch. Dr. Legris, sighing with relief, met him at the door.

"Is something wrong, Doctor?" Father Chiniquy asked, somewhat out of breath. "Achille said Euphemie fetched you, and he seemed to think something happened to Marie. I put him in charge of the demolition work and hurried over here."

Dr. Legris assured him, "Marie is all right now. I'm afraid she tried to take her life by slashing her wrist. I gave her a sedative so she's sleeping now. It's Evaloe I am worried about. He's beside himself with remorse. I gave him an ultimatum. I said he had to put Marie in an institution or I would have to take the children away."

"Where are the children?"

"Bernice Allard took them home with her. She said Euphemie can watch them there. I have advised against their staying here. I think Evaloe had better get his mother or someone to stay with Marie."

"I agree," said Father Chiniquy. "Let me talk to Evaloe. I think I can relieve the torture of his soul."

"I was just going for you. I must get to my office now. I will look in on Marie later."

What had only moments before been the heaviest of burdens seemed much lighter for Euphemie to bear in the comforting presence of Father Chiniquy. They went down the short hall to the kitchen where Evaloe sat at the table with his head down on his folded arms in a picture of despair. Euphemie excused herself, saying, "Excuse me, Father, I will go collect some clothing for the children. My mother said we could keep them at our house."

"An excellent plan. Don't go yet, Miss Allard. There's something I want to say to both of you."

Evaloe raised his head and glanced quickly at Euphemie, who turned away from both of them to clean up the lunch dirty dishes Evaloe had stacked on the kitchen cabinet.

"Won't you sit down, Father?" Evaloe's voice broke. "I suppose you heard about Marie?"

"Yes, my son. The doctor told me. I met him on the way in. He's worried about you, too, Evaloe. He said Marie is sleeping now so I will talk with her and pray with her later. Right now, I want to talk with you."

Evaloe poured out his heart. The pastor listened patiently to the facts he already knew—what a good woman Marie is, what a wonderful wife and devoted mother she had been and how she had changed since the baby was born. The birth had been touch and go and the doctor said they were lucky to save both baby and mother. Marie seemed all right at first, and then she started to change. She lost interest in everything-- the baby, Mina, her home, her husband and her appearance....

Tears filled Evaloe's eyes. "Dr. Legris thinks the toxemia permanently affected her brain. Oh, it's all my fault. I wanted a son so bad. She had a hard time when Mina was born. We should never have had another."

Euphemie remembered Evaloe's joy when he first told her the new baby was a boy.

"Don't blame yourself, Evaloe," Father Chiniquy advised. "Marie wanted that baby as much as you did, and he is fine little boy. If Marie had had a heart attack, I think you would not have tormented yourself like this. If she had died from a heart attack, you would have mourned and missed her, but you would have said it is just the way things happen. If she had survived a heart attack, you would have been grateful to God and set out to do everything possible to help her fully recover."

"But it wasn't a heart attack."

"No, Marie had a brain attack. A woman who has been a devoted wife and loving mother suddenly changes because the poison of toxemia attacks a portion of her brain. More often than not, I am told, death results, sometimes for the baby, sometimes for the mother and often for both. Marie and Stephen are alive. Let's thank God for that. Then let's call on Him for help and do everything we can to bring Marie back to health again. We don't know that the brain damage is permanent."

"But she tried to kill herself. Isn't that a crime? She will be condemned forever to purgatory."

Euphemie had thought about that, too.

Father Chiniquy.shook his head emphatically. "Purgatory is an invention of the priests of Rome. Since I left the Church of Rome for the Church of Christ, I have spent many hours reading and meditating on the Gospel. You know, I have not found a single word about purgatory. From the beginning to the end of the divine book, we learn that it is through the blood of the Lamb, shed on the cross, that our guilty souls can be purified from their sins."

Euphemie had stood quietly drying dishes during the conversation. She almost dropped a cup. She said incredulously, "No purgatory, Father?"

"I know both of you have retained the views taught to you by the Church of Rome since your childhood. I, too, had that training. As a priest, I said many, many masses for the souls whose loved ones paid for the prayers. Read the Testaments I gave you, dear children, and you will find that I am right. Marie will not be condemned to purgatory."

Euphemie still had her doubts, but Evaloe, in his agony, reached out for the comforting belief.

"Oh, thank you. Thank you."

Tears ran down his cheeks.

"Dr. Legris advises that Marie be put in an institution for a while," he added sadly.

"I trust Dr. Legris' judgment. It will be hard for you and for her. Remember, you are not alone. You have family, friends, your pastor and, most of all, your blessed Savior. Let's kneel, right here in your kitchen and ask His blessings on Marie, you, the children and this home."

They knelt.

Father Chiniquy prayed for Marie's return to health, for Evaloe's strength in time of need, for the welfare of the children and for the understanding that God has no purgatory.

Evaloe said, "Amen."

Then he added, almost with anger, "I wish no one had to know about what Marie did today. What will they say—the old women on the corners, the old men hanging around the blacksmith shop?"

Father Chiniquy pulled a slender volume of Psalms from the skirt pocket of his cassock. "Let me read you David's Psalm for Deliverance from slanderers: 'Have mercy upon me, O Lord, for I am in trouble; mine eye is consumed with grief, yea, my soul and my belly. I am like a broken vessel for I have heard the slander of many; fear was on every side while they took counsel together against me. But I trusted in thee, O Lord. I said, "Thou art my God." Oh, how great is Thy goodness! Thou shalt hide me in the secret of thy presence from the pride of man; thou shalt keep me secretly in a pavilion from the strife of tongues. Thou heardest the voice of my supplications when I cried unto thee.'"

Father Chiniquy closed the Book of Psalms and asked, "Do you have the Bible I gave you, Evaloe?"

"Yes, Father. Right here."

He picked it up from the kitchen cabinet.

"Let me mark some passages for you. Read them and spend a few moments in quiet prayer. You will find a great strength."

Euphemie marveled that this man could so calmly deal with the sorrows of his parishioner while at that very moment his career, his reputation; all he had worked so hard for were in serious jeopardy. He marked the passages, listened a moment at Marie's door and then departed from the sad house to join the jubilant group on the church lawn busily tearing down the platform, chopping up the confessional box and lowering the cross from the steeple.

Euphemie tiptoed about collecting clothing for the children. Before she left the house, she returned to the kitchen intending to reassure Evaloe that all would turn out well and that she would take very good care of the children as long as he needed her. She found him gently snoring, sitting at the table with his head down on the open Bible. She blessed Father Chiniquy for the peace he had brought poor tormented Evaloe. In her compassion, she leaned forward to kiss his bent head but thought better of it. She gently closed the door behind her with the premonition that nothing would ever be the same as it was before that day. Never before had any tragedy touched her so personally. She wondered if she could ever smile again.

The days passed slowly. Every day, Euphemie's father brought home news. Apparently no one knew about Marie's attempt to take her life. It was common knowledge that she was having serious mental problems, but the church's confrontation with the bishop overshadowed all other news.

On the heels of the August 3 excommunication, Father Chiniquy founded the Christian Catholic Church on August 22. All those who joined the new church were aware this meant they were personally excommunicated from any Roman Catholic Church and therefore deprived of sacraments, marriage, spiritual contact with other Catholics and, finally, Catholic burial. Among the transformations were the disappearance of statues, auricular confession, holy water, Latin Masses, fast days, vestments along with discontinuance of belief in purgatory, indulgences, mediation of the saints including Mary, and papal infallibility.

There was growing antagonism among the colonists. Friends and even members of the same family with different persuasions no longer spoke to each other. The faithful 15 or 20 families that elected to remain with the Church of Rome were incensed at the desecration of the steeple cross and the confessional box. They banded together to sue the apostate and his followers for the possession of the church. It was hard to believe a colony could change from a peaceful, bucolic settlement to quarreling, spiteful factions with each group claiming to be the favored of God. Euphemie thought God must surely be angry at the turmoil all in the name of Christianity

Marie's parents, upon receiving the doctor's personal recommendation, agreed to the arrangements for Marie's commitment. In less than two weeks after Marie was taken away, Evaloe stopped by Allards to suggest that Euphemie and the children move back to his place. The Allards offered no objections to having their unmarried daughter live in the home of her cousin's husband to care for his children. Such was often the case when a mother died in childbirth or from cholera or diphtheria. Euphemie, wishing they had not been so willing, begged for a little more time. She wondered if she would be worthy of the trust her parents had in her. When Evaloe bent down to give Stephen a goodnight kiss, his hand brushed hers, and her heart skipped a beat lest her parents suspect how much that touch meant to her. She took the children off to bed, listened to their prayers and read to them until she heard Evaloe depart.

Chapter IV
The New Confession

The next day, Euphemie timidly approached Father Chiniquy's study in the church. Francis Bechard was leaving as she entered. Remembering his performance at the meeting, she smiled at him.

He said formally, "Good Day, Miss Allard," and stood aside for her to pass.

She supposed he was wondering what had brought her to Father Chiniquy's study. She would have been surprised to know what thoughts were going through his head. The young teacher had an eye for a pretty girl, and he admired Euphemie's trim figure, her thick auburn hair and her warm brown eyes. Her complexion had a healthy glow instead of the sallow tint of so many French girls he knew. She had a prim, tiny mouth in repose; but when she smiled, her lips were full and generous. He had been thinking ever since he came to the village he would like to court her when he had set aside enough money to afford a wife. He had heard rumors that Evaloe Morais was sweet on her. Although he was quite certain Evaloe would be true to his wife, ailing as she was, he could understand how having a nursemaid around like Euphemie could be a temptation.

Father Chiniquy greeted her warmly. "Well, Miss Allard. Good Day. Good Day."

He rose from his chair behind his big polished oak desk and hurried around the desk to hold the chair when she sat down on its very edge as if poised for flight. He was unfailingly polite. To ladies, in particular, his manner was very courtly.

He hesitated a moment, waiting for her to state her reason for her visit. Sensing her reticence and embarrassment, he asked gently, "Is there some special reason for your call, or did you just drop by to say 'Good Day'?"

Since she was not in the habit of just dropping by her priest's study to say "Good Day," the suggestion made her smile. The smile soon faded, and she regarded him for a minute or two without speaking. His was such a familiar face. The dark, slightly curly hair trimmed just below his ears receded from his brow in a deep widow's peak. His thick eyebrows did not meet in the center like her father's but arched slightly over the dark brown eyes that looked at her with such compassion. He was clean-shaven and the tiny cleft in his strong chin came and went as he smiled slightly and then looked at her soberly. A skin-colored wart on his right upper lip was not offensive. It called attention away from the dominating eyes to the strong yet gentle lips. His face was muscular and powerful, reflecting his driving will and intellect.

She said timidly, "Is it true we can no longer come to confession?"

"Not exactly," he said with instant understanding. "We all need a place to unload the burdens of our hearts. The only difference now is in procedure. We can either kneel by our bedside and confess directly to God, or if he feel a need for human contact, we can meet vis-à-vis, so to speak, with our pastor."

"I need a confessor," her voice was barely audible. "Won' t you hear my confession?" she begged

He had returned to his chair. He got up to close the door of the study. On his way back to his desk, he stopped and laid his hand gently on her shoulder.

"Let us not call me a confessor. Let's say I am your counselor, your comforter."

"I don't want my parents to know."

She remembered that priests could not reveal what was told them in confession, but she was not sure how confidential her confession would be with a counselor or comforter.

"Of course not. The discussion between a pastor and his parishioner is as private as any information passed through the confessional box. If you do not wish your parents to know, whatever you tell me will not reach their ears unless you later request me to tell them."

She twisted her handkerchief and said nothing.

He moved his chair around so he was half-facing her. Instead of looking at her, he stared out the window and waited.

Burdened with a heavy sense of guilt and convinced her confession would be kept secret, Euphemie decided to tell what was on her heart although she felt uncomfortable in the new setting and longed for the dark privacy of the confessional box.

She began, "Has Evaloe Morais spoken to you about taking the children back to his home?"

"Yes, he is a sad and lonely young man, and he sorely misses the children."

"He wants me to return, too, and stay there to care for them and to be his housekeeper."

Father Chiniquy continued to scrutinize the trees through the window as he nodded. "A very wise choice. The children love you, and I can see that you love them. God knows they need that kind of love."

"It's true," she agreed. "I love them dearly. That's why I would never want to do anything to hurt them."

"To hurt them?"

"Oh, I don't know how to say it. We never did anything wrong, you know. Neither Marie nor little Mina were ever given cause to suspect... but, oh, Father Chiniquy, Evaloe and I...love each other!"

She had said it. The words spoken out loud sounded even more dreadful than the thought held in her mind.

Father Chiniquy sat very still until she controlled her sobs.

Then she said, "I cannot go back there. I am afraid someone will suspect. We have been so careful to avoid any shameful action, but we both know the other's feelings. Oh, don't you see, Father, I cannot bear to see Mina and Stephen put in an orphanage or pushed around from foster home to foster home..."

Father Chiniquy turned his chair around and sat with his elbows on the desk and his chin resting on his interlaced fingers. Although short and stubby in stature, he had long slender fingers. In spite of the carpentry work he had done in the past six years to help colonize the village, his hands were supple and graceful though calloused and suntanned.

He looked at her tenderly. "Young lady, I am glad you shared your concern with me. There is no reason to blame yourself for loving Evaloe. He is a wonderful young man, beautiful on the inside as well as handsome on the outside."

"But he is my cousin's husband," she sobbed.

"Indeed. And according to what you have told me, you have done nothing to infringe on Marie's rights. What you may be taking for romance could be simply the turning toward each other so often experienced by those caring for a sick person over a long period of time. Then, too, you and Evaloe share your love for Mina and Stephen, and that brings you close together. Or, if your feeling for each other has advanced beyond that stage, you are still not up against an insurmountable problem. If I were to judge, I would say your big concern is not with the past in which you have managed to keep your passion in check. Is that correct?"

"That's right. We have never had any secret meetings or anything like that."

"But your feeling for each other is very deep and with Marie out of the house, you worry that your love for each other will overpower your discretion?"

"We would not want it to."

"Have you discussed this with Evaloe?"

She shook her head.

"Oh, no."

"Then this love has never been declared?"

"But it is there. I'm not imagining it, Father. Please don't think it is a silly girl's fantasy. It's not something I wanted to happen."

"Sister Allard, I am convinced you are not imagining this. Up to now, you have faced your problem without much human support, and no doubt there have been times when you have felt you could not bear it. Let me now share that burden. From this moment on, I am interested in your problem. As best as possible, I want you to cease worrying about it. Instead, confide in me. Our concentration will be on the present and the future. Together with God we will seek an appropriate solution."

"Oh, Father, I am so ashamed to burden you with my petty problems when you have so many big, big worries right now."

"Yes, I do seem to be beleaguered with problems, and I want you to pray for me. But never hesitate to confide in me. I will always have time for you. Remember, we are going to solve your problem together."

"Oh, thank you, Father. I feel so much better already."

"Let's plan, now, for a solution. I have been giving the matter of the Morais children some thought already. As you may know, I often go hunting and fishing with Evaloe's father. He has been very concerned about the welfare of his grandchildren. Marie's parents in Canada would take them, of course, but Evaloe wants them to stay here with him near enough for Marie to see them now and then if possible."

"Oh, he couldn't stand to part with them."

"I know you are right. His mother and father still have six children at home in that little farmhouse so they cannot take on two more. But this is what I suggested to Evaloe's father. Evaloe is a carpenter so why not have him add an ell to the farmhouse? There's plenty of wood growing right there on the farm. His mother and the older children could care for his little ones while he is at work during the day, and he could be with them at night."

"Did Mr. Morais like that plan?"

"Yes. He said he would speak to Evaloe. In fact, Evaloe's salary added to the income from the farm would help solve some of Ed Morais' problems. Farmers are really in sad financial straits this year."

"So Evaloe would not need me for a housekeeper and the children would not be neglected," she sighed with relief.

"And Miss Allard, here's something else I've been thinking as we sat here. I told you I have problems. One of them is that after Bishop Duggan's visit, my housekeeper, Miss Amiot, informed me that she cannot break with the Church of Rome, the church of her family. She feels she can no longer care for my household. In fact, she is leaving today. As you know, I built my parsonage big enough to entertain visiting dignitaries and to house new immigrants temporarily as they arrive from Canada."

Euphemie was only half-listening, but she sat bolt upright at his next statement.

He said, "I need someone to look after the household so I can be free to take care of the ever-increasing concerns of the church. If we can arrange for Evaloe to move his family in with his parents, would you consider being my housekeeper?"

Euphemie was shaken by the suggestion. Whatever could he be thinking? To care for a sick cousin and two babies and run the household in a humble cottage was one thing. Father Chiniquy's parsonage was as big and magnificent as some of the beautiful homes in Montreal. She knew he often entertained clergymen and other important people who came from churches on the East coast to learn about the great temperance movement he had started when he was in Canada.

"I couldn't. I just couldn't."

"I think you can. I know you can. There's nobody I would like so much. But don't decide today. Go home and think it over. Talk it over with your mother and father."

"But I don't want them to know about Evaloe and me."

How could she tell one part without the other?

"Of course not. That subject need not be mentioned. I'll tell you what I will do. Let me talk to your father and tell him I am in dire need of a housekeeper. I will ask him if he will approach you to see if you might like the position."

The new turn of events left Euphemie in turmoil. She was at once relieved and agitated. She was hesitant and doubtful of her ability to accept such responsibility. But maybe it would be a good thing....

"Perhaps," she said more to herself than to Father Chiniquy, "if Evaloe and I don't see each other, perhaps...."

"God will find a way to work things out, young lady. Don't forget that God controls the smallest as well as the greatest events of this world. I dare say there is not a single fact in my eventful life that has not taught me there is a special providence in our lives. You will be so busy you will not have time to..."

Euphemie broke in, " To covet my cousin's husband?"

"No, I was going to say to miss the children too much. You may have them visit you any time. Or you may ride out to the farm any time in my buggy. After all, the Morais farm is only a mile out of town."

"But I haven't said I'd take the job," she protested.

True, Father Chiniquy had provided a solution to her problem, but he had presented her with a new choice so overwhelming she could not believe it was happening. That he wanted her was very flattering, but she did not share his belief she would be quite capable of filling the position.

He got up from his chair and helped her from hers.

"I am hoping you will say yes. I need you, Miss Allard. Before you go, let's pray about it."

"But, Father, you haven't given me any penance to do."

"Do you mean so many 'Hail Marys' to recite? No, and I am not going to assign any. Your penance is to sort out your feelings and your responsibilities and come up with a solution pleasing to God."

Chapter V
Out of the Depths

At the end of the prayer, Father Chiniquy rose from his knees and pulled Euphemie to her feet. He walked with her to the door and reassured her that all would work out well if she put faith in the Lord. She walked home not thinking for the first time in weeks of Evaloe and his children. What, she wondered, would life be like as a housekeeper for an excommunicated priest? Did she really know this man who could solve her problem so easily while handing her another decision that might change her entire life. He was so sure of himself even in the face of opposition from powerful bishops. He must have nothing but pity if not contempt for his floundering parishioner.

Little could she suspect what ecstasy turning to agony he was experiencing at that very moment. Immediately after she left his study, he turned the key in the door and joyfully dropped to his knees near his desk. He rested his hands on the edge of the desk, leaned his head on his hands and poured out his gratitude to God for helping him in this new type of counseling for the guilt-tormented. His joy was short-lived and quickly replaced by great confusion when he considered the enormity of the task before him.

He felt a tremendous responsibility. He realized he would have to guide his people into regions entirely new and unexplored. The trouble and difficulties, which Luther, Knox and Calvin met at almost every step, were to be met by him. Although they were giants, they had many times been brought low almost to the point of discouragement. He questioned whether he had enough knowledge, wisdom and experience for the task before him.

"Dear Lord," he prayed. "My tiny success has not blinded me to the reality of my deplorable isolation from the great masses of the clergy. With few exceptions, they are speaking of me as a dangerous man and lose no opportunity to shame me and show me their contempt and indignation for what they call my obstinacy. In this sad hour, there are many clouds on my horizon, and my mind is filled with anxiety."

For more than hour he cried to God in vain. No answer came.

He cried for a ray of light to guide him. He wept. He felt that God, too, had forsaken him. To add to his distress, the thought crossed his mind that by giving up the Church of Rome, he had given up, as Bishop Duggan had pointed out, the church of his dear father and mother, of his brothers, of his friends and of his country. In fact, all that was near and dear to him would be sacrificed. He did not regret the sacrifices but didn't know if he could survive them.

"My God," he prayed fervently, "A war will be declared against me. The Pope, the bishops and priests all over the world will denounce and curse me. They will attack and destroy my character, my name and my honor in their pulpits. My best friends—my own people—even my own brothers are bound to look upon me with horror, as an apostate, a vile outcast. I cannot even look for protection from Protestants because much of my priestly life was spent writing and preaching against them."

Having descended to the depths of despair, his ebullient spirit began to bubble again. His mind rushed forward to the new struggles and new difficulties. Despair gave way to planning.

He arranged with his Lord, "I must form an army and raise a banner in Your midst around which all the soldiers of the gospel will rally. Jesus Christ, Himself, will be our general. He will bless and sanctify us. He will lead us on to victory."

As if by signal, his first recruit banged on the door.

"Charles, are you in there? Open the door."

It was Achille, always impetuous, always in a hurry.

Charles rose stiffly. He must have been there on his knees over two hours because the sun was already low in the west. He turned the key and opened the door for his brother. Achille was four years his junior, an inch or so taller and much stockier. His work had always involved outdoor physical labor. His body was blocky and strong. Charles had to admit the full beard suited him.

"Why are you all locked up in here? It's getting dark. Why don't you have a light?"

It was difficult for Charles to adjust to the hearty noisiness of Achille after the deep emotional experience he had just gone through.

"Just wanted a little privacy," he said, 'to kind of think things through."

"Well, I'll go. Nothing urgent, anyway. It can wait."

Achille turned to leave.

"No, no, Achille. Don't go. You are just the one I want to talk with."

"About what?"

"Let's hear what you have to say first."

Charles assumed his place behind his desk and motioned for Achille to occupy the chair Euphemie had vacated a few hours earlier.

"I was wanting to tell you that Lucy finally agreed to leave the Church of Rome, so we and our children are with you all the way."

Tears came to Charles' eyes. He pushed back his chair so quickly it fell over. He went around the desk and threw his arms around his brother.

"You cannot know what unspeakable joy your decision has given me. Thank your darling Lucy for me from the bottom of my heart. May the Lord add his blessing."

He squeezed Achille's shoulders.

Achille said earnestly and sadly, "But I don't think Louis and Edna can be persuaded to change. I have talked and talked, but Edna finally told me to get out of her house, and Louis said I had better leave."

This was not news to Charles. He was disappointed but not surprised. Louis, the youngest of the family, was always the quiet one. Although he was not impetuous like Achille or a reformer like his oldest brother, he was quietly obstinate and had been set in his ways even as a little boy. His wife had never been especially fond of Charles. Both she and Louis were extremely upset by Charles' departure from the established procedures of the church. Charles hoped Louis and he and Achille could remain friends. His mother's heart would have broken had she lived to see the day when her boys no longer were friendly with each other, especially over the matter of religion that she had so diligently drilled into them.

Charles discussed with Achille the plans to go to Kankakee City and legally break all ties with the Church of Rome. They promised to meet again the next day. Achille let himself out, and Charles continued to sit contemplatively at his desk in the gloaming. He had not yet lighted the kerosene lamp.

Odd how the memories of his mother persisted!

Chapter VI
Seeds of Doubt

Ah, if his mother were still alive, what would she think of him now that he was at war with the very church she held so dear? She could never have dreamed when she helped him, before he was eight years old, to memorize large portions of the French and Latin Bible that such learning could be the foundation of a break with Catholicism for him.

When he was a boy, few people had Bibles. The Chiniquy copy was one Charles' father had received before he left the Theological Seminary in Quebec to study law and become a notary. Charles remembered the rainy Sabbath days when the neighboring farmers, unable to go to church because of inclement weather, gathered at the Chiniquy home. They often lifted him to the dining room table and asked him, an eight-year old, to deliver from memory long parts of the Old and New Testaments. On nice Sundays, farmers waiting near the church door in their buggies would ask him to recite some chapter of the Gospel. Most of the people could not read and were delighted with his recitations. He had learned the history of the creation, the fall of man, the deluge, the sacrifice of Isaac, the history of Moses, the plagues of Egypt, the history of Samson, the most interesting events in the life of David, several Psalms, all the speeches and parables of Christ and the history of the suffering and death of Jesus as narrated by John.

Charles reflected that he could still recite large portions of those scriptures learned at his mother's knee so long ago. One of his most vivid memories of his father was of the day the new priest in the Murray Bay area came to the Chiniquy home. He was born in France and had been condemned to death under Robespierre. He had found refuge with many other French priests in England. From there, he made his way to Quebec and had become the bishop of Murray Bay. The Chiniquys were interested in his story. Charles listened with rapt attention to the tales of persecution. Suddenly the priest's tone changed. He demanded to know if the Chiniquys were reading the Bible to their children. He said it was his painful duty to take their Bible and burn it.

Charles was stunned. Burn their Bible! It was their most treasured possession.

His father, although French on his mother's side, was the son of a fearless Spanish sailor, originally named Et Chiniquia. He sprang to his feet and demanded that the priest leave. Charles had never seen his father so angry. The priest left immediately. Charles ran to kiss and thank his father. He jumped on the table and recited in his grandest style the fight between David and Goliath, feeling in his own mind that his father was David and the priest was the giant whom the little stone had knocked down.

Looking back, the apostate wondered if doubts had been planted by his early schooling. Because there was no school in Murray Bay, Charles, when he was nine years old, was sent to live with his mother's sister in St. Thomas. His Aunt Genevieve and her husband had no children, and they treated him like a son. He remembered his first schoolteacher, Mr. Allen Jones, who was born in England where he received most of his schooling. He had taken additional study in Paris and was an excellent teacher both in English and French. The children from the best families of St.Thomas studied under him although he was a Protestant and the local priest opposed his school. Perhaps the first glimmers of doubt about the Catholic Church were seen then.

Three years passed without his seeing his family. He was seldom homesick but in the summer of 1821, he became very restless and homesick with a special longing to see his father. He was permitted to go home for a short visit. He remembered the date vividly. It was July 17, 1821. He spent the afternoon and evening by his father's' side joyfully showing how he could do algebra, geometry and spelling.

"You have learned so much in such a short time," his father said proudly.

Charles thought his father looked older but seemed in good health. He was shocked when his father died in his sleep that night. It was about four o'clock in the morning when his mother screamed. Charles ran to his parents' room where he found his father stretched out on the floor and his mother in her nightgown and cap lying in a faint across his father's dead body. The doctor later diagnosed he had died from heart failure.

Because his mother was so devastated she could not walk along in the funeral procession, Charles manfully concealed his grief and stayed home with her to comfort her.

A few days after the funeral, his mother heard from her two sisters. The one with whom Charles had stayed in St. Thomas said, "We have no family and God has given us the good things of life. Come live with us."

The other sister, married in Kamouraska to Hon. Amable Dionne, wrote, "We have lately lost our only son. We wish to fill the vacant place with Charles, your eldest. We shall bring him up as our own child, and before long he will be your support."

It was decided that his mother would move with Achille and Louis to live with her sister in St. Thomas while Charles would live with the Dionnes in Kamouraska. They auctioned their things. Charles had carefully concealed his father's Bible, but it disappeared during the sale of the household goods. He never knew if his mother relinquished it or if some of their relatives, believing it their duty, destroyed it.

Charles left on a sloop to Kamouraska while the others crossed the wide St. Lawrence River on board a schooner. It was a sad parting.

Upon his arrival, Charles told his aunt and uncle he would like to become a priest. Delighted, they arranged for him to study Latin under the vicar of Kamouraska. Beginning in 1822, he attended the College of Nicolet and completed the course in August 1829, and immediately started theological study at Nicolet. A Professor Leprohan took a liking for him, and Charles used to sit near him under the giant pines of the campus. They discussed the numerous mysteries, difficulties and responsibilities of being a priest. The professor often spoke of the difficult art of knowing the characters of the men by whom a priest is surrounded in order to become a source of blessing and usefulness to them. Charles was proud to have him for his mentor.

One day Charles asked him, "Whom do you consider the best among the ecclesiastics and professors who have labored under you while you were director of Nicolet College these past twenty years?"

The Rev. Leprohan gave the question mature consideration, and then he said, "The answer is Mr. Fluet. Never have I seen a man so gifted in all the virtues that make a good Christian and a perfect gentleman."

Charles agreed. "He was a friend of mine when he was a professor here. I remember how he was constantly referring to the New Testament."

"Yes, his knowledge as a theologian and a philosopher was above everything I have seen among my acquaintances. To those moral qualities, the good providence of God has given him some of the highest physical qualities of the body. He was the most handsome man at the college."

Charles added, "And his was one of the sweetest and most melodious voices."

The Rev. Leprohan agreed. "He was one of our most accomplished professors. When he left for Sandwich, we felt very sad indeed. We comforted ourselves that he was doing vast missionary work in west Canada."

Reflecting on that conversation, Charles recalled further that two days later he met The Rev. Leprohan coming from the mail line.

"My God," the professor cried. "This is not possible. It cannot be! I have just received the most deplorable news about Mr. Fluet. Remember we talked of him only a few days ago?"

"Of course. What is the news?"

"You could never guess it."

After a moment's thought, Charles said, "The most incredible and saddest news that can come to me is the Mr. Fluet has become an apostate and that he has turned Protestant."

"This is most strange," replied the professor. "You are correct. Fluet is an apostate. He has just publicly abandoned our holy religion." He added with sadness. "He declares himself to be a Protestant"

The news spread rapidly all over Canada. No French Canadian Roman Catholic priest had left the church for 60 years. The humble people of the country as well as the highly educated of the city had come to the conclusion that their religion of Rome was on such sure foundations nothing could shake it.

Little did Charles dream back in 1831 during his college days that less than 25 years later he would join his old college friend as an apostate, outcast from the Church Rome, not yet accepted by the ranks of Protestantism.

Charles wondered if Professor Leprohan was still living and if so, what his reaction would be to the news about Charles' break with the Church of Rome. Had he, perhaps, suspected that his young friend, always so questioning, might someday question too much? Charles had often been chastened because of his questioning attitude in and out of the seminary classroom.

His mentor cautioned him. "I have repeatedly warned you against the habit you have of listening to your own frail reasoning when you should only obey as a dutiful child. Were we to believe you, we would immediately set ourselves to work to reform the Church, throw all our theological books in the fire and have new ones written, better adapted to your fancy. What does all this prove?"

Charles did not answer.

The professor continued, "Only one thing and that is that the devil of pride is tempting you as he has tempted all reformers and destroyed them as he will you. If you do not take care, you will become another Luther."

He shook his finger at Charles. "Do you not see the danger of your position? On one side are all our holy popes and ten thousand learned Catholic bishops, all our learned theologians and priests, backed up by our two hundred million Catholics drawn up in an innumerable army to fight the battle of the Lord. On the other side, what do I see? Nothing but my small, though very dear, Chiniquy.

"Is it not just as absurd for you to try to reform the church by your small reasons as it is for a grain of sand which is found at the foot of the great mountain to try to turn that mighty mountain from its place or the small drop of water to attempt to throw the boundless ocean out of its bed or try to oppose the tides of the Polar seas? Take my friendly advice, my son, before it is too late. Let the small grain of sand stay at the foot of the majestic mountain! Let the humble drop of water consent to follow the irresistible current of the boundless sea, and everything will be in order."

Charles, the man, pulled himself from the dreams of his past and started home. Dusk lingers long in Illinois in early September, and night was slowly closing in as Charles locked his office door and left the church. He kept his office locked to protect records and correspondence, but the church doors were never locked. Any parishioner was welcome to stop in for a few moments' contemplation and prayer.

He headed across the church lawn toward home. Instead of going past his stable and grape arbor, he took a route he often chose through the cemetery bordering the church. In the six years he had pastured his flock, he had comforted many mourners whose loved ones, including infants and children, lay in the burial ground under markers bearing assorted epitaphs, some very simple, some more elaborate

He moved from gravestone to gravestone. It was getting so dark he could not read the names. No matter. He knew them all, anyway. He wondered if the dead were alive if they would have joined with him or against him. Some, he suspected, would have been against him judging from the actions of their heirs. Indeed, he would not put it past Will Amiot and Jess Leveque to disinter their parents and move them elsewhere, out of the bailiwick of the devilish apostate, as they called him.

Chapter VII
The New Housekeeper

With saddened heart, he turned toward his house, which looked, dark and uninviting with no welcoming lamp.

He had often said, "There is no greater happiness for a man than approaching a door of his home at the end of the day knowing someone on the other side of the door is waiting for the sound of his footsteps."

He would miss Miss Amiot's cheery presence. He let himself in and touched a match to the kerosene lamp in the kitchen. On the table was a note left by one of his flock, Mrs. Saidon, telling him she had put a pot of barley-vegetable soup on the back of the stove. Her note rested on a plate of gaufres, the sweet waffle-like cookies the French women made so often. He smiled as he read the note, happy that Mrs. Saidon's cooking ability far exceeded her ability to write and spell.

He had thought he was not hungry, but he ate two bowls of the hearty soup. He restricted himself to one cookie. The slenderness of his youth was a thing of the past, and he had learned that over-indulging in the rich, buttery gaufres stretched his waistline. The women of his parish were always trying to feed him. French women are noted for their cooking. His Ste. Anne parishioners were no exception.

After his meal, he walked down the street to talk with the Allards. They were sitting on their front porch talking to two other persons. A lighted lamp in the front window threw a shadowy light on the porch.

When he drew close, he was glad to see the visitors were Achille and Lucy. He felt they would champion his cause.

They welcomed him warmly and insisted on getting a chair for him, but he said he was only going to stay a moment and sat down on the top step. He quickly got to the reason for his visit.

"You know, of course, Miss Amiot is no longer my housekeeper as of today," he said.

"Yes," replied Bernice Allard. "We heard that. I guess her father really forced her to make that decision."

Lucy spoke up with disgust. "Seems to me she's old enough to make her own decisions. She must be almost 35."

"Nonsense," said Achille, goading her. "You women all need a man, be it father or husband, to tell you what to do."

Charles was used to their bickering. Lucy had a tendency to be a woman suffragette, much to Achille's chagrin. Charles rather admired her for it.

Hastening to forestall a full-blown argument, he said, "Whether she decided herself or had her decision made for her does not concern me. What concerns me is I need a housekeeper. Bernice, do you suppose Euphemie would consider taking the job?"

Bernice, seldom without words, was speechless, but only for a moment.

"Euphemie? Our Euphemie? Oh, I don't think so. She's caring for Evaloe and Marie's children. She is putting them to bed right now. We are keeping them here, you know. Poor darlings!"

"Yes, I know. What a blessing for Evaloe to have such dear relatives. But I understand he is planning to add an ell on his father's farmhouse and move in with his parents."

"Oh, is that right?" asked Joe. "We hadn't heard that. Seems odd he did not mention it. He came by here only yesterday and asked us if Euphemie could keep house for him and care for his children."

Lucy laughed. "Seems Euphemie is everyone's choice for housekeeper. Does she get any say in the matter?"

"Of course she does. Evaloe may not decide to do that, but his father told me today he hoped they could work things out. I think Ed Morais is having trouble making ends meet with all those mouths to feed."

Joe Allard asked, "So now he wants three more to feed?"

Charles explained. "Evaloe's salary would help pay for the food they don't raise on the farm. The older children could watch over Mina and Stephen during the day, and Evaloe could be with them at night. When Marie gets better, her children will be close enough to visit. When she improves enough, God willing, to be released, it will be handy for her to have the older children help with her little ones."

Achille said, "I can't believe Ed Morais figured that out all by himself. Charles, did you have a hand in those arrangements?"

"Well, Ed did discuss the plan with me, and it seems like a good one. If it works out, Evaloe won't need Euphemie to care for his children. If and when that happens, do you think she would consider working for me?"

"Euphemie would be perfect for the job," Lucy said definitely. "She's good looking, educated and a lovely girl."

"I agree she is all those things," said Bernice with pride. "But, Father, do you think she is mature enough for that position. You have so many important visitors."

"Absolutely. She will make a charming hostess."

Charles felt Euphemie's mother could be easily won over, especially since her good friend, Lucy, had voiced her approval. He decided to work on Joe by assuring him that he would hire additional help for Euphemie to do the laundry, cleaning and extra cooking for guests. He hinted that her salary over and above her room and board would be more than she could earn elsewhere. He also promised that Euphemie would have access to any horse and buggy in his stable any time she or her parents wanted to use them. John Mason, his capable groomsman, would have all responsibility for the care of the horses and the stable

Euphemie had tiptoed down the stairs and sat on the bottom step within earshot of the front porch. She heard her father's promise to think about the matter for a day or two.

She heard Achille say, "Charles, you won't keep Euphemie long. A girl like her will soon get married."

To Euphemie's amazement and embarrassment, her mother confessed, "I've really prayed about that, but Euphemie doesn't seem to be interested in any young man. I even made a novena in her behalf this year because she is 23 and still unmarried."

Euphemie held her breath. If ever Father Chiniquy were going to betray her by letting it slip about Evaloe and her, this would be the time.

Instead, he said, ""I will be glad to have her as long as she wants to stay." Changing the subject, he asked Joe, "Did Achille tell you about our plan to go to Kankakee City and break all ties with the Church of Rome?"

Strangely enough, it was Achille, the impetuous one, who offered a word of caution.

"Charles, are you sure that is what you want to do? You will make many enemies. Enemies don't bother me much, but then I am not a priest."

"It looks as I am not a priest either," Charles said dryly. "I shall never be able to give you any idea of my sadness when I consider that I am opposed by my bishop and the whole clergy in the reform I consider the only plan of salvation. I will admit I was frightened at first, not only by the wrath of the clergy who will hunt me down, but still more of the ridicule of the whole country which will overwhelm me in case of failure. God alone knows the tears I have shed, the long sleepless nights I have passed in studying, praying and meditating on the scriptures"

Euphemie was surprised to hear him admit wrestling with his decision. He always seemed so sure of himself. Rather than being disappointed in him, she found herself liking him better. Perhaps he did not regard her as a ninny for her irresolute behavior, after all.

He continued, "I feel God is in my favor, and I will succeed in this reform."

Therein lay the difference between him and her. He considered the consequences, prayed about them, made up his mind and went forward confidently. How she envied his strength and confidence!

Achille prophesied, "You'll become the Luther of Illinois. Look what you did for the cause of temperance at Beauport. At the beginning, what could have seemed a more hopeless cause?"

"How did that all get started?" asked Joe. "I remember the big bonfires and the parades, but I never did hear about the beginning. Did you request being sent to Beauport?"

"No, just the opposite. Many times, I had said to the other priests, when talking about our choice of different parishes, I would never consent to be curate of Beauport. That suburb of Quebec was too justly considered the very nest of drunkards of Canada, and what a shame! It is a beautiful area with fertile soil, inexhaustible lime quarries and forests near at hand to furnish wood to nearby Quebec City, but the people were classed among the poorest, most ragged and wretched of Canada. Almost every cent they were getting at the market went into the hands of the saloonkeepers. The Rev. Mr. Bewgin, who was their cure since 1825, had accepted the moral principles of the great Roman Catholic 'Theologia Liguouri,' which says a man is not guilty of the sin of drunkenness so long as he can distinguish between a small pin and a load of hay."

Euphemie, still sitting unobserved on the stairs, almost gave herself away by giggling.

Achille chuckled, "A small pin and a load of hay? Yes, I would say a man is really drunk if he cannot make that distinction."

"In September of 1838," Charles continued, "I received a letter from my bishop appointing me bishop of Beauport. I appealed but in vain. I was told I had already disappointed my superiors by refusing to become the first bishop of Oregon. I was made to feel that I had committed a sin by obstinately refusing that post, and God, as a punishment, had given me the very parish for which I felt such repugnance."

"But you really cleaned up that place," Achille said proudly.

"I had not been there three months when I decided to organize a temperance society. I not only prayed almost night and day during many months, but I studied the best books written in England, France and the United States on the evils of intoxicating drink. I also took a pretty good course in anatomy in the Marine Hospital under the learned Dr. Douglas. The temperance reformation grew and spread throughout Canada. To praise me for such work seems a kind of blasphemy when it was so visibly the work of the Lord," Charles said modestly.

"The other clergymen did not appreciate what your were doing, did they?" asked Lucy.

"No, they did not. The press, both French and English, were unanimous in their praise. But when the Protestants of Quebec were blessing God for that reform, the French Canadians, at the example of their priests, denounced me as a fool and heretic.

"I sent messages to four of the neighboring curates requesting them to come and see what the Lord was doing, but they refused. The indignation of the bishop knew no bounds. In fact, he referred to the reform as a ridiculous temperance society. He said, 'Had you compromised yourself alone by that Protestant comedy—for it is nothing but that—I would remain silent, in my pity for you. But you have compromised our holy religion by introducing a society whose origin is clearly heretical. Last evening, the venerable Grand Vicar DeMars told me that you would sooner or later become a Protestant and that this was your first step.'"

"Perhaps DeMars was a prophet," said Achille.

"I answered the bishop by saying, ""About the prophecy of Mr. DeMars, that I have taken my first step toward Protestantism, my only answer is that the Protestants alone praise me when the Roman Catholics priests condemn me. To me, that proves that Protestants, on this question, understand the Word of God and have more respect for it than we Roman Catholics. Instead of remaining on the lowest step of the ladder of one of the most Christian virtues, temperance, we must raise ourselves to the top where Protestants are reaping so many precious fruits."

Lucy was intrigued by the story. "Did things soon change in Beauport?"

"Yes, the public aspect of the parish changed considerably. Debts were paid, the children were well clad, seven thriving saloons were closed and their owners forced to take other jobs. Peace, happiness, abundance and industry took the place of fighting, blasphemies and squalid misery. We opened the seventh school and from that day on the children of Beauport have received a good education. "

"You must have been proud." Bernice commented.

"For me Beauport had turned into an earthly paradise, and there was only one desire in my heart—that I should never be removed from it."

"Then why did you go to Kamouraska?" asked Joe.

" I was sent there."

Bernice asked, "Wasn't Kamouraska your birthplace? Surely you liked going back there as a priest."

He sighed. "It was not that I loved Kamouraska less, but that I loved Beauport more," he paraphrased Shakespeare's Brutus. Euphemie recognized the quotation and wished she could let him know she shared that knowledge with him.

Charles stood up. "I must be going. Let me know Euphemie's decision as soon as you can."

Bidding them good night and God bless he left them, his mind turning quickly to the days ahead while those he left on the porch continued to reminisce about Beauport.

Joe asked, "Remember how we used to go to Beauport to see those bonfires?"

"Oh, yes," recalled his wife. "The merchants took all their barrels of rum, beer, wine and brandy to the city square and set fire to them. The men, women and children gathered round to shout and sing."

"I liked it," Achille added, 'when the merchants gave Charles an axe to chop up the last barrel of rum."

"The noise," said Bernice, "of the crackling barrels mixed with the raging fire was scary."

Lucy had not found it so. She said proudly, "But people really rallied round Charles. Over 40,000 signed the petition for him to present to Parliament to make rum sellers responsible for the damage caused families of drunkards. People in carriages and on horseback went to meet him as he rode into town and those on foot brought tree branches to form an arch for him to travel through."

Bernice nodded. "He well deserves the title 'Apostle of Temperance' given him by the Bishop of Montreal."

Euphemie had seen the Column of Temperance erected halfway between Quebec City and Montmorency Falls. She knew it had been blessed by a bishop from France, but she had never heard the other stories. She was overcome with timidity and was fearful she could never serve such a great and important man.

Stephen cried out in his sleep. She stole back up the stairs to comfort him. He went back to sleep at once. She was tempted to go to her parents and tell them she simply could not be Father Chiniquy's housekeeper. But then, she reasoned, they would wonder how she knew about it. She decided to wait until they mentioned it.

She undressed, put on her nightgown and robe and braided her long auburn hair. Looking at herself in the mirror over the dresser, she wondered if she dared accept the job. Father Chiniquy had said he was positive she could do it. Did he really think she was capable or was he trying to save her from her longing for her cousin's husband? He had suggested that their feeling for each other was something other than romance, a drawing together of two people who shared the care of a very sick woman and her two dependent children.

It was more than that, she knew, at least for her. So many things about Evaloe thrilled her—the smell of his clothing when she gathered it for the wash, the tanned firmness of his muscular forearms, his large hands so capable with a saw and hammer and yet so tender and loving when hugging his children, the merry twinkle in his brown eyes when Stephen did something funny. Could it be she was ready for love, and Evaloe, a lonely man whose loving wife had turned against him, was an object on which she could shower her heretofore-unexplored emotions? Was his response truly romantic, or was she reading love into a response that was merely gratitude. Perhaps, he, like her mother, thought of her as an old maid. Was age 23 too old for an infatuation?

Whether their love for each other was real or a thing of her imagination, it must never be expressed or exposed. She must do everything in her power to keep it from flowering. She must think of Evaloe as only a good friend, husband of her cousin and father to Mina and Stephen. If he moved to his father's farm, the children would no longer be her concern. She must find something else to do.

Despite her mother's novena in her behalf, Euphemie found none of the unmarried young men in the village the least bit attractive. Evaloe spoiled them for her. Her love for him was like a disease, something that had come upon her unbidden. It filled almost every waking moment, day and night. In the sunshine and in the darkness she thought of him. Day by day, minute by minute, she was obsessed with her love for him. Was she to go on forever like this, or was there a cure? Had Father Chiniquy found an antidote?

She knelt beside her bed and prayed for guidance in the decision she knew her parents would put before her the next day. She was beginning to believe Father Chiniquy's offer might be her salvation. Had she heard what her parents and their friends were saying on the front porch, she might have wondered if she were jumping from the frying pan into the fire.

Achille remarked, "Charles has had some really rough times. Somehow, I think this is going to be the biggest challenge. He's up against a powerful group."

"All will turn out all right," said Lucy confidently. "Remember when he was on trial because that priest's sister made those awful false accusations about his amorous immoral advances toward her? We thought when they moved the trial to Urbana, he would be ruined."

"Abraham Llincoln saved him from that. I was so relieved when he could prove she had been paid to lie. What a wonderful lawyer!" Bernice commented.

Joe observed, "Charles has been fortunate in his choice of lawyers. When he was accused last year of setting fire to the Bourbonnais church, without a good lawyer, he could have been convicted no matter how innocent. Instead the priest who accused him was sent to jail."

Lucy got up. " We could sit here and talk all night about Charles' eventful life, but we must be going."

She kissed Bernice.

"Tell Euphemie we think she ought to accept Charles' offer."

Achille added his approval. They walked with arms entwined down the wooden sidewalk to their home three doors away.

After they left, Euphemie's parents contented themselves with the idea that the charges against Charles were but fabrications of his enemies to hurt his honor and his standing in the church and in the community. Since he had been exonerated from all charges, they saw no reason to worry.

Their typical French awareness of a bargain too good to pass by told them that the offer to be Father Chiniquy's housekeeper was a fine opportunity for their daughter. She had been reared in good schools in Canada. She deserved a better lot than scrubbing and cooking in some other woman's cabin or cottage. The parsonage had a large library, lovely artwork, beautiful furniture, a well-stocked larder and new stables for excellent horses. Since many of Father Chiniquy's visitors were young, unmarried seminary students, his home would be a place where Euphemie could meet some nice young man to marry.

The Allards had no way of knowing that the new reform would attract religious leaders from all parts of the United States and from foreign countries as well. Had they known, they may have felt the responsibility would be too great and the exposure to such radical ideas too dangerous for their daughter.

Chapter VIII
Plans for the Party

Euphemie's parents helped her move into the big house. Evaloe had taken the children to his mother's home two days earlier. If he noticed that Ephemie was cool and reserved toward him, he did not let on. She promised to visit Mina and Stephen often. They left without a backward glance, eager to get out to the farm and play with the new kittens. Euphemie was glad to see them happy, but their eagerness to be on their way made her sad. She wondered if Evaloe was going to miss her. After wishing her well in her new position and thanking her for all she had done for the children, he, too, left without looking back.

Her room in the parsonage was off the kitchen on the ground floor. It was good-sized, about 14 feet square with an alcove large enough to hold her clothing as well as store the wooden tub she used for bathing. She found a place near the window for the sewing machine her mother had insisted she bring with her. Sewing for her was a pleasure, not a chore. Since she was 15, she had made her mother's dresses, her father's shirts and all her own clothing. Not every household had a sewing machine. Euphemie was glad she didn't have to sew everything by hand.

Father Chiniquy, knowing he would be away for the day making preparations for the trip to Kankakee City to break with the Church of Rome, had shown her the house the day before. She had been to parties there but had never toured the house. It was so much finer than any of the other homes in the village there was no comparison. He had sent to New

England for the plans, and the best craftsmen in the village contributed their skills to make their pastor's home a real showplace.

The great room in the center of the ground floor ran the length of the house and was over 15 feet wide. Serving as a hallway, it could also be converted to a large dining hall. On each sidewall were two tables with drop leaves flanked by chairs upholstered in flowered velvet.

"When we have a big party," Father Chiniquy explained, "we move these tables together and add extra leaves as necessary for the size of the crowd to form one big table. That way. we turn this hall into a banquet room."

The second floor rooms opened off a mezzanine that ran around the great hall. From the floor of the hall one could look upward past the mezzanine to the very top of the house.

"Did you ever see anything like this?"

He was like a little boy showing off his toys. In the ceiling was a big skylight with panes that could be slid open by means of long braided cords to permit fresh air and sunshine to filter to the open space 20 feet below. The walls of the mezzanine were hung with beautifully framed pictures and tapestries done by artists he casually mentioned. None of the names meant anything to Euphemie. She resolved to learn about art and artists.

The second floor was reached by two stairways—a sweeping carpeted one from the great hall and a narrow one with a carpet runner on the treads leading up from the kitchen. The master bedroom had polished oak floors partially covered with a multi-colored rug. The predominant color of the room's furnishings was red. The four-poster bed and the armoire were made of black oak. The huge armoire had doors of plate glass mirrors with side mirrors like wings folded back on brass hinges against the sides of the armoire.

"If I need a three-way view," he explained, "I just unhook the back edge of these side mirrors and swing them out to combine with the front one for a full-length all-around reflection."

When he demonstrated how it worked and moved her so she could see her reflection, Euphemie was embarrassed to find she looked very broad from the rear. She mentally resolved to eat less. She was particularly fascinated with his bathtub designed by one of his friends in Montreal.

It stood in a small room by itself except for a little heating stove and a peculiar looking pump.

"This is how it works," he said. "I bring several jugs of water upstairs—one of cold water and the others filled with warm water from the cook stove reservoir. I attach a jug at a time to this petroleum pump. It pumps the water up this pipe and sprays it down over me in the tub. I always finish with a jug of cold water."

Euphemie shivered and laughed.

"Would you like one" he asked. "I could send for one for you, and it would be here within a month. You would really enjoy it. The warm waters tumbling down over the body are so relaxing."

She blushed as she and he shared a mental picture of her nude body being rained on by the overhead sprinkler. In boarding school she had been taught it was immodest to take a tub bath without a bath gown spread over the tub to cover all but a girl's head.

"No, no, no," she insisted. "I brought my own wooden tub from home."

"As you wish," he said. "See this pipe that leads out the window to the lawn below? I dip the water from the tub into this trough-like container and it flows on down to the lawn. In the water I put a few of these metal disks with scripture references printed on them. They, too, flow down to the lawn. I encourage the children to look for the disks when they come to church. They take them home, look up the passages, memorize them, and then they return to recite the verses for me and exchange the disks for coins."

"What a clever way to get the children to learn scripture!"

"They like it. I like it, too. Helps me get acquainted with the children and helps them get acquainted with me."

The kitchen was well equipped, and Miss Amiot had left everything in excellent order. The walls beside the stove were lined with shelves. The shelves on the side by the cellar stairs were bigger and farther apart than the ones toward the window. On these shelves were placed every material used for cooking, all the table and cooking utensils and all the articles used in housework. They were so arranged that with one or two steps the cook could reach all the things she needed.

"Most kitchens have just the one window, but our plan called for two windows making for a better circulation of air in warm weather by having one open at the top and the other at the bottom. You will notice the light is better for working here."

The flour barrel almost filled the closet. Beside it was a form for cooking with a molding board laid on it. One side of the board was used for preparing vegetables and meat; the other for molding bread. The sink had a pump for well water and another for rainwater. There were shelves for storing cornmeal, white and brown sugar and a tin of molasses with a tight cover and a cork in the spout. A small cooking tray near the stove held pepper, salt, and a knife and a big spoon.

Euphemie could hardly believe all this was to be hers to use and maintain.

The day after Euphemie moved in, Lucy Chiniquy came to call. Euphemie had always thought of her as her mother's friend. She was a likeable, lusty sort of woman, a perfect wife for the adventuresome Achille. Euphemie felt an almost reverential awe for this woman who seemed to rise above every storm of life.

From the first day in the parsonage, Lucy became Euphemie's friend and not just a friend of her mother. Despite the difference in their ages, Lucy insisted that she be called by her first name. In moments of close camaraderie, she called Euphemie "Euph" or "Phemie." The younger woman had never had a nickname before, and she found it awkward at first.

Women of entirely different temperaments and age often form firm beautiful friendships by working together on projects that require their utmost effort and talent. Such a project sprang full-blown into the new Lucy-Euphemie relationship. Father Chiniquy and Achille announced ever so casually that the 15 men chosen to go to the courthouse with them on Thursday, two days away, would be returning for supper at the parsonage. Father said he had told them to bring along their wives and children, a group of about 50 in all. Many others were to go along, but only 50 would be invited to the supper.

"Only 50!" Euphemie was panic-stricken, but Lucy was undismayed. She led the way to inspect the pantry supplies and the contents of the milk house. She prepared an order for Achille to take to the farmer who supplied their table with milk, butter, eggs and farmer's cheese. She told Euphemie that Father Chiniquy at one time kept a cow to supply him with those items, but he sold it to pay lawyers for his defense in a legal action brought against him a year or so before.

"You are lucky," she said. "You won't have to milk the cow or churn butter."

"Lucky indeed!" thought Euphemie. She hated cows.

Back in the kitchen, Lucy asked, "Euphemie, how are you at baking pies? We will need about a dozen."

"Terrible," admitted Euphemie. "I confess I haven't made a dozen pies in my whole life. Mama almost always makes the pies at our house. She taught me how, but I cannot do it today, not a dozen."

"Then let's ask your mother to do it for us."

Euphemie hesitated.

Lucy said, "I'll ask her."

Euphemie was surprised later to learn how flattered her mother was to be asked.

Lucy said she would boil beans and bake them and also bake ten loaves of bread. She thought they ought to serve smoked pork from the smokehouse and use maple syrup to candy yams they found in the fruit cellar.

When Lucy left, Euphemie went to her room to finish unpacking. One of the sweaters she had worn at Evaloe's house held the familiar pungent odor of pine shavings and varnish, an odor that filled Evaloe's house whenever he worked in the lean-to shop next the kitchen where he fashioned fiddles in his spare time. Euphemie had loved to hear him whistle the merry French tunes of *Alouette* and *Sur Le Pont* as he worked, almost as if he were impregnating the tunes into the pine sounding boards. He could fashion beautiful fiddles, molding the curved edges with his strong big hands that strangely enough could deftly fashion the delicate fiddle bridges.

Euphemie had taken violin lessons at the Academy in Montreal and she, on occasion, played a tune on her neighbor's fiddle. The fiddle was the Frenchman's music maker. Seldom was there a picnic or family get-together without one or more fiddlers there to liven the evening.

Evaloe's fiddles were in big demand, but the price he could get for them was far too little for the amount of time it took to make them. He would have liked earning his living at fiddle making. However, he found it necessary to chop trees into planks and build them into houses during the day. He took time for fiddle making only at night. As he cut wood during the day, he set aside the choice pieces of pine for the sounding boards and the supplest strips of maple for the curved frames. He said the virgin timber made fine fiddles.

Euphemie embraced the sweater, burying her nose in the fragrant yarn. She was both chagrined and grateful that she had not thought about Evaloe at all that afternoon. "This busy life will be good for me," she thought to herself. Remembering how quickly she had become involved, she add ruefully, "But I didn't really expect to be entertaining 50 people for supper two days after I moved in."

Chapter IX
Sharp Tongues

On the day of the hearing, Lucy invited Euphemie to go with Achille and her to Kankakee City, but Euphemie felt duty bound to supervise the activities in her kitchen although Father Chiniquy had engaged two women to help cook, serve and wash the dishes.   The crowds began to assemble at nine o'clock. By ten, a large group in their buggies had gathered around the church.

Euphemie walked over to the churchyard to watch the departure. Evaloe was there. Just being near him and hearing his voice filled her with longing. Composing herself, she inquired sedately in the presence of others about the children and Marie.

So many people arrived to accompany the pastor and his committee, Euphemie began to wonder if there would be anyone left in the village. Before departure, Father Chiniquy quieted the crowd and explained again the purpose of the trip and expressed gratitude that so many had made the momentous decision to join him in his break with the Church of Rome.

He told them that upon their return he wanted them to bring their rosaries, crucifixes and prayer books and pile them in a huge pile on the corner of the church cemetery. The cross from the top of the church steeple and the confessional box were already chopped up and ready to be tossed on the bonfire, which would be lit at dusk. There was no sadness or regret in his voice. He had made his decision and was going forward with his plans completely convinced he was in God's favor. Euphemie marveled at the man's confidence and audacity.

His enthusiasm was contagious. The crowd took off in high spirits as if headed for a carnival. Euphemie could not believe that so few shared her misgivings. She was torn between her loyalty to her new employer, who was also her pastor and family friend, and her inbred loyalty to the symbols and teachings of the Catholic Church. She felt her life had suddenly been turned upside down and she was experiencing a bad dream.

She felt a pang of regret as Lucy and Achille went by in their buggy. Evaloe was riding with them. How she wished she had yielded to Lucy's insistence that she leave the dinner in charge of the cooks Father Chiniquy had hired for the day. As she watched, Achille stopped at the edge of the crowd and offered Emilie Soucie a ride. Euphemie bit her lip to keep from crying. She had never been in love before. Jealousy was new to her. She experienced possessiveness that she would never have thought herself capable of feeling. Why did Emilie have to go with them?

She returned to the house and checked the table setting again. Imagine having china place settings for 50! She and Lucy had found three such sets in the large pantry. They had chosen the floral pattern that looked lovely on the big table in the great hall. Father Chiniquy had said to set the children's table with the same china because this was their day, too.

"It's a day they will always remember," he predicted.

The cooks, Mrs. Fregeau and Mrs. LaCrosse, arrived about 11 to peel potatoes and put the pork roasts in the outside oven. They also brought along three bags of corn on the cob, which Lucy and Euphemie had not included on the menu. They immediately set about the task of shucking the corn. Euphemie offered to help. They didn't need her help, they insisted, so she wandered out in the yard toward the stable. The horses were carefully penned in. The stable boy had gone part way with the crowd as she remembered he had asked permission to do. She thought of hitching a buggy to the gray mare and riding out to see Mina and Stephen. She missed them so much. However, she decided she would not abandon the house to those domineering women. After all, it was her kitchen now, put under her charge by its master.

She patted the horses, fed them some sugar cubes and went back to the house to choose something to read from the library. Reading was one of her favorite things to do. She had had little time in the past few months to indulge in that luxury. It dismayed her that among all that selection she could find nothing to interest her restless mind.

She went to her room and picked up her rosary, a dainty beautiful rosary given to her on her first communion day by her grandmother. It had been a comfort through many trying times during her school days and during the long, perilous journey by covered wagon from Canada to Ste. Anne. She did not have the heart to throw it on the bonfire pile to be burned like the popping barrels of burning whiskey her father had described several nights before. She knelt beside the bed with the rosary in her hands and clicked through the beads, perhaps for the last time. If Father Chiniquy said rosaries must be burned, then they must be, hers included. She did not think it incongruous that she called upon the saints to give her courage to defy the priests she had been brought up to fear and respect.

Mrs. LaCrosse called to her to ask if Father Chiniquy had given any specific time for supper to be served. Euphemie rose from her bedside, carefully put away the rosary and went into the kitchen. Mrs. Fregeau assigned her the task of slicing bread and cutting pies.

They gossiped freely in front of her as if she were but a child and would not understand. They talked about the bonfire and mentioned that at first they were indignant that Father Chiniquy had insisted on burning perfectly good rosaries and prayer books that could be given or sold to someone else. They did not seem to share Euphemie's attachment to those things and would apparently have gladly parted with their rosaries and prayer books for a price. Her father always said a Frenchman could live a week on what a Scotsman throws away. With the Scot's reputation for thrift, that would mean the French were mighty frugal. She smiled to herself.

She stopped smiling and almost cut her finger on the sharp bread knife when Mrs. LaCross said, "Father Chiniquy is always doing something with fire. He built many big bonfires in Canada to do away with barrels and barrels of whiskey. They said you could get drunk just attending the fire and smelling the fumes. They also say, you know, that he set fire to the church in Bourbonnais when he was filling in there for that Father Cajeault."

"That was just a rumor," Mrs. Fregeau said. "Why would he do that when he put 300 dollars of his own money to finish the building? Besides, the building was not insured. What would be the point?"

"You are right. The building was not insured. I know that for a fact. Tom's brother was going to take care of the insurance on Monday. His company would not insure the building until it was completely built. Father Chiniquy, the men from Bourbonnais and some helpers from Ste. Anne finished it on Saturday night in time for the Sunday services. It burned Sunday afternoon."

Mrs. Fregeau said, "They put that priest in jail for starting the rumor about Father Chiniquy causing the fire. He was supposed to pay Father Chiniquy some money, remember? But somebody helped him escape. They say he is in Canada now. That's what the rumor is, anyway."

"There will be plenty of rumors," said Mrs.LaCrosse. "Wait until people in other towns hear about the bonfire here tonight."

"Euphemie, you might not be safe here," warned Mrs. Fregeau. "You had better have your papa teach you how to use a gun. Father Chiniquy has many enemies."

"Surely no one hates him enough to hurt him," Euphemie said. "I'm not one bit afraid."

She was thinking their wagging tongues might do more harm than anything. Despite the fact that only moments before she had questioned Father Chiniquy's demands to burn the rosaries, she now felt extremely defensive about him and resented even a hint of criticism of him from Mrs. Fregeau and Mrs. LaCrosse.

They did not linger long on the subject of Father Chiniquy, however. Their agile tongues went on to discuss other juicy bits of gossip. Euphemie was about to cut into the second apple pie when Mrs.. LaCrosse asked, "Did you see Evaloe Morais ride off with Achille and Lucy? Wasn't that Emilie Soucie with them?"

Euphemie could feel the nape of her neck getting warm. The flush spread to her cheeks.

Mrs. Fregeau replied, "Oh, I suppose with Marie in the insane asylum, he's bound to squire around some of the other girls. He's certainly a handsome devil. But I can't think why Emilie's mother is letting her run with him."

Euphemie spoke up quickly, "She isn't running with him. She is just riding in Achille Chiniquy's buggy."

She slashed the last hunk of apple pie into two wedges.

"Father Chiniquy wanted every buggy filled. They asked me to go, but I felt I was needed here since I am the housekeeper of the parsonage now," she said pointedly. She slapped down the knife, strode to the stove, inserted the shaker and gave the coals a hearty shake

"Here," cried Mrs. Fregeau. "Don't do that. We have the coals banked just right for the corn kettles."

Euphemie jerked the shaker one more time.

Mrs. LaCrosse asked in an insinuating tone, "So they asked you to go along with Evaloe? You should have gone. You two would have had a good time."

Euphemie caught the suggestive glance that passed between the two women. She wanted to slap them.

Instead, she said, "I am going out to see how the roasts are doing in the outside oven. "

She knew they resented her tending the food they had "put over," as they said, and that is why she took a long-handled fork with her to poke at the meat. They had taken over her kitchen, criticized her employer and their pastor and gossiped about her friend. They had even intimated that there was something between Evaloe and her. Or was she too sensitive on that issue? By her actions, had she indeed given them grist for their gossip mill?

While she was testing the roast, John Mason rode up at a fast pace on a black stallion. He had stationed himself as a lookout on the hill called Mt. Langham, the highest point around, located about three miles north of town on the route to Kankakee City. He announced that he had seen the caravan of buggies headed for Ste. Anne and they should be in town within an hour.

Euphemie went inside to tell the cooks the crowd was on its way. They assured her they could manage without her and suggested she go to the church to help the welcoming party on the church lawn. With mixed emotions she followed their suggestion.

She filled a ewer with warm water from the cook stove reservoir and went to her room to bathe. She changed into her new lavender checked gingham dress, backcombed her hair on the sides and reinserted the big celluloid pins. She pinched her cheeks and bit her lips to bring a little more color to her face. She smiled back at her reflection in the little mirror over her dresser. She turned eagerly to meet the caravan, eager for the news and eager for a chance meeting with Evaloe.

Chapter X
The Bonfire

A straggly group had assembled on the church lawn. Anyone who could get away had gone to Kankakee City. Of course, the families who were still faithful to the Church of Rome remained in Ste. Anne, but they stayed in their homes or on their farms. Since they had no local priest and had to be serviced by priests from St. Mary's or L'Erable, 15 miles away, they had no permanent leader. Although backed by the greatest power on earth, they were isolated in the little village and so few in number, they could cause little tempest—not at that time, anyway.

A table made by laying boards across two sawhorses had been set up on the church lawn by a few of the stay-at-home converts. Their wives had brought doughnuts and cider to serve the travelers. They dared not serve anything intoxicating because Father Chiniquy was very adamant in his rules against drinking. Euphemie suspected, though, that many a colonist had a jug or two of homemade French wine tucked away in the corner of his cellar for private medicinal or other use. Her father did, she knew.

Euphemie offered to help, but there was nothing for her to do. It seemed to her she was not really needed anywhere. She should have gone with the caravan.

At last they arrived. Euphemie was caught up in the excitement. Achille and Lucy Chiniquy's buggy was one of the first. Emilie Soucie was with them, but Evaloe was riding on a wagon with some men and boys. They were boisterously singing an old French hymn and waving banners proclaiming, "Goodbye, Church of Rome."

Euphemie was pleased to see Evaloe having a good time. Life had not been pleasant for him of late. She was doubly pleased that his companions were men and boys and not the bold Emilie Soucie.

Evaloe and his group jumped down from t he wagon and ran to Father Chiniquy's buggy. They lifted him to their shoulders and carried him triumphantly to the cider table

"Ave Father Chiniquy! Ave Father Chiniquy!" they cried.

He struggled to get down, raised his hand for silence and said, "My dear ones in Christ. Do not praise me. I am but a humble vessel of the Lord. It is to our precious Savior we owe our praise. Let us join in singing *Te Deum.*"

He sang the first phrase alone and the crowd joined in. They finished the hymn in lusty voice and waited for him to say Grace before they attacked the cider and doughnuts with gusto.

Euphemie moved back from the table and stepped on the toe of someone coming up behind her. She fell back against that person and felt herself caught against a rock of a chest and wrapped in a pair of powerful arms. Her nostrils flared at the familiar woodsy fragrance. It could be no one but Evaloe. His embrace was quick, and to the casual observer was merely a helpful steadying hand for one who had stumbled. All through her body Euphemie could feel a desire so intense she was seized by a sudden trembling. Was it her imagination or did she detect a tremor in his muscled arms? She knew she should pull away from him lest others like Mrs. LaCrosse and Mrs. Fregeau might guess her secret love.

With tenderness, he said, as he let her go, "That's my toe, you know. You should have been there. Euphemie. You should have heard Father Chiniquy. What a convincing argument he gave the judge! Our crowd filled the entire courthouse lawn."

Could it be the tremor she felt in his arms was only the stimulation of the exciting events of the day and had nothing to do with her presence?

"I wanted very much to go, but I felt I was needed here." How many times she was to say that in her life! "Was there any trouble?"

"Some. A bunch of Catholics from Kankakee City tried to block our way on the edge of town, but when they saw the size of our group, they threw a few rocks and eggs and sort of hung around on the edges. Our men were ready for them. We had crowbars and pitchforks."

"You did? Did Father Chiniquy know that?"

"Yes. He said no guns, but he did not object when he saw us loading the other weapons for self defense."

Father Chiniquy dismissed the crowd to go home to do their evening chores. He reminded them to return at dusk with their rosaries and prayer books to burn on the bonfire. Euphemie tardily remembered her responsibilities and hurried ahead of the crowd to the parsonage. The 15 committee members and their families had made arrangements to have their chores done by neighbors. They soon meandered over to the parsonage lawn.

Euphemie's resentment toward the two cooks changed to admiration and appreciation when she saw how efficiently they handled the meal service. They kept things going in the kitchen while she and Lucy waited on the tables. Father Chiniquy deferred to her on every question about the meal and complimented her in front of everyone. She felt very important. She realized, that without the expertise of the cooks in the kitchen and without Lucy's planning, she could never have managed to serve the hungry adults and noisy children. She resolved to learn how to supervise big dinners so she would truly be in charge.

She lingered in the kitchen after the meal on the pretext of helping with the dishes, but Father Chiniquy insisted that they all go, Mrs. Fregeau and Mrs. LaCrosse, as well, to the bonfire. He said the dishes could wait until later. He asked John Mason to carry some boxes he and Euphemie had packed earlier. One of them held priest's clothing he intended to toss on the bonfire. He had ordered four tailor- made suits from Chicago to replace the priestly apparel, but they were not yet ready. His one black suit, hastily made by the local tailor, had to suffice until the delivery, but that did not change his plans to publicly burn the robes he had once so proudly worn.

Euphemie, frugal person she was, had requested him to lay aside the least worn robes, suggesting that she and some of the other seamstresses of the village could make warm clothing for the school children from the fine fabric. Father Chiniquy, his practical self, ever mindful of the near poverty of his flock, winning over his dramatic self, agreed that she had a good plan. Euphemie was glad she had screwed up her courage to make the suggestion. She was proud that he acted on it without a hint that it was unseemly for her to make it. All but his oldest priestly robes were folded into boxes and sent to the sewing room. For the fire, he gathered boxes of tracts and other flammable printed materials.

By the time Euphemie made her way across the lawn to the church, twilight was beginning to lower. The sun had already disappeared from sight leaving the western sky a soft dusty rose. The cicadas were chorusing their good night anthem, a kind of plaintive, tuneless song swelling then ebbing with long silences between choruses. Euphemie, when she first came to Illinois, had imagined the woods east of the settlement to be a cathedral where the cicadas worshipped with the long pauses between choruses caused by their organist flipping through the hymnal to find the next number.

The pyramid of pine branches burned brightly. Enthusiastic young men, a few women and the children were tossing in kindling made earlier from the confessional box and the wooden cross from the church steeple. Euphemie saw her parents in the crowd and was saddened to see them approach the fire and toss in their things with no apparent hesitation or remorse.

The excitement was contagious. The pine branches crackled and popped. The chopped boards burned quickly. Convert after convert approached the fire and threw in the vestiges of their Roman Catholic religion, some making the sign of the cross from habit, some wearing looks of determination and a few looking very sad. The flames shot forth toward Heaven as if to praise God for the marvelous reformation. The smoke, a curious mixture of black almost angry clouds and white playful puffs, swirled with the changing evening breeze. As it changed directions, so, too, did the people, moving out of its range first to the right and then to the left and sometimes stepping back from the heat when the flames licked at a batch of papers and books not yet consumed. Someone was ringing the church bell, and its mellow tone pealed out over the noise of the fire. Antoinne Corriveau started singing hymns. Many joined in. Euphemie felt she was witnessing a spectacular chorus scene from a play with the singers moving to the right and to the left, the sound of their voices wafted on the same breeze that swirled the smoke. Looking across the crackling flames at the faces of the shifting crowd, she was struck with the thought that purgatory would be like that, filled with familiar faces and figures moving restlessly about trying to find a cool spot midst the crackling, popping eternal flames.

Father Chiniquy insisted there is no purgatory, but try as she might, she could not dispel the belief so instilled within her from childhood. It was not a belief she wanted to retain. How much more in keeping with her concept of God would be an afterlife with no purgatory! She was content to let the pagans burn in Hell, but for God to require his faithful to suffer the agonies of purgatory lessened only by the fervent prayers of priests and relatives seemed heartless.

She tossed her prayer book on the fire and saw the flames lick it. She gave the crucifix a last kiss and flipped it gingerly toward the fire where it fell short of the flames. She hoped against hope it might not burn. Much to her dismay, Ambrose Allain came by with a big rake and scooped all the materials at the edge into the flaming inferno. He stirred the books so their pages would catch fire.

He shouted over the noise, "Have to tidy up a bit, Euphemie. Look at those books burn. Isn't that a sight?"

She could not answer. What did he know of the heartbreak of seeing books burn? He could not read, could not even sign his name—had to use an "X" on all the deeds and legal papers that required his name. His father and brother and he were the first settlers in Ste. Anne, and they had acquired many acres of land, which they later sold to other colonists. Euphemie's father bought his land from Ambrose.

Father Chiniquy, with face uplifted to the darkening sky, joined in the lusty singing. On the last chorus of the second song, he raised his arm for attention. The crowd quieted; the sexton stilled the bell, its last tone lingering in the air and fading away just as Father Chiniquy, his powerful voice carrying beyond the fringes of the crowd, shouted in exaltation, "My dear brethren. Praise be to God. What wonderful cause for celebration we have tonight! We have broken with the Church of Rome."

The crowd cheered.

"Our fellow countrymen who saw fit not to join us have said that for us God may as well be dead. As I look out at your faces, I know that cannot be so. God is not dead. He lives in you. God loves you. You must have faith in the Lord. We need only look to Jesus Christ to show us how to discover our best selves, how to evolve for ourselves a moral code and standards. We need only follow his matchless example."

He looked around lovingly at his flock. "Peace be to you, brethren, and love with faith, from God, the Father, and the Lord Jesus Christ. This is a new concept, and for some it may be more difficult than for others. You must learn to LET GO. Turn away from symbols that men have made so important and turn to the simple salvation bought by God's own son. LET GO! Let faith take over your life. LET GO! Let God be your salvation."

With each exhortation to let go, Father Chiniquy shook out a priestly robe and tossed it on the lively flames. The robes were made of wool and at first refused to succumb to the fire; then, without bursting into flames, they began to smolder and shrivel, giving off a terrible odor of burnt wool

"What a stink!" someone cried. Everyone laughed.

Euphemie could not stand it. She ran back to the parsonage and into her newly acquired room. She fell on her knees beside her bed and prayed, repeating the prayers she usually said with her rosary. She clasped her empty hands so tightly they hurt.

She rose, rinsed her face with the last of the water in the ewer, changed into her work dress and went to the kitchen. Mrs. Fregeau and Mrs. Lacrosse found her there half an hour later busily washing dishes.

Chapter XI
Frayed Cords

The news of the Chiniquy religious reformation spread over the continents of America and Europe. Euphemie, busy learning the duties of a parson's housekeeper, was astounded at the amount of mail arriving each week. Letters of inquiry came from every denomination—Episcopalians, Methodists, Congregationalists, Baptists and Presbyterians asked for details of the reformation. Some letters were accompanied by booklets to induce Father Chiniquy to join their particular denomination. In less than six months, more than one hundred ministers of Christ and prominent church laymen of different denominations visited the parsonage, some staying a day while many others stayed a week or ten days to study for themselves the new religious movement.

Euphemie surprised herself, and her parents, by quickly becoming very efficient in meal planning and preparation as well as providing overnight accommodations for so many.

One of the first to arrive was the Right Rev. Bishop Helmuth of London, Canada. He was the learned Dean of Quebec, well loved and honored in Great Britain and Canada. He arrived the day after the bonfire. Father Chiniquy was in his study at the church. Euphemie gave the visitor a glass of cool fruit juice and left him in the library while she went to fetch her employer.

On the way to the church, she noticed something shiny on the periphery of the still smoldering ash heap of the bonfire. She kicked the object away from the ashes and bent to pick it up. It was a section of a rosary with a crucifix attached. She blew off the ashes and wiped the crucifix with her apron. It was her very own crucifix. She knew it was hers because on it were the letters "E" and "A" she had scratched the day of her first communion. She remembered getting spanked when her mother noticed the scratched initials on the beautiful little cross. She looked around and found no one nearby. She touched the crucifix to her lips and then tucked it in the bodice of her dress where it rested, still quite warm, between her breasts. It was not an unpleasant feeling. She smiled happily.

She did not find Father Chiniquy in his study so she looked in the chapel. She was glad to see that the 14 beautiful pictures—all fine works of art given to Father Chiniquy by wealthy friends in Montreal—were still hanging on the walls. They represented the Way of the Cross, and each was surmounted with a cross. Prior to the reformation, one of her favorite devotional exercises was to kneel before them and say, "Oh, Holy Cross, we adore thee." Earlier that week she heard Father Chiniquy tell Achille he might throw them on the bonfire, but Achille said he knew where he could sell them for a fine price, and the colony could certainly use the money.

She loved the paintings. She was glad to know that someone somewhere would be able to enjoy them as she had. Lucy had told her Achille thought they would eventually remove the statues of Sainte Mary and her mother, Sainte Anne; however, they felt that some of the people were still too young in the new faith to bear parting with the statues. Euphemie was almost ashamed to admit she should be included in that group.

When she entered the chapel, Father Chiniquy was standing behind the pedestals that held the statues. At first, she did not see him. Then she spied him with his pocketknife in his hand. He was bending over the cords that held the statues in place. The acoustics were good, especially since the chapel was empty.

She heard him say, "My good ladies, you must come down from your high position. God Almighty alone is worshiped here now. If you could walk out of this place, I would politely invite you to do it. But you are nothing but mute, deaf, blind, motionless idols. You have eyes yet you cannot see. You have ears yet you cannot hear. You have feet yet you cannot walk. What will I do with you now? Your reign has come to an end."

He did something to the cords. Euphemie thought for a moment he was cutting down the statues. She hid her face in her hands to keep from witnessing their fall. Nothing happened. Then she heard him say, "Now, my good ladies, take care of yourselves, especially when the chapel is shaken by the wind or the coming in of the congregation."

Not wanting him to know she had seen and heard, she tiptoed out as he climbed down from the altar. She re-entered, calling as she came in, "Father Chiniquy. Father Chiniquy."

He was near the pulpit by that time and answered, "Yes, Miss Allard. What is it?"

"You have a caller, the Rev. Helmuth from London, Canada."

"So soon? I was not expecting him until next week. Thank you. You made him comfortable, I trust."

"Yes, Father. I gave him some cool fruit juice in the library and left him looking over your collection of Bibles."

"Good!"

He hurried past her. The crucifix, nestled between her breasts seemed heavier and bulkier. She hoped he would not notice. She waited until he closed the outside door before she went down the aisle to look behind the pedestals. What had he been doing? The cords were still intact. But wait! They seemed to be badly frayed halfway up. Yes, that is what he had done. He had cut four of the six strands of the silken cords that held the statues in place. Why?

That afternoon, four more ministers arrived, two from Chicago and two from Michigan. Euphemie was busy preparing beds and meals for them She gave little thought to the cords until the following Sunday morning

She sat with her parents in their regular family pew about halfway down on the right side of the center aisle. As usual, they were early because her mother insisted on being there at least a half hour before the service began. The other worshippers arrived a few at a time and seated themselves quietly in their family pews each man had carved, some more elaborate than others, out of walnut wood from the nearby forest.

When Father Chiniquy entered the side door and approached the pulpit, the worshippers took that as a signal to fall on their knees to pray. Euphemie knelt, arranging her new pale blue moiré dress to avoid any unnecessary wrinkling or soiling. She had always been proud and careful with her clothes. Now that she was Father Chiniquy's housekeeper, she was even more particular about her appearance. She was so preoccupied she did not immediately notice the falling statues. Her first awareness was caused by the murmuring of the congregation usually so reverent and still as they waited for Father Chiniquy's prayer.

"Oh, My!" her mother whispered and crossed herself in apprehension.

Euphemie followed her mother's horrified gaze and saw the statues of Sainte Mary and Sainte Anne teetering and about to fall forward, apparently dislodged from their pedestals by the sudden motion of the worshippers falling to their knees. Euphemie watched fearfully for what seemed an eternity. The two statues rocked back and forth several times and then fell simultaneously with loud crashes and broke into fragments, parts of Ste Mary's blue gown mixing with the white fragments of Ste Anne's robe.

Like everyone else, Euphemie was startled by the crash. She was too stunned to move when others about her rose from their knees and started laughing. A flying fragment hit the back of the pew in front of the Allards. A piece of blue china fell at Euphemie's feet. She instinctively grabbed it and held it tightly in her fist.

When someone said, "How foolish and blind we were to put our trust in those saints to protect us when they cannot take care of themselves," she wiped away a tear. Two saints had fallen in front of her. That was sad enough, but sadder still was the realization of the hoax Father Chiniquy had deliberately played. He, too, fell from the pedestal on which she had placed him. She was confronted by a sudden irreparable loss of something uniquely precious. She could not measure the magnitude of the deed and was taken over by waves of nausea. She recognized that he was not a saint, merely a man of common clay not above maneuvering to make a miracle seem to happen.

When he confessed that night on her parents' front porch of having many a sleepless night wrestling with his decision to leave the Church of

Rome, she gladly accepted the knowledge that he was, on occasion, like the rest of his flock—unsure of what to do. Knowing that about him made her like him even better than before because he seemed more human. But this deed! What he did was a secret about him she would never, never in her whole life tell anyone. It was a secret that was to color her life-long relationship with this man about whom others would write in years to come, "Was he saint or devil?" Instinctively, she felt she had been spying on him, like a person on the outside of a house looking in on one who thinks he is alone. He, in his unawareness that she was watching, displayed a self no one else suspected. The feeling that she knew him better than anyone else gave her a sense of power over him that she reluctantly accepted.

Like a child who learns there are no fairies, Euphemie mourned for the saint that Father Chiniquy once was. Like the statues of the saints lying fragmented on the chapel floor, her former image of him could never be put back together again .She dropped the fragment of china clutched in her fist and was unaware it had cut her hand. Blood dripped on her new dress.

Armed with her new knowledge, she felt she must become Father Chiniquy's caretaker and shield him from his critics. If the truth were ever out, he would be ruined—ruined by the wrath of the clergy and the ridicule of the world. She alone could make or break him. With the power went responsibility. No, no one must ever know what she saw Father Chiniquy doing with his penknife that afternoon in the empty chapel. The girl became mother to the man, and in a sense, she traversed the painful passage from girlhood to womanhood.

Chapter XII
Ends of the Earth

Hardly ever was there a time when there were no overnight guests. One such evening occurred early in October. Euphemie let in two visitors, one at a time, and their visits were spaced an hour apart

The first visitor was Hector Goyette, whom she knew. He had come from Canada with his family in the same group with the Allards. He had not, however, joined in the reformation and was one of the staunch members of the Church of Rome who took their wives and children every Sunday to Ste. Mary's to worship in the Catholic Church,

Euphemie, wondering what his purpose was in calling on Father Chiniquy, led him to the library and returned to the kitchen to prepare some coffee in the event her employer called for it. She could hear Hector's loud voice. Father Chiniquy, quiet at first, raised his voice to a loud pleading tone.

Hector said belligerently, "Well, we are going and nothing you can say will stop me."

"But the trip will take you six months by wagon train. Oregon is clear over on the Pacific coast. Why don't you wait until spring?"

"It's better to travel frozen ground than mud. You taught us that when we came here from Canada in the dead of winter."

"Hector, there have been many reports of new attacks by Indians on pioneer wagons. No matter how big your wagon train is, there could be a great deal of danger and terror in store for your family. Besides that, such a trip is expensive. You will have neither job nor farm when you get there. You will ruin yourself financially."

Hector banged his fist on the wooden arm of his chair and said, "You are right when you say I will expose my life and the very existence of my family; you are also correct when you say the expense of crossing that immense territory could ruin me financially; but God knows the motives which prompt me to leave this place and go so far away. I know He will protect me."

"I wish I knew your motives."

"That is what I came tonight to tell you. So long as you were faithful to your vows and a good priest of Rome, I was among your devoted friends and nothing was more pleasing to me than your presence in my home."

"Yes, my dear Goyette, we spent many a wonderful evening together. I always enjoyed your wife's fine cooking."

"We liked your company, and we were among the most faithful to attend your church services."

"I remember it well."

"But now you are an apostate. I know very well it is your intention to make us all Protestants. My family is already shaken. I feel myself unable to answer your arguments and resist your efforts. I see only one way of escape from your influence and bad example."

"My dear Hector, for the love of God, don't go. Stay here and join us."

"Absolutely not!" Hector shouted. "I am going to put such a distance between you and me that I shall never hear any more of you. When there is a continent between us, I will have nothing to fear from your efforts."

"Oh, Hector, you are making such a mistake."

"I don't see it that way. If I lose my fortune, I shall at least have my faith. If I have to die on the plains of the West, God, who knows why I go there, will give me and my family a better life in the hereafter."

Father Chiniquy said regretfully, "Hector, I can see you have made up your mind, and we Frenchmen are pretty stubborn once we set our sights on something."

Euphemie heard him open the desk drawer, the one with the squeak, which she kept forgetting to oil.

"My dear friend Hector, please accept this Bible as a last token of our old friendship. It is a Roman Catholic Bible and you are allowed to read it by your church."

"Never! It is because you too much read this dangerous book that you are lost today. I will NEVER read it. You may keep it."

He must have started toward the door because Euphemie heard him say, "Tell Euphemie to get my hat. I am leaving here, and I hope never to see you again. I would go to the ends of the earth to get away from you,"

Father Chiniquy's voice was choked with emotion. "My dear Hector, for God's sake don't refuse such a gift. It is the very testament of our Lord Jesus Christ. Do not reject it. Take it with you."

"NEVER!"

Hector was in the foyer and he called out, "Euphemie, where did you put my hat?"

He shouted back over his shoulder to Father Chiniquy, "And don't think I am the only one. Just wait. Some of those you think most loyal are going to wake up to what a mistake they have made."

He accepted his hat from Euphemie and shook it under her nose. "And, young lady, that includes you and your mama and papa."

He stomped out of the house, slamming the door behind him.

Euphemie turned from the door and started to enter the library to ask Father Chiniquy if he wanted a cup of coffee. She hesitated at the threshold because she saw he was kneeling beside the desk holding the rejected gift in his hands. Tears rolled down his cheeks. She wanted so much to go to him and comfort him. Instinctively, she recognized that the rejection by one of his oldest friends created a deep hurt and privacy was needed to deal with it.

Would Hector's prophesy about her and her parents ever come true?. She thought not. Her father, and her mother, too, were staunch followers of Father Chiniquy. As for herself, she was loyal to him but not yet a firm believer. Perhaps she was living proof of the theory, "Give me a child and let me train him up a Catholic, and he will always be a Catholic no matter what name he takes on himself."

She walked quietly to the kitchen, placed the coffee pot on the back of the cook stove and went to her room.

Chapter XIII
Absolution Offered

Soon a knock on the front door called Euphemie to the front part of the parsonage again. She thought it might be Hector Goyette returning to apologize and accept the Bible. Instead, when she opened the door, she found herself face to face with the Rev. Mr. Mailloux, the grand vicar of the bishop. She remembered him well because he had often visited her school in Montreal. It was he who led the caravan of clergymen to Ste. Anne on that never-to-be-forgotten day when Bishop Duggan failed to persuade the wandering sheep to return to the fold.

From force of habit, she paused to genuflect before politely asking the vicar to wait in the foyer until she called Father Chiniquy. She returned with her employer. The two men—the vicar and the ex-priest—greeted each other courteously but formally. Euphemie excused herself. She was so nervous her knees trembled.

On her way to her room, she heard the Rev. Mr. Mailloux say, "I feel happy to be the bearer of a message which I hope will put an end to the awful scandals and sad divisions...." They went in the library and closed the door.

Euphemie shut the door to her room and collapsed near her bureau. She pulled open the second from the bottom drawer and fumbled through her underwear until she touched the crucifix she had hidden there. She held it to her heart and leaned her head on the open drawer. She tried to still the loud pounding of her heart.

Suddenly, she heard a rap on her door. It was Father Chiniquy.

"Miss Allard," he called.

"Yes, Father." She opened the door.

He said, "I forgot to tell you Mrs. Morais asked if you could go out see Mina and Stephen this evening. John will hitch up the buggy for you. Try to get back before dark."

At any other time, Euphemie would have gone eagerly to the Morais farm, but she longed to know what the Rev. Mailloux wanted. Had he come to invite Father back to the Church of Rome? If so, would he go? He had seemed rather glad to see the vicar. She wondered what she wanted him to do. Until that moment, she would have said, "Go back. Go back." For some reason, she was filled with ambivalent feelings. Is that the way a mother feels, she wondered, when her man child must reach a momentous decision?"

Mina was playing in the farmyard with Evaloe's young sister when Euphemie arrived. Stephen was ready for bed. They were delighted to see her. Mrs. Morais looked surprised when Euphemie told her Father Chiniquy had delivered her message, but she, too, was glad to see Euphemie.

She said, "Mina really misses you. She talks about you all the time."

Euphemie cried out silently, "Does Evaloe miss me? Does he ever talk about me?"

She hugged Mina and Mina gave her a big wet kiss. Stephen was a darling baby, and Euphemie loved him dearly; but Mina was her favorite. Evaloe was still working on the addition to his father's house, and he worked until there was no more daylight. Euphemie lingered a little longer than she should have so she could talk with him. It was a joy to watch him work, the muscles of his strong back rippling under his homespun shirt wet with sweat. When she said she had to go, he insisted on riding his horse ahead of her buggy until she got to the parsonage drive. Mina rode with her and returned with Evaloe on his horse.

There was no time for a word alone or a caress, but it was an evening Euphemie enjoyed and she thought Evaloe liked it, too. Was that to be her lot in life, a few casual moments snatched now and then with another woman's man? Why couldn't she have met Evaloe first? Marie could have had any number of suitors. She would never have missed him.

In parting, Mina begged her to return often to the farm.

Evaloe said, "Please do." Then he added, "The children miss you, Euphemie."

"And, you, Evaloe, do you miss me?" she was afraid to ask.

The Rev Mr. Mailloux had left. Father Chiniquy was sitting at the kitchen table drinking coffee.

He said, "Oh, I am glad to see you are back. No trouble, I hope."

"None at all."

He apologized. "I am sorry to have made up that story about Mrs. Morais. I could see the vicar wanted to be alone with me. I suspected the reason for his visit. He asked me to return to the Church of Rome. I remember when it fell my lot to make that offer to Mr. Fluet, who had been my teacher at Nicolet College."

"This Mr. Fluet was…" she fumbled for the word. She could not bring herself to say "apostate." It sounded so evil!

"An apostate like me? Yes. It was back in 1831, before you were born, as a matter of fact. I had two more years at seminary when I learned that he left the Church of Rome. He was a missionary in western Canada at the time. He was the first French Canadian Roman Catholic priest in 60 years to leave the church.

"Twenty years later, in the spring of 1851, I was headed for Illinois. The Bishop of Chicago had asked me to come to Illinois to direct the tide of French speaking emigrants from France, Belgium and Canada in order to form a New France. The Bishop of Montreal asked me to stop on my way to Illinois at Sandwich on the River St. Clair near the United States border. I was to try to get Mr. Fluet to go back to the church. I reminded the good bishop that Fluet was married."

"Married? A priest married?"

"Remember he no longer considered himself a priest. He was married and had three children. I told the bishop we could not invite him to abandon that woman and the children to starve to death. It was decided to offer him $10,000, which I took with me.

"It is customary, then, to invite…ah…apostates to change their minds?" Euphemie asked.

"Oh, yes. The Rev. Mr. Brassard, curate of Longuieul, accompanied me as far as Sandwich. There we learned from the judge of Sandwich that

Mr. Fluet earned extra money to augment his clergyman's small salary by serving as a notary and working for the judge, a Catholic. The judge believed that were Mr. Fluet alone, our job would have been easy because, though a Protestant and an apostate, Mr. Fluet once or twice a week sent bouquets from his beautiful flower garden to be put on the altar of the Catholic Church."

"He did that?"

Father Chiniquy seemed to think it was all right for an apostate to send flowers every week for the altar of the Catholic Church. Surely he would not be too angry that she, a mere follower, had found and treasured her scorched crucifix.

"That is what the judge told us. He also said that Mr. Fleut's wife, a most honorable woman, would fight like a lioness to tear the hand that would take her children from her or deprive her of her husband."

'Did you meet her?"

"No, we did not. We approached Mr. Fluet. He was not surprised to see us. He was surprised we had waited so long. He said he would not make a decision without consulting his wife. The next day, he returned to say he could not break the happy ties of married life and fatherhood. His wife, when told of the money, had said, 'Go tell them there isn't enough gold in Canada, nor in the whole world, to tempt me to trample under my feet the blessed crown of wife and motherhood which the great God has given me.'"

"She must have loved him very much," said Euphemie, thinking she could love Evaloe that much.

"Yes, he was in that respect a very fortunate man."

He drank some coffee before he said, "The Reverend Mr. Mailloux tonight spoke of the honors and dignities I received while a priest and said he had been sent with the promise that the venerable bishops will do still more for me if I go back and submit as a dutiful priest. He asked my forgiveness for what he and the Bishop of Chicago have done to me. He assured me he is still my friend."

":Oh, I am so glad."

"I would not be honest were I to deny his words made a profound impression on me. My poor human and sinful heart was not indifferent to the honors, dignities and riches which would be in store for me the rest of my life if I were to accept the message of peace from the Roman Catholic bishops of Canada."

Euphemie was embarrassed by his frank discussion of his innermost feelings. She went to the cupboard for a cup and poured herself some coffee at the stove. The cream and sugar were on the table, but she hesitated to reach for them. She took a sip of the black coffee that was so strong she shuddered.

"Here," he said, rising gallantly. "Sit down and help yourself to the cream and sugar."

She realized he had been through two emotional interviews that evening—first Hector Goyette and then the Rev. Mr. Mailloux. She was flattered that he trusted her enough to unburden himself in her presence. She hoped she could fulfill his needs. Strangely enough, she was not uncomfortable in the reverse role of counselor.

He went on, convincing himself as well as her that he had made the right decision, "I would have fallen prey to the Tempter had not the dear Savior come to my aid. At that moment, a grand solemn divine spectacle struck the eyes of my soul. I saw my Savior on the summit of the high mountain where the devil had taken Him to show Him all the kingdoms and glory of the world. As a flash of lightning, it passed through my whole body, transforming me into a new being. Instead of a stubby little Frenchman, I was an unconquerable giant, though I knew my strength was not my own strength."

Euphemie wanted to tell him he always seemed like a giant to her.

He continued. "I told the Rev. Mailloux I appreciated the sincerity of his motives in bringing me the message from the bishops of Canada. I told him that had I left the Church of Rome for worldly motives, I would surely accept. I told him to tell the good bishops that though they should offer me all the dignities and incalculable treasures of the Church of Rome, I would not take them in exchange for the treasure I have found in the Bible. I handed him the Divine Book."

"Did he take it?"

"No, indeed. Rising to his feet, he took a step toward me and shook his finger at me. 'Miserable apostate,' he cried. And he uttered a rage of threats

"I answered, 'I am not shaken any more by your threats than I was by your glittering promises of human glory and honor. I am a servant of God. If it is His will that I suffer, I will suffer for the cause of the Gospel.' Taking his hat and cane, he left the house so fast I could hardly accompany him to the door."

Father Chiniquy drained his cup. Euphemie was trying to think of something comforting to say. Before she could speak, he began to chuckle, "At least Mailloux had the grace to admit when I questioned him about O'Regan that I was right in branding that fellow a scoundrel. You remember I told you the Pope had banished him to an extinct bishopric called 'Dora'? Well, he consoled himself in his misfortune by retiring to England and then to Ireland where he established a bank with questionable funds."

"Oh, I am so glad you don't have to ever worry about his coming back. I was so afraid for you."

He reached across the table and patted her hand, "Don't you fret your pretty head about me. Forgive me for burdening you with my problems. It has been quite an evening. You will do me the favor of keeping the vicar's visit and our little talk absolutely confidential?"

"Oh, I will," she said fervently. "That is one thing Papa said I must do when I took this position. He said, 'You must treat everything you hear or see as sacred and confidential as if you were a doctor or a'"

"I suppose he said 'a priest.'"

She blushed. "Yes."

"Well, pastors keep secrets, too".

"I know," she said demurely. She was confident he had told no one about her confession of love for Evaloe.

Seeming to read her mind, he said as he walked toward the dry sink with his dirty cup "By the way, how did you find the Morais children and their papa this evening?"

Chapter XIV
The Gift

The next morning when Euphemie entered the kitchen to prepare breakfast, she found Father Chiniquy already there. He was wrapping in plain butcher's paper the Bible that Hector Goyette had rejected.

He said, "Miss Allard, later on this morning, I want you to take this package to Mrs. Hector Goyette as a farewell gift from me in memory of the many wonderful meals I have eaten at her table. I believe Hector said he was leaving about ten today to go to Kankakee City to make final arrangements for joining the Oregon caravan."

Euphemie understood very well without his saying so that the Bible was to be delivered during Hector's absence. She delivered the Bible as directed. Mrs. Goyette insisted that she stay awhile. The house was empty except for the bare essentials necessary to keep a family of five going until they joined the wagon train. In the kitchen there were a few boxes that were used for seats because the kitchen chairs were already packed.

"Most of the things we are taking with us are in the wagon, " Mrs. Goyette said. "The mister is so anxious to get going, he couldn't wait to pack the wagon. Would you like to see it?"

Euphemie did not know much about wagons in general, but she did remember the one in which her parents and she had ridden from Montreal. It was a trip she hoped never to repeat although there were some good times around the campfire at night. The Goyettes had been in their caravan. As she remembered, the Goyette wagon was one of the smaller ones and not too well equipped, a mistake Hector had not made this time.

"My man got the best wagon he could buy," Mrs. Goyette said with pride. "He fixed it up nice. But I wish we were staying. We were doing so well here. If we had spent the money on a new steel plow to replace the wooden one and built a new tool shed, it would have been better for us. I like it here."

"Oh, you'll like it in Oregon, Mrs. Goyette."

"If we ever get there. There are fierce Indians on the way and the trail will be hard. We were told to sell our horses and buy oxen, but my Hector can't see it that way. He says he does not want to be an old man before he gets there and oxen are too slow. Even with horses, it will probably take six months."

"I am sure you will be perfectly safe from Indians by traveling with a caravan. How many wagons in all?"

"I think there are 20 families signed up."

"What do the boys think about the move?"

The Goyettes had three sons, aged fourteen, twelve and five.

"Oh, they are excited about it, and of course the two older ones are glad to get out of going to school. I am taking their school books along. I told them they have to study on the trail."

"That's a good plan. Don't forget to take the Bible Father Chiniquy gave you."

Madame Goyette answered evasively, "I laid it in my trunk."

Euphemie did not know if that meant she would take it, but she was certain the Bible would not go along if Hector Goyette knew about it.

Mrs. Goyette said wistfully, "Do thank the good Father for me. I miss him so much. I just cannot understand how a priest can turn on his own church the way he did. We always thought he was so wonderful and would have followed him to the ends of the earth. But now, it seems we are going to the ends of the earth to get away from him."

Three days later the Hector Goyette family left Ste. Anne never to return. Father Chiniquy didn't learn until years later that the Bible he gave Mrs. Goyette went with them on the venturesome trip to Oregon.

Chapter XV
Tête à Tête

In her spare time, which was very limited, Euphemie ripped up one of the cassocks Father Chiniquy had packed away to be made into children's clothing. She carefully preserved the ornate braid to use at a later time on a Sunday dress for her mother. Using a warm iron over a dampened tailor's press cloth, she steam pressed the pieces of fine wool. She discovered the fabric was richer and prettier on the reverse side. It was all wool, lightweight and drapeable. She decided to make a school coat for Mina, but she was certain the coat would not be warm enough without an extra warm inner lining. When she went to the Morais farm for Mina's old coat to use for a pattern, she asked Evaloe if it would be possible to line the coat with beaver fur.

Beaver fur was plentiful around Ste. Anne, which had been called "Beaver Mission" by its first white settlers before the arrival of Father Chiniquy and his band of French Canadians. Two good-sized streams, one a bit bigger than the other, were called Big and Little Beaver. They meandered through the farmland south of Ste. Anne with a hundred or more beaver lodges in each creek. Evaloe and his father were fine trappers and expert skinners. Their beaver pelts were rough cured—scraped clean of all flesh and sewn with deer sinew to willow frames to dry. At times in the Morais farmyard there were 20 or 30 beaver skins hanging to dry. Evaloe had learned how to cure the fur so it could be used for clothing.

Without this final process, the skins had an offensive odor and the fur itself was not pretty.

Euphemie carefully ripped Mina's outgrown coat into sections to use as a pattern. Later, she planned to make the least worn portions into a jacket for Stephen.

In the afternoon of the day she took the Bible to the Goyette home, she stretched out the pressed wool fabric on the great hall rug. She laid the pattern pieces on the fabric and shifted them around, being careful to have the grain of the fabric running the same way on all pieces. She wanted to make each section bigger than the pattern to allow for the recent growth of the little girl as well as for the bulk of the fur lining. She shifted the pieces here and there, anchoring them with weights she had made by covering padded half-bricks with scraps of cloth from her piece bag. She had very few pins, and the brick weights did a fine job keeping the pattern from slipping during the cutting.

She was so concerned about being able to get the coat from the fabric pieces, she was not aware of Father Chiniquy standing in the doorway. He thought she made a pretty picture, crawling about the cutting floor, arranging and re-arranging the pieces of dark green material from Mina's old coat on the pieces of black fabric from his robes.

"You are just the person I am looking for," he said. "I see you have your work basket handy."

His voice startled her and she jumped up, smoothing first her dress and then her hair. A few stray locks insisted on falling across her forehead into her eyes.

"Oh, Father. You frightened me."

"I am sorry. I never want to be frightening—especially to pretty young ladies. I just pulled a button from my new suit. Very poor tailoring, I'd say, and I wondered if you would please sew it on for me."

"Of course, Father," she said. "They should have used heavier thread to sew on a button with a metal shank."

She picked up her workbasket from the floor and sat down with it in her lap. It was divided into sections neatly filled with threads of different sizes and colors, bobbins, needles, and a few pins, buttons, a tape measure, scissors and a thimble. She selected a needle and a spool of heavy black thread. She stretched out a length of thread, snapped it off between her front teeth, wet the end and expertly guided it through the needle's eye. She held the needle in her right hand and pulling one length of the thread taut with her left, she rolled her fingers around its tip and quickly made a knot.

"That always has been a mystery to me," he commented.

"What has, Father?"

"How you ladies can tie a one-handed knot like that."

"Oh, is that hard for you to do? There's really nothing to it. I will show you how sometime."

She reached for the coat and the button. In a minute the button was sewn firmly in place with just enough play in the thread to permit easy buttoning. Rather than search for her scissors in the workbasket, she bent over the thread and bit it off.

"Won't you ruin your pretty teeth that way?" It was a reproof and a compliment.

"I should have used the scissors," she admitted. "But I was in a hurry,"

"I did not mean to interrupt your work. Please go ahead."

"I didn't mean I was in a hurry because of me. I thought you were going someplace."

"Well, no, as a matter of fact, I am not. This is one of the few times I have little to do. How is the coat for Mina coming?"

"It is going to be nip and tuck. I think I will have to use a facing instead of a hem," she said dropping down to the floor beside her pattern. 'You see, here, if this were just two or three inches longer…'"

"You are telling the story of my life. Always too short. See, if I had been a tall man, there would have been no problem."

Euphemie was embarrassed.

"No, no, no," she said. "It will be fine. I just meant that it would have been nice to have had a big hem to let down for next year. Mina is growing so fast. She will probably be tall like her father."

"Lucky girl," he said sincerely.

She seemed to be getting in more and more trouble. She shifted the sleeve pattern and set a brick weight on it. She reached for the scissors and started cutting.

"This is lovely fabric," she said to change the subject. "Much nicer than your new suit."

"Yes, it is," he agreed, pulling a chair away from the wall and turning its back to her, he straddled the seat and rested his chin on his hands folded on the back of the chair. He looked down at her as she snipped away at the cassock he had once been so proud to wear.

"I rather hate giving up the trappings of priesthood," he said candidly. "As you know, I am a short man, but when I donned my cassock, I felt ten feet tall. I regretted throwing my robes in the bonfire as much as you regretted throwing in your rosary."

She stopped cutting. He knew.

"You thought I did not know how much that hurt you," he said gently. "A pastor knows his flock and suffers with them."

She started cutting again. With head bent low, she murmured, "I've been wanting to talk to you about that."

"About what?"

He liked to hear her speak. Her voice, so low-pitched and vibrant, struck a responsive chord, and he found himself responding to its warmth. She told him how she had found the charred crucifix still fastened to bits of the rosary and how she had hidden it in her bureau drawer. By the time she finished the story, the garment was completely cut out. She crawled full circle around the fabric and was on her hands and knees before him.

She put the scissors down, leaned back on her heels and clasped her hands in front of her mouth. She closed her eyes and said in a very low voice, "I feel more and more guilty about it every day. But you see, it was given to me by my grandmother and she is dead now."

He looked down at her tenderly.

"Don't feel guilty, my dear babe in the new faith. You naturally cling to the things you were taught to revere as a child. Only seven years ago, when I preached in the Cathedral of Montreal, one of the sermons that made the most visible deep impression on my congregation was on the Virgin Mary's powers in heaven when interceding for sinners. The object of my sermon was to show that Jesus Christ cannot refuse any of the petitions presented Him by His mother, that she has always obtained the favors she asked her Son Jesus to grant her devotees. I was honest, and I sincerely believed what I said. But when night came, before bed I took my Bible as usual and knelt before God in that neat little room I occupied in the bishop's palace and studied the scriptures. Strange to say, I felt a mysterious awe as if I had entered for the first time a new and most holy land."

Euphemie rolled to a sitting position, smoothed her dress around her and sat very quietly. It was hard to believe that this man who had preached in the Cathedral of Montreal and resided in the bishop's palace was sitting here astride a chair chatting with her in such a casual manner about controversial topics. She sat raptly listening to his telling about the long night of scripture and soul-searching that terminated with his going at breakfast time in search of Bishop Prince. He had been a friend since they were in Nicolet College together. He told his friend that his night's study and prayer had convinced him that since Jesus is our best friend, our most powerful and loving friend, we should go directly to Him in prayer and not through Mary, who was definitely inferior in power, love and mercy.

"Bishop Prince was shaken by my revelation. He said, 'I hope you are not yielding to the temptation to become a Protestant as so many of your enemies whisper about you.' I answered, 'It is my hope that our merciful God will keep me, to the end of my life, a dutiful, faithful priest. However, I cannot conceal from you that my faith was terribly shaken last night.'

"And that was the beginning of my questioning the power of Mary for intercession. After much research and prayer, I am convinced I cannot believe in a doctrine that tells us the heart of the Good Shepherd is so cooled and irritated against His erring sheep that He would forget them or cast them off if the Holy Virgin were not there to remind Him of what He has suffered for them."

He looked down at Euphemie with tenderness.

"Was the rosary your only memento from your grandmother?"

"The only one except a baby ring," she said as she tugged at a gold chain around her neck. She pulled out a tiny gold circlet.

"Oh, for a moment I thought you were wearing the crucifix."

"No, Father. It is in my bureau drawer. But I will go get it now and give it to you to destroy."

"Not at all. Keep it as a treasure to help you remember your loving grandmother. The reason I asked the congregation to throw in their rosaries was to give them a concrete act of commitment. You have done the act. What you have retained is just a souvenir, so to speak, of times gone by."

Chapter XVI
Rumors Afoot

Their intimate discussion was interrupted by a loud knock on the front door. Euphemie scrambled to her feet, upsetting her workbasket in the process. She opened the door to Ephraim Therrien and Christophe LaFontaine, who breathlessly asked if they could speak with Father Chiniquy.

When he appeared at the door behind her and invited them in, they said, "Oh, good, you are here. Father, there are rumors spreading today against your character faster and worse than the prairie fire which came near destroying the village three years ago. If you cannot stop the rumors, we have come to tell you in the name of many that you will have to leave the colony."

Euphemie thought they acted like the mice in the nursery story that were elected to hang the bell on the cat.

"What rumors?" asked Father Chiniquy as he ushered them into the library and shut the door. Euphemie returned to the great hall, collected the spilled contents of her workbasket, folded her sewing and put it away for stitching another day.

Suddenly the library door opened and the two men and Father Chiniquy left the house in a hurry, without a word to her. She was consumed with curiosity. She assumed the rumors had something to do with the burning of the Bourbonnais church or the bonfire in Ste. Anne. She peeled the potatoes for the evening meal and set them in a pan of cold water. A roast was cooking in the oven.

She walked to her parents' home to see what they had heard. They were reluctant to tell.

At last, her mother said, "It's just the old rumor often started by the enemies of priests."

"What rumor?" she persisted.

Her mother hesitated.

Her father said, "They are saying that while in Canada, Father Chiniquy fathered some illegitimate children. About a dozen, they say."

"Illegitimate children? A dozen? Do you get children by the dozen like eggs in a crate?"

"Euphemie, don't be flippant," her mother cautioned. "This is a serious charge. They say he was interdicted and forced to leave Canada for that reason. We do not believe it, of course, but if those who are making the charges are not proved to be liars, Father Chiniquy could be in trouble— much trouble. He must stop them."

"Don't mention that we told you this," requested her father. "We don't want Father Chiniquy to know we heard it."

She promised not to reveal they had heard the rumor. She walked back to the parsonage. Her father had said, "Now, don't worry about it, My Pet. There is not a word of truth in it." She supposed it could have happened. Father Chiniquy must have been very attractive to women in his younger days

"He is short," she thought. "That does not seem to matter to some women. Papa is an inch or so shorter than Mama, but that doesn't seem to bother Mama, who walks along erect and proud beside him." She, herself, preferred taller, muscular men. More like Evaloe.

She resolved never to mention height again in front of Father Chiniquy because she gathered from the conversation that afternoon he was sensitive about his short stature. Even at fifty years old, he had a sparkle in his eyes and a manner that charmed the ladies in the congregation, even some of the younger ladies. There was something about him women found attractive.. She found him absolutely charming in an informal setting like that afternoon, yet it was difficult to imagine him involved with women in a sexual way—and a dozen times? With perhaps a dozen different women? Ridiculous! He would never have broken his priestly vows of celibacy. By the time she reached the parsonage, she was so thoroughly convinced of his innocence, she was irate that anyone could start such rumors and even more irate that others would listen and pass them on.

In the meantime, Father Chiniquy and his two informers searched out the priest named Father Deneau, who had started the rumor. He was in Ste. Anne to visit his sister, Mrs. Antoine Aime.

Father Chiniquy said, "Please tell me, before these two witnesses and your brother-in-law here, if you know that, when in Canada, I had a great number of illegitimate children and if you have ever told that story anywhere."

Father Deneau answered, "No, Sir. I never said any such thing."

His brother-in-law asked angrily, "How can you say that? Last night in the presence of 20 witnesses, you said Father Chiniquy had about a dozen illegitimate children in Canada."

The priest protested. "I did not say that he had. I said I had been told that he had."

Father Chiniquy demanded, "Now, Sir, can you say to my face that I have been interdicted and turned out of Canada by the bishops?"

"No," Father Deneau said reluctantly. "I cannot say that for I know the contrary. I know the bishop has given you as a token of his esteem a silver chalice to say mass."

Antoine Aime accused with fury, "That's a lie. Only last night you told us the bishops had turned Chiniquy out of Canada. What are you trying to do?"

Turning to depart, Father Chiniquy said to the priest, "That is all I wanted—your admission in front of witnesses that those rumors are false. Goodbye, Sir, and goodbye to you, Antoine. In the future, be certain you know what you are saying is true."

Ephriam and Christophe urged him to sue. They said they could find at least 30 witnesses who had heard the accusations.

"No, my friends," he said. "I prefer to follow the example of Christ and forgive."

Euphemie had been home only a few minutes when he returned, apparently undisturbed.

He said, "I had to help settle an argument for Ephraim and Christophe. It is a good thing I had that button sewed on my coat. I always feel a person has more authority when he has all his buttons."

Euphemie felt he could have acted with authority if he had gone in his long underwear. In the times ahead he would need all his buttons, all his faith and all his courage because his enemies would be legion and powerful.

Chapter XVII
Hard Times

One Thursday morning, Bernice Allard walked over to the parsonage to talk with Euphemie.

"Your father," she said sadly, "is so downhearted. He is afraid he is going to lose the harness shop."

"Oh, Mama, why?"

Euphemie was concerned. She was well aware of the plight of the farmers, but her father farmed only a small piece of land. His primary source of income was his harness shop. Because two bad early frosts the previous autumn had made it difficult for the farmers to salvage even enough of their crops for seed, some families had very little to eat and would have starved had they not used up their home-canned fruits, vegetables and meats. In the spring, the rains came early and washed out the fall plantings. Some farmers had saved back enough seed to plant again, but another three weeks of rain washed out that planting. Euphemie knew that many families had mortgaged their land to buy food and fuel. Those who were still paying on their farms were forced to take out second mortgages at extremely high rates of interest, often, she had heard, as high as 20 or 30 per cent

Bernice explained with resignation, "It is not only the farmers who are hard hit. They can't pay all their bills. You know how tenderhearted your father is. He tells them to pay their mortgages first and buy food and shoes for the children and pay us when they can. I don't know where he thinks we are going to find money for our mortgage payments."

"Oh, Mama, I wish we could help. Father Chiniquy sold two horses and a buggy and mortgaged this house to keep up the church. There has been no money for his salary or for other church expenses. He heard yesterday that his enemies in Bourbonnais bought up his notes to ruin him. He is almost beside himself with worry, not only about his own problems, but about those of all his flock."

Almost as if to belie her statement, Father Chiniquy entered the back door and called out cheerily, "Well, Good Day, Mrs. Allard. How are you? Look, Ladies, at what I received in today's mail."

He held up a check. "It is from my old friend in Canada, George Sunderland from Prince Edward Island. His congregation heard of our work, and they want to be part of it. They sent this check for $500. It is like manna from Heaven," he said gratefully.

But $500 did not go far to ease the woes of over 500 families. It occurred to Father Chiniquy that other places not visited by such calamities of nature as had ruined the economy of his parish might come to the help of the poor French Canadians.

He discussed the idea with the pastor of the Presbyterian Church in Kankakee City, who gave him a letter of introduction to the Rev. Mr. John Leyburn, editor of *The Presbyterian* of Philadelphia. He assigned his clerical duties in Ste. Anne to Henry Morrell, who was studying for the ministry. He went by train to Philadelphia.

He secured a modest room in a hotel and presented his letter of introduction to Dr. Leyburn, who was polite but very cool. Father Chiniquy felt, for the first time in his life, like a beggar. As a priest, he had always had plenty, not only for himself but also for those around him who were in need. The editor told him they had helped a man claiming to be an apostate less than a month before and he had turned out to be a fraud.

He said, "I do not want to discourage or rebuff you, but you are intelligent enough to understand that, because of that experience, there will be mountains of prejudices against you and your mission of charity for your starving people." He told Father Chiniquy of a noonday prayer meeting he could attend and suggested he introduce himself there giving his name, position and trials in as few words as possible.

Father Chiniquy hurried to the church. At twelve noon he sat in one of the front pews of the crowded church. As soon as he could find an opportunity, he got up to speak on the first six verses of John 15. He had not yet given his plea when the president rang a bell to stop him and said, "We are not allowed to speak more than five minutes."

Disappointed and confused, he sat down convinced he had made a fool of himself before the English-speaking crowd. He saw expressions of pity for his poor English spoken with a strong French accent. If only he could have addressed them in French!

He felt his first appearance before the Philadelphia crowd was a failure. He returned to the editor's office. Although Dr. Leyburn was displeased to see him there again, he said, "I was upset with the rudeness of our president today at the noonday prayer meeting. As you are a stranger and a Frenchman not yet quite familiar with our English language, he ought to have given you at least ten minutes to speak."

Father Chiniquy asked the editor to give him the names of the principal ministers of the city. Dr. Leyburn hesitated and then complied, extracting a promise not to reveal his name when the ministers were contacted. It was late afternoon and too late to contact anyone that day. With barely enough money in his pocket to pay his hotel bill, he walked to his hotel rather than take a carriage.

The next day he started out. He had been told not to present himself at the door of a minister until after eleven o'clock. Since he had to walk two miles to the home of the first minister, he left the hotel at ten. The long streets were bordered with houses three to five stories high. The day was hot and humid with scarcely any breeze. He stopped at a house along the way to ask for a drink from their pump. Although the drink helped him, the next mile seemed even longer.

Much to his surprise and embarrassment, he was refused entrance at the first parsonage by a haughty maid. He had more than a mile to go to the next home. It was half past one when he reached his destination. There he was told by the servant girl to return at three o'clock. He asked if he might sit and rest in the shade inside the doorway, but the girl slammed the door in his face.

He had another mile to go to the next minister. His feet hurt so much he could hardly step. For more than six years, he had been treading the cool grass of the prairie. Trudging on the hot city walks caused his feet to blister so badly the skin broke open in several places. It was as if nails were piercing his heels and the balls of his feet.

At the third house, he was told the minister was just leaving for the country and could not see him. When he begged for just a few minutes of the clergyman's time, he was stoutly refused. He left before he was forcibly ejected. The brief rest made his blisters even more painful. He had had no breakfast and no dinner. He had been walking in the hot sun about five hours. He felt faint. Everything went round in circles and he fell down unconscious.

When he awoke, a woman bending over him said, "Aren't you Father Chiniquy who spoke at the prayer meeting yesterday?"

"I am, Madam."

"Are you so sick you cannot walk?"

"Madam, my feet are so blistered I cannot take another step. I have been walking in the hot sun since this morning without stopping to eat."

At first, it was feared he had suffered a sunstroke. His benefactor called a carriage and took him to her doctor who examined his blistered feet. He spread a linen cloth with ointment made of beeswax and tallow and made it into a small dressing. With a pair of sharp surgical scissors, he made an aperture in the blisters not already broken and carefully laid the dressing on the blisters. He gave his patient some salve and dressing and advised him to stay off his feet and change the dressings as often as three times a day.

The woman who rescued him took him to her hotel room to recover. She was, he learned, Miss Rebecca Snowden, an heiress who spent much of her fortune helping the poor. After she saw that he was fed and rested, she helped him change the dressings. She was in her late forties, a tall English woman with a long, ugly face and a big beautiful heart. That evening, when her patient felt better, she provided him with paper and pen to write some letters. He wrote to Euphemie, who felt a twinge of jealousy when she read what a wonderful nurse Miss Snowden was. Euphemie had begun to think of him as her charge. He told her how ashamed he was of his poor English at the noonday prayer meeting. He asked her to make arrangements with the teacher, Francis Bechard, to tutor him in English.

Euphemie's maternal instinct was aroused. Anger made her lash out at the ignorant people who had made fun of her Father Chiniquy simply because he was not fluent in their language. Why, he was a wonderful speaker in his own beautiful French, a language more eloquent than any other. He said he wanted her to take lessons in English also so she would be able to converse with any English-speaking guests he might entertain in the parsonage.

"Let them learn French," she thought defiantly. But she followed his instructions and showed the letter to Francis. He said he would be happy to tutor Father Chiniquy and encouraged her to join the class.

In the meantime, Miss Snowden took Father Chiniquy in her carriage to the noonday prayer meeting at the same church where he had been rebuffed the day before. Using her influence with the ministers in Philadelphia, she asked the group to arrange to have a special meeting. She helped her patient hobble to the front pew and sat beside him

After the preliminaries of the prayer meeting were over, a Mr. Stuart gave the history of Chiniquy's conversion and depicted the spectacle of the suffering of his flock from the loss of crops. Over $1,500 was put in the collection plate started by Miss Snowden, who dropped in $200. It was agreed that Chiniquy should address the churches of Philadelphia, one each evening and that collections should be taken for his starving people.

He remained 17 days in Philadelphia and from there went on to New York City and Boston where he met even greater success, thanks to letters of introduction from Miss Snowden.

When he returned to Ste. Anne with $55,000, he also brought with him barrels of food and clothing donated by the kind hearted Protestants in those eastern cities. A crowd met him at the Kankakee City depot. They took him to the church where others waited eagerly to thank him and bless him. Euphemie attended the meeting and was happy to see how grateful the desperate parishioners were. How she wished Father Chinquy could bask forever in the sunshine of their gratitude!

She regretted he would soon be at his desk where he would learn of the criticism heaped on him during his Eastern campaign. The wrath of the Catholic clergy was beginning to manifest itself. The bishop had brought a suit against him to win back the church building. The Kankakee City papers published an editorial about him entitled "The Chiniquy Humbug," and a private circular printed in Canada was being distributed asking aid to fight against Chiniquy and his Satanic work *The Chicago Press and Tribune* and *The Chicago Daily Times* denounced him as an imposter. They warned, "Father Chiniquy's parishioners are probably better off than they have ever been in their lives. They are not suffering for any of the necessities and many are enjoying the luxuries of life. True, they are in debt for their land; true, they are poor; true, they must study economy to make ends meet; but the same things are true of half the men in this and every other state. The pretense that they ought to be singled out as objects of special charitable effort is a bold invention of Father Chiniquy himself." The Bourbonnais newspaper published a list of 1600 names of Catholics who subscribed to a fund for Father Desaulnier, pastor of a Bourbonnais church, to use in his work against the schism.

Euphemie wished there were some way she could protect her employer from learning what had been done in his absence. She knew she was powerless. To her surprise, Father Chiniquy was not upset by the articles written about him. He said he had been expecting things like that to happen. He was, however, deeply saddened by the list of Bourbonnais subscribers, many of whom had been his friends.

"That Isaac Desaulnier could lead the fight against me cuts me to the quick," he told her. " At one time we were united by the bonds of sincerest esteem and friendship. He was my classmate in college. He later became president of St. Hyacinthe College."

Euphemie had little time to think about Rev. Desaulnier. When Father Chiniquy was home, the visitors came and went. There was little time for anything but her housekeeping duties.

Chapter XVIII
The Chiniquy Committee

Although his days and evenings were crowded with meetings and duties, Father Chiniquy always took time from his busy schedule to counsel a distraught parishioner. Evaloe sought him out one day in his study at the church to tell him that Marie's parents were distressed about their daughter being confined to an insane asylum. They were convinced if she stayed there, she would never have a chance to recover. They consulted a doctor in Montreal who had treated such patients with success. They were most insistent that Evaloe take Marie to Montreal to be treated at the doctor's sanitarium. They offered to pay part of the expenses and to provide a home with them for Evaloe and the children. The doctor said it was important for Marie to have her husband and children near her.

"So when are you leaving, my son?" asked Father Chiniquy.

"Leaving? I cannot possibly go. I have no money set aside and our crops are ruined. We have some beaver furs to sell, but that won't bring near enough."

"How much will you need?"

"Over $500. But it is ridiculous to talk about."

"Not really. Possibly I can arrange it."

"Oh, no, Father. That is not why I came to you. I only wanted you to help me explain to Marie's parents that I want to do everything possible to make her well, but I cannot manage this, not this year." He sighed. "I hope to God next year is a better year."

Father Chiniquy insisted that Evaloe take some of the money the eastern Protestants had contributed. He assured him those sympathetic Christians would have wanted their money used that way. He did not tell him $500 was the amount he had set aside to pay off the mortgage on the parsonage.

The arrangements were made. Evaloe's parents were sorry to see him and the children leave, but they wanted what was best for Marie. His mother was pregnant again, and she was glad to have the extra room Evaloe had added to their small house.

Euphemie had mixed emotions about their going. She would miss the children and certainly she would miss Evaloe .She was somehow relieved he would not be near to arouse the longing she tried to suppress. She was hopeful the treatment would restore Marie's health because the children needed their mother; yet she knew with Marie back home, there would never be a chance for a romance between herself and Evaloe. Perhaps there would not have been anyway because Evaloe was such a good man he would never commit an act of unfaithfulness. Euphemie would not have wanted him to be different.

These were the thoughts of her calmer moments. There were other times, tormented times, when the thought of his long absence was unbearable. Not to see him, not to hear his voice, not to smell his woodsy fragrance, not to wake each day and wonder if she might see him that day would be torture. Despite her inner turmoil, she managed to maintain outward propriety when Evaloe brought the children to say goodbye. Her self-possession almost deserted her when Evaloe shyly presented her with a gift wrapped in beaver skins.

"I want you to have this," he said, awkwardly thrusting it in her arms. "A little something to remember us by."

She folded back the beaver skins exposing the most beautiful fiddle she had ever seen, its maple gleaming with a soft patina coaxed to the surface by hours of hand rubbing. The f-holes were exquisitely carved. She ran her fingers lovingly down its smooth curving surface. Tears of joy ran down her cheeks.

"Don't cry, Aunt Euphemie," said Mina. "It's pretty, the prettiest one Papa ever made."

"You are so right, My Pet," she said. "I am crying for joy because it is so beautiful and because you gave it to me."

"It's a different pattern than I have ever made," Evaloe explained. "One I heard about from an old inmate when I visited Marie. He used to be a fiddle maker. He drew this pattern for me of a violin called 'The Alard.'"

"'The Alard'? You are teasing me."

"No, I am not. The old man said it was one of the most famous Stradivarius violins. I think that is the name. Have you ever heard of Stradivari?"

"Oh, yes. The greatest of all violin makers."

She added, "Up to now." She tucked the instrument under her chin and cuddled it to her shoulder.

He laughed and so did Stephen. It pleased Stephen to laugh. He was carrying the bow, and he whipped it around like a knight brandishing a sword. Evaloe rescued the bow, but before he handed it to Euphemie, he said, "The old man told me, too, about a different kind of varnish, an oil varnish. I tried different things and came up with a walnut oil and varnish mixture. It needs strong sunlight and lots of time to dry. I was afraid it would not be ready to give to you before we left. I had never thought too much about varnish before, but the old man said varnish is one of the most important things to produce a superior tone, and the old masters used to guard their varnish formula very carefully. Here, Euphemie, try it."

" I am a poor one to test the tone," she said, but she drew the bow carefully across the strings, tightened the stops a little and tried again.

"What a glorious sound," she exclaimed.

"Play something, Aunt Euphemie," begged Mina.

Remembering Evaloe's whistled tunes as he worked, tunes she felt he impregnated in the instruments he created, she played the rollicking *Alouette*, timidly at first and then with gay abandon, filled with the joy of life. The children danced about and sang along. Evaloe looked on with pride. Father Chiniquy came on this scene as he cut across the churchyard toward the parsonage.

"Well, well," he said. "May I join in?"

He took Mina and Stephen by the hand and circled about with them. Mina soberly danced, but Stephen hopped about so wildly he fell down.

"Look, Father, at this beautiful fiddle Evaloe made for me. He says it is called 'The Alard,' patterned after a violin made by Stradivari."

She handed it to him for inspection. He accepted it carefully as if indeed it were a rare old Stradivarius.

"'The Alard'? It seems to me I have read about it. The French name brought it to my attention because I thought most of the famous violin makers were Italian—Maggini, Rodini and Amati and his famous pupil, Antonio Stradivari. I wonder if Hortense Alard inspired Stradivari.

Noting they had never heard of Hortense, he added, "She was one of the great lovers of all time who wrote unabashedly of her amorous affairs. She may have been one of your ancestors."

Euphemie blushed. She was certainly not a Hortense, but she longed to think this fiddle had been designed for her by a man who loved her.

Father Chiniquy said sincerely, "Stradivari could not have done better." He turned the fiddle all about, admiring its beauty. "And Paganini could not have played better for two such inspired dancers," he smiled at the children."

He noticed the unusual finish and questioned Evaloe about the varnish. When he learned Evaloe had formulated a varnish formula using walnut oil so plentiful in their colony, he was intensely interested.

"You must patent that formula," he advised. "It may make you a fortune."

"And who is in greater need? Evaloe laughed. "Seriously, Father, I will get a job and pay back the money to the Chiniquy Committee as soon as I can."

"Don't worry about it. We are confident you will repay when times are better for you. God grant it will be soon."

He relinquished the fiddle to Euphemie, kissed the children on both cheeks and shook hands with Evaloe

"All arrangements are made for you to take Marie by train to Montreal. Let us know how you make the trip. I wish you well, my son. Just think, my little ones, you will soon be riding on the choo choo train."

While Evaloe and Father Chiniquy talked, she slipped away to take the fiddle inside to a safe place and to get the gifts she had for the children. She had a toy soldier that had belonged to her brother for Stephen and for Mina she had a beaver muff she had fashioned with a tiny coin purse. She also picked up the box of sandwiches and cookies she made for the train ride. She wished she had a gift for Evaloe. She had not dreamed he would bring her a gift. She might not be able to see him, hear his voice or smell his fragrance, but with the fiddle cradled on her shoulder, she would feel his presence. It was truly a gift of himself.

When she told him with regret that she had nothing to offer, he said sincerely, "Euphemie, you have given us so much already. I do not know how we could have managed without you. The children love you and are so pleased you like their gift."

So it was a gift from the children? Of course. A married man cannot bestow such a present on his nursemaid. Was that indeed how he thought of her or was it how he was making himself think of her? No matter! He had fashioned the beautiful fiddle just for her, and she would treasure it always.

Despite the warnings of the Chicago press that Chiniquy was an imposter, the Protestants of New York City and Boston invited him to return three months later. He also went to Washington, Baltimore, Pittsburgh, Montreal, Toronto and Springfield, Massachusetts. Wherever he went, committees were formed under the name of The Chiniquy Committee. Help came also from England, Scotland and Germany. Back home, The Chiniquy Committee of six men with Achille in command paid off mortgages and distributed the food and clothing.

The long winter months stretched endlessly for Euphemie. She forced herself to read and study art and art history as well as daily scriptures outlined by Father Chiniquy before he left. Sewing gave her some relief from depression, but her real solace was her new fiddle. Strangely enough, it was not so much of Evaloe she thought as she practiced over and over the music Father Chiniquy obtained for her. She looked forward to Father Chiniquy's pleasure when he returned to find she had mastered the selection he picked for her. During the brief interval he was home between his Eastern campaigns, he was most complimentary about her amateurish performance and assured her over and over she was capable of becoming a truly fine violinist who could do justice to such a rare and beautiful instrument.

His joy on learning that she had musical training as well as talent and love for music surprised and pleased her. His own talents so overwhelmed hers she felt insignificant in his presence. His confidence that she could do whatever he chose for her to do was beyond belief.

She practiced long hours and at first signed off every practice with the rollicking *Sur le Pont* or *Alouette*. The fiddle seemed almost to play them by itself as if indeed the tunes were built into it by its maker. It was fun to play so freely and easily after trying to master the difficult sheet music. The practice sessions bore fruit and the old masterpieces became familiar. Euphemie often did not think to play Evaloe's favorites. When occasionally she thought of Evaloe, she was surprised and relieved to discover her longing for him had dulled. Her life had taken on a new dimension, and she longed for her employer's return. Whenever he was in town, the pace of her life at the parsonage picked up considerably, almost to a frenzy. Euphemie found herself looking forward to those times with pleasure.

When Father Chiniquy returned to Illinois, he was again met at the Kankakee City depot by a crowd. More than one hundred buggies and wagons loaded with people, old and young, with flags in their hands were in the caravan. They stopped at the church to sing some beautiful old French hymns and thank the Heavenly Father for His mercies. Father Chiniquy told them about his successful trip, and they told him how they learned their mortgages had been paid. John Perrault, spokesman for the group, said, "The brokers told us either you or members of your committee paid our mortgages. Now our colony owes not a single cent more to the moneylenders of Kankakee City. We have no words to tell you our joy, our gratitude to God and to the benefactors who have saved us from complete ruin.".

Ephemie was proud and excited. Father Chiniquy stood ten feet tall. He did not need priestly robes to make him mighty.

He said, "Just as our Christian friends of the East have paid our debts to the last cent, so our Heavenly Father sent His Son Jesus to pay our debts. In both cases, the debts have been paid and the debtors saved from their creditors without paying a farthing."

A voice from a back seat said, "The comparison is not quite correct." It was Jacques Martin speaking.

"What do you mean, Brother Martin?"

"Well, when our Savior died, he did not ask us to sign any obligation to repay other people, but the Chiniquy Committee has forced us, I for one, to sign a paper by which we promise to give certain rent according to what was given us to support a high school or a college in our midst."

Euphemie could not believe her ears. Was this the way to respond to the wonderful charity Father Chiniquy had secured for them? Everyone began talking at once. Father Chiniquy silenced them by raising his hand.

"My good brother," he said, addressing himself to his critic but meaning for all to hear and heed. "These admirable Christians of the East are Protestants as you are today. They believe, like you, that they were sinners and through their sin contracted a heavy debt to God, so great a debt it was impossible for them to pay. Then God sent his Son to pay the debt. These eastern Christians believe that God put on them the obligation to love you and help you as He helped them."

A rumble of approval went through the congregation. Euphemie sighed with relief.

He continued, "But do not forget it. By accepting Christ and His Gospel for your guide, you have accepted the obligation to do to each other what Christ has done for you. You must bear the burden of each other. The strong must help the weak; the rich must help the poor. The fathers, more than ever in the past, must consecrate their resources, not only to the material but also to the moral and intellectual advancement of their children, don't you agree?"

"Amen. Amen."

"This is why the committee has wisely invited you to take public obligation to consecrate repayment of the monies sent you to the support of a high school or a college where your own children will learn to become good citizens and good Christians and, hopefully, ministers of the Gospel."

"That's what we want for our children."

"We can't object to that plan."

"Get the school started."

He gave them a few moments to comment. Then he reminded them, "Notice the payment is not in favor of strangers and people a long distance away, but it is a favor to yourselves, for your children are surely a part, if not the better part, of yourselves."

With a short prayer and the singing of another hymn, the crowd was dismissed. Euphemie was glad to see that, but for a few dissidents, the members of the congregation were in accord with Father Chiniquy. Ten feet tall was not tall enough to describe her pastor and employer. He was indeed a giant!

Chapter XIX
The Fever

During Father Chiniquy's absence, Francis Bechard conducted a small class in English for Achille and Lucy Chiniquy, Joseph and Irene Pallissard, Euphemie and Dr. and Mrs. Legris. Euphemie invited all of them including the teacher to the evening meal the day of Father Chiniquy's return. They promised to use only English during the meal as a surprise for him. Euphemie set the table for eight because it was not her custom to eat with Father Chiniquy and his guests.

That night, however, he commanded, "Miss Allard, get your plate and come sit with us. You were a member of the class and you need the practice as well as the others."

At first, they remained true to their intention to speak only English, but as Father Chiniquy told of his adventures in the eastern cities, they wanted to ask questions. Except for Francis and Dr. Legris, their vocabularies were too limited. Less than halfway through the meal, other than saying, "Please pass the butter" or "Thank you for the biscuits," they reverted to their native tongue.

Euphemie was self-conscious at the beginning of the meal, but everyone was very friendly and she soon relaxed. Francis was especially charming and witty. She found herself laughing a great deal. He loved her laugh, so throaty and genuine; not a foolish giggle like that of many girls he knew. Everyone commented on the delicious meal of fricasseed chicken and dumplings, buttered carrots, biscuits and maple sugar custard.

Euphemie was becoming an excellent cook, using imagination and skill to create dishes from the limited supply of food caused by the crop failure.

While the others were enjoying dessert, Father Chiniquy left the table and returned with a large package.

"This is for you," he said to Euphemie.

"For me?"

"Yes, open it now."

She tore off the wrappings and found a black violin case. Everyone exclaimed at the beauty of the soft Venetian leather and the richness of the brass hinges and clasp.

"Look inside," Father Chiniquy said eagerly.

She opened the catch and lifted the lid. The case was lined with royal blue velvet, exquisitely soft and puffy like a down comforter.. She caught her breath when she realized this beautiful gift was really for her.

"Go get your fiddle. Let's see if it fits."

It was a perfect fit and "The Alard" looked ever so elegant lying there, its gleaming golden patina contrasting yet blending with the soft matte finish of the cloudlike blue velvet.

"While you have the fiddle here, let's hear a tune," Father Chiniquy suggested.

Euphemie shook her head.

"Not in front of everyone," she whispered.

They all insisted until reluctantly she relented, tuned the strings, drew the bow tentatively across the strings and began to play. Surprise and delight were registered on the faces around the table. Father Chiniquy acted like the proud father of a child protégée. His evident pleasure inspired her. She cradled the instrument under her chin and drew the bow like a caress across the strings, her eyes half-closed in dreamy pleasure. How could she know the envious thoughts shared by Father Chiniquy and Francis Bechard, each imagining her loving treatment of the fiddle as an expression of love for Evaloe, its maker.

After the applause and compliments, Dr. Legris turned to his host and asked, "Do you feel well, Father? You look so flushed."

There's a doctor for you," Father Chiniquy joked. "Never can relax. Always trying to drum up business for his pills and potions."

The doctor persisted. Father Chiniquy was forced to admit he was burning with fever and suspicious he might be coming down with an influenza sweeping the eastern cities.

"But then, on the other hand," he added. "I am probably only exhausted because I have followed a most rigorous schedule. As much as I hate to admit it, I am getting older. One or two days' rest will find me as good as new."

The guests left early except for Dr. Legris. Euphemie prepared the bed and Father Chiniquy wearily climbed in it.

"Dr. Legris recommends that you take some whiskey or brandy, but I told him there is none on the premises. Papa has some homemade brandy, for medicinal purposes only," she hastened to add. "I could run over there for some."

"No, absolutely not," he said as the doctor entered the room. "You know better, Doctor, than recommend that to me. You will have to read my *Manual of Temperance* again or have you ever read it? Did I ever tell you how my manuscript for that manual was lost and found again? I was pastor at Kamouraska at the time. I had worked for four months to complete it. I finished it and rolled it up in its crudeness and sent it to a publisher in Quebec City by schooner. The schooner's captain was named Bechard."

The doctor looked at him questioningly.

"A week later," Father Chiniquy continued, speaking rapidly, "Captain Bechard was at my door. He looked 20 years older. His schooner had wrecked on the rocks of the St. Lawrence River between Berthier and St. Valier. It was a miracle he and his crew escaped. He was picked up unconscious on the sand where he had been hurled by a furious wave. The little roll of manuscript I had given him was lost. He had placed it in his small black trunk that had gone to the bottom of the river. The money he had earned and was taking to Quebec City to pay off his debts was lost also. I gave him 25 pounds to help replace his schooner. He promised to get twice that much from his rich uncle. We knelt and prayed together, and I asked him, 'Where do you think I can find your small trunk with my papers?'"

Dr. Legris put his hand on Father Chiniquy's brow.

"He is talking like a man with a terrible fever. He is almost out of his head. He keeps talking about a Captain Bechard. He must be thinking of Francis Bechard, the teacher. I will go home for my bag and be back in a few minutes with something to bring down this fever so he can rest."

Farther Chiniquy turned to Euphemie, determined to go on with his story.

"I am not a rambling idiot. I am telling a true story."

"Yes, Father," she said soothingly. She dipped a cloth in a basin of cool water, wrung it out and bathed his hot forehead and cheeks.

He continued, "Captain Bechard, and that was truly his name, said he had searched for four days and found nothing. I hitched my horse to my buggy and went toward Quebec City. The roads were very bad, and it took me two days to reach the first house in St. Valier. 'Have you heard anything of the wreck of Bechard's schooner?' I asked. 'Ah, yes. It was a complete wreck. It was dashed on the rocks and torn to pieces.' I persisted, 'Have you found anything on shore?' They said nothing except a little trunk that was entangled in the mud and branches. They let me look at the trunk. In it was my manuscript completely unharmed by the water. I took it myself to the publisher in Quebec City. Some weeks later I received a letter from The Rev. M. Ballargon, curate of Quebec. He wrote, 'Your marvelous little book, *Manual of Temperance*, has just been delivered. I read it and went to my parishioners and said, "After the Gospel, this is the best book you can read. It is written by Father Chiniquy, and I hope in a few days to hear there is a copy in every home in Quebec, and in fact, in all of Canada."' The result was that within three days, three thousand copies were sold, and I hope ten thousand more will be sold."

Dr. Legris returned.

"There you are, Doctor. I see you, too, have found a little black trunk." He was trying to be jocular, but he was so weary and feverish, his words made his doctor and Euphemie concerned instead of amused.

The doctor mixed some powder in a glass of water and directed his patient to drink all of it. He did and fell back on the pillow completely exhausted.

He was desperately sick for four days and nights with the fever rising and falling but never reaching a normal temperature. Euphemie nursed him faithfully, taking a little time to sleep only when Lucy came to sit beside him   At times, he knew her, but other times he called her Miss Snowden and complimented her gallantly on what a good nurse she was. Euphemie knew he was not responsible for his feverish words, but she could not help being jealous of the "other woman" in his life.

On the fifth night, his fever broke, and he was bathed in perspiration. He opened his eyes and looked around

"I am cured. Give me something to eat. I am hungry. And no more chicken broth, please. I want something solid, something I can chew."

Euphemie went to the kitchen and returned in a short time with some good boiled beef, some thin buttered toast and a cup of steaming, fragrant tea all neatly and prettily arranged on a tray set with a dainty cloth and the best china.

Dr. Legris insisted that he stay in bed two days longer. During that time he told Euphemie how much he appreciated her ministrations.

"A man is fortunate to have such a nurse," he said. "A good nurse is a true artist. Ah, the softness of her touch, the music of her gentle voice, the quietness of her footsteps, the sense of security and rest inspired by her kind and hopeful face, the promptness and attention to every want—humoring the patient's caprices and listening to his reasonable and unreasonable complaints!"

"But you took me for Miss Snowden," she could not resist saying.

"I did? How could I? There is no comparison. She is tall, old and ugly with a voice as raspy as a wood saw. She is kindhearted and generous, but I could never mistake you for her, my dear."

She could think of nothing to say.

He asked, "Was I talking wildly and out of my head?"

"Once in a while."

"I am seldom sick. Years ago, however, I had a bout with typhoid fever. For 13 days I was desperately ill. I saw visions. At one time I was suspended from the top of a mountain by a thread with my head hanging down. Another time my enemies were attacking me with daggers and swords. I was so sick and the inflammation of my brain was so terrible the least noise, even the passing of carriages or the walking of the horses on the street outside my room, caused me real torture. On learning of this, my friends immediately covered all surrounding streets with straw to prevent the possibility of any more noise."

"How thoughtful!"

"On the thirteenth day, the doctor said, 'He is dead or if not, he has only a few minutes to live.' The words echoed in my ears, and I had fears of being buried alive. With much anxiety, I turned my thoughts and my hopes toward Sainte Anne and Sainte Philomene. Sainte Anne was the object of my confidence since the first time I saw the many crutches covering the walls of La Bonne Ste. Anne du Nord Church. Sainte Philomene was a new saint whose body had miraculously recovered from a fatal illness and the world was filled with the noise of her miracle."

"Oh, yes, I know of Sainte Philomene," Euphemie said.

"I saw above my head Sainte Anne and Sainte Philomene sitting in the midst of a great light. Sainte Anne was very grave and very old. Sainte Philomene was very young and beautiful, sort of like Miss Snowden and you, don't you see?"

Euphemie blushed at the understated compliment.

"They were both looking at me with such love and kindness, I felt myself drawn to them by a magnetic power. The vision disappeared and I was cured. Later several competent physicians assured me what I called a miraculous cure was nothing but the turning point of the disease when Nature either kills or cures the patient. My so-called vision was but a dream of my sickly brain at the supreme crisis of the fever."

Achille stood at the threshold of the sick room.

"Are you well enough to have company?" he asked.

"I am feeling fine, but I am a prisoner in my own home, held here by the policeman, Dr. Legris, and his deputy, Miss Allard. Come in. Come in."

He was delighted to see Achille and get on with the many items of business they needed to discuss. Euphemie excused herself to take care of the household duties she had neglected during her days and nights of nursing.

"And how are things with the Chiniquy Committee?"

Achille reported, "We have been very busy. We have distributed almost all the food and a great deal of the clothing. You made quite a haul this time."

"When I told those good Christians how our people wept and praised God when they received the first donations, they were eager to send more."

"I used the money," Achille said, "to finish paying off the mortgages. We had some left, and we put it in the bank until we learn what you want done with it."

"Did all the men sign the promise to repay the money by contributing to our school?"

"Yes, they finally came around, " Achille said ruefully. His brother suspected that Achille must have used a little friendly persuasion on some of the stubborn Frenchmen.

The Chiniquy Committee was not a new organization. It had merely taken on the new chores of distributing the gifts from the eastern states. It was formed in 1851 to help build the colony. At first, it was made up of Charles and Louis Chiniquy and the three Allains—Michael and his sons Antoine and Ambrose. Achille joined the group in 1853 when he returned from the gold mines of California to what his brothers described as the gold mines of the Illinois prairie.

The committee held extensive acres of land in the new settlements of Ste Anne,. Ste. Mary's and L'Erable. Tenancy was the only way some farmers could guarantee themselves a crop during their first year. The committee pledged to deed the claims to squatters if they found purchase money during the first six months or a year. To seal the bargain, they gave a bond for a deed to the settlers in the form of a loan. The committee claimed to have the lowest interest rates in Illinois, but it was labeled by Father Chiniquy's enemies as the "Societe des Tondeurs" (Society of Fleecers.) It was publicly accused of terrorizing those who opposed them.

Achille was in high good humor. "Guess we won't be called 'The Societe des Tondeurs' now."

Charles was too weak to match Achille's robust enthusiasm. He smiled wanly and said, "Only our enemies used that term. Our people were happy enough to have our help in keeping claim jumpers away and helping them get started."

"And grateful they should be," insisted Achille. "Some were too poor to even pay two dollars rent per acre. I have to confess I did not like your idea of share leases, but it is working out."

Father Chiniquy had talked long and hard to get the others on the committee to agree to his plan. He admitted, "I thought for awhile we had over reached by using our farm land as collateral to buy more property in the village."

"Achille said, "Me, too. When the tenants could not pay their rent, we were in bad straits. It is lucky for us those Easterners had big pocketbooks."

"And big hearts! Praise the Lord!"

Achille stood up to leave.

"Don't worry any more about our notes. They are all paid off. First, I distributed the money to the village residents. They paid me their back rents. I hurried over to the Kankakee City banks just in time to pay our obligations and thumb my nose at our enemies who had hoped to foreclose and ruin us."

"Oh, wonderful! Thank you, Achille, my dear brother."

He was still running a slight fever. The excitement of hearing the good news made him sweaty again. He mopped his brow with the handkerchief Euphemie had tucked under his pillow.

"Are you expecting another flood?" asked Achille, smiling.

"Why do you ask that?"

"Well, I thought maybe you were going to get an ark ready like old Noah."

"An ark?"

"Yes, One of the boxes you brought back with you is labeled *'Bois d'arc'* (wood of the arc). I looked inside. The box is filled with seeds. Are you going to grow arks?"

"No, no. No," laughed his brother. "That seed is for Osage hedge. I purchased it in Baltimore for only 20 dollars a bushel. They tell me the price is really going up. You remember we talked about using it for fences. The Osage is sometimes referred to as the *'bois d'arc.'*"

"Is that the kind of wood Noah used for his ark?"

"No one knows for certain. *The King James Version of the Bible* says God commanded Noah to use 'gopher' wood. I am told that Osage is disease-free and unattractive to pests with the exception of marauding gophers. So perhaps that is what 'gopher' wood was, although I am inclined to think Noah used a conifer such as cypress or cedar. The name—the wood that bends--may have been given the wood by the old French trappers because of its supple, tough quality. The name is euphonic and probably captured the fancy of the seed sellers."

"So you want to get hedge rows growing here to replace rail fences. Do you think it better than wire fences?"

"I don't know. Wire rusts unless it is painted and it has to be stretched taut to make a secure fence Winter frosts cause the heavy posts to heave, and the wire has to be tightened each spring."

"I have heard several objections to hedge," Achille countered. "In the first place, the seedlings are hard to get started in this climate. In the second place, it takes at least three years to get it going. And thirdly, the gaps in the hedges frequently do not fill up, the plants turn into trees, and the livestock find gaps they can pass through."

His brother nodded. "Yes, I am aware of all those arguments. But I was told in Baltimore that we should use the English method of hedging called the 'plashing' technique—partially cutting off the plants a few inches above the ground to bend and thoroughly entwine them. Some farmers plant as close as three inches apart; others as far as twelve. As for the seedlings, I thought we could glass in our southwest sun porch and use it as a greenhouse to get the seedlings ready for next spring. Let's talk about it later. I must not be as well as I thought. Suddenly, I am very, very tired."

Achille left quickly, and his brother fell asleep almost immediately.

Chapter XX
The Chiniquy Church

On the next Sabbath, Father Chiniquy, not yet strong enough to preach the sermons, was surrounded by loving well wishers when he attended the morning service. It was a service given over to joyous thanksgiving and praise to God for the salvation of the village from economic ruin and for the recovery of their beloved pastor from the ravages of fever.

Later that day at a meeting of the elders, Father Chiniquy brought up a topic that had been troubling him for many months, the name of his church. At first, they had adopted the name "Christian Catholics." The press, however, always referred to the reform group as "The Chiniquy Church," a name Father Chiniquy did not want. He reported to the elders he had been asked in Philadelphia and other eastern cities, "Do you call yourselves 'The Chiniquy Church?' Why do you not connect yourselves with one of our great Protestant denominations? That denomination would take you by the hand and help you through your difficulties."

He looked around at the men who had been chosen church leaders by their peers. He said, "I told them that joining one denomination is a difficult thing for new converts from Rome. We observe so much dissension among Protestant churches. We see the good Episcopal Church so much opposed to what she calls dissenters that she will not allow ministers of other Protestant churches to speak in her pulpits; we find the Presbyterians divided into two fiercely fighting camps, the Old School and the New School; a little further we find the Lutherans with their crucifixes and so many other ways of Romanism assuring us they are the best branch of Christ. At a little distance, we see the Methodists telling us a different story. We find the Baptists who go down in their water baths. There are more than one hundred different Protestant denominations, many fighting like wild cats."

Elder Therrien spoke up, "Maybe we are better off rid of all of them."

"I entertained that thought, too, Elder Therrien. But as I was heading for church this morning, I crossed the backyard of the parsonage and stopped to rest a moment in the cool shade of my grape arbor. I opened by Bible to 15th Chapter of St. John and read with prayerful attention the words of Christ to his disciples, 'I am the Vine; ye are the branches.'

"Looking around at the arbor, I noticed for the first time that there was not one single grape branch like the other branches. The variety reminded me of the branches of the Protestant church. I noticed that though all the branches are quite different in appearance, they all are loaded with splendid grapes for they were all perfectly united with the vine. There are varieties of views among the many denominations. So long as Jesus is the vine, I believe that, rather than risk being regarded as just another religious sect known as 'The Chiniquy Church,' we would be wise to unite ourselves to the vine through one of the established branches. The only thing necessary is that we be well united with the vine."

He looked around at the elders who seemed to agree with him.

"I want your opinion on our uniting with the Presbyterian Church. We have a sacred link with the French Huguenots, the martyred Christians of France who so heroically shed blood for Gospel causes. Many of our French Canadian converts have the same names as those heroic soldiers and probably have the blood of the martyrs running in their veins."

The elders unanimously decided to join the Presbyterian Church if that organization would accept the convert church. The congregation-at-large was informed of the decision and gave its whole-hearted approval.

The six elders accompanied Father Chiniquy to Chicago to respectfully request the Chicago Presbytery to allow them affiliation with the international Presbyterian Church. Euphemie's father was one of the elders. He later told his wife and daughter how the pastor and elders were questioned about their religious views and their new religious movement.

"I thought they were going to turn us down," he said. "They finally agreed to take us in. We all breathed a big sigh of relief when the moderator said, 'Here is our *Westminister Confession of Faith*, which you will adopt and declare yourselves faithful children of the Presbyterian Church.' Imagine our surprise when Father Chiniquy shook his head sadly but firmly and said, 'Mr. Moderator, please withdraw that book and put the Bible in its place as the standard of our faith and life.'"

Euphemie gasped, "What happened then?"

"The moderator was aghast," her father continued. "'Mr. Chiniquy,' he said, and he was angry, 'we cannot do that. Our custom is that the *Westminister Book of Faith* is the standard to which the new members pledge. We cannot change the rule. You think you can come to us on your own terms. You are sadly mistaken. We cannot, we will not change our rules to accommodate you.'"

"So we are not going to be Presbyterians?" Euphemie's mother asked.

"That's what we thought then. Now, we don't know. A very distinguished white-haired man spoke up. Everyone seemed to respect him. He said he and some other leading Presbyterians had felt for some time that the Westminister Confession is now cumbersome for this age. He said he wasn't in favor of abandoning it, but he felt it should be simplified. He recommended that the board consider among themselves a few days before making the decision."

"Was that all right with Father Chiniquy?"

"Oh, yes. He said he would gladly wait."

Two weeks passed before the letter arrived from the Chicago Presbytery granting the Chiniquy converts admission to the Presbyterian Church and granting special permission for them to lay their hands on the Bible instead of the *Westminister Book of Faith.*

Euphemie was not surprised. Others might marvel that a great international church would bend its hard-bound rules to accept a band of converts from Rome whose leader refused to abide by their standard method of acceptance, but Euphemie was confident all along that Father Chiniquy would get his way. Her father said the Presbyterians conceded because it was a feather in their cap to get an entire colony of ex-Catholics in their fold. Euphemie was certain Father Chiniquy's persuasive powers caused the Presbyterian elders to make the Ste. Anne colony an exception.

Members of the Chicago Presbytery made their way to Ste. Anne by way of Kankakee City where crowds of people gathered to escort them to Ste. Anne. The chapel was crowded with converts from the village and surrounding towns. The members of the Chicago Presbytery addressed them and received all of them as newborn children of the great Presbyterian family.

Father Chiniquy requested he henceforth be addressed as Pastor Chiniquy. He said, "When I appeared before the eastern congregations, they introduced me as The Reverend Mr. Chiniquy, but when they spoke directly to me, they called me Pastor Chiniquy. I liked that. Since I am no longer a priest, I prefer you call me Pastor Chiniquy. It may take awhile for you to get used to it, but soon it will come naturally to you."

At the end of the ceremony, the sexton rang the big church bell and its melodious tones were the accompaniment for the group singing. Euphemie and the other women preparing refreshments in the church kitchen joined in the chorus, "Glory to God in highest; and on earth peace, good will toward men."

Euphemie, no longer a timid maiden lingering on the fringes of church activities, was in charge of the women preparing the refreshments. What a feast of thanksgiving it was!

In Kankakee City, over one hundred heads of families also broke with the Church of Rome and formed the French Presbyterian Church of Kankakee. It, too, was accepted into the Chicago Presbytery. The Reverend Mr. Chiniquy was the leader of both churches although he was often absent from both pulpits for months at a time. During those periods, young ministers or capable laymen took his place. .

Euphemie, often exhausted but never dismayed, loved the excitement and activity in the parsonage. At times, during Pastor Chiniquy's frequent absences, she served as hostess to those who arrived unannounced to see for themselves what the reform was all about. Many young ministers, although disappointed in not finding Pastor Chiniquy there, were smitten by the apostate's charming housekeeper. Had she given them any kind of encouragement, they would have become her suitors.

"Think of that," exclaimed Pastor Chiniquy one morning over his breakfast coffee. "We now have two hundred heads of families in Chicago, forty five in Ottawa, fifteen in Joliet, forty in Middleport and about two hundred more in Indiana and Michigan."

Euphemie shared his delight but feared for his health. He spared himself very little time for sleeping and usually ate on the run unless he dined with guests. She worried over him like a concerned mother.

"I know what you are going to say," he said, smiling. "I agree with you. This is too much for one man to do. I must get a preparatory college started, modest as it will be at first. I need able Christian leaders to help me in what promises to be a great evangelism."

She could not see that the establishment of a preparatory college could be any immediate help; indeed, it would only add more duties to his busy schedule. She found herself worrying more and more about him. He seemed oblivious to the insults and accusations that were hurled at him wherever he went. He never mentioned it, but she had been told his life was threatened in every city and town where he lectured. At home, the Ste. Anne Catholics had no place to worship and they were bitter. The lawsuit brought by their bishop to regain possession of the building and land it was built on was pending. In the meantime, the Ste. Anne Catholics either worshiped in homes or traveled to Ste. Mary's or L'Erable.

"I wish," she told her employer, "that all the Ste. Anne Catholics would move to Ste. Mary's or L'Erable and stay there."

"Whoa, there!" he said, as he pushed his chair away from the breakfast table. "Let's not be so generous as to turn L'Erable over to our enemies. Achille and I have big plans for that little town on the Iroquois River. Ask Lucy to show you sometime the map we drew up. L'Erable could become a great port if we are successful in our plans to dredge the Iroquois to make it navigable. It connects with the Kankakee River and on to the Illinois and Mississippi rivers and on to the Gulf of Mexico. When Bishop Vandervelde asked me to colonize this area, he said it could become the granary of not only the United States but also the whole world. Now is the time to plan how to get that grain as well as beaver pelts to the big markets. Chicago seems to be a growing town with some geographic advantages, but we believe L'Erable could give it a great deal of competition. The

Chiniquy Committee owns large tracts of land along the Iroquois Someday soon we should get that project started."

Euphemie shook her head in disbelief.

"Is there no end to the things you hope to accomplish? You should have been made twins or maybe ten of a kind."

She tried in every way she could to make life easier for him. It pleased him to hear her play the fiddle. Although he often asked her to play for guests, her greatest joy came from playing for him alone on those rare occasions when no one else was around. He closed his eyes then and lay back in his big chair in complete relaxation. On one such occasion, after an especially difficult week, he quoted from I Samuel, "And it came to pass that David took a harp and played with his hand; so Saul was refreshed, and was well, and the evil spirit departed from him."

Those were moments Euphemie cherished

Chapter XXI
Treachery in Canada

One blustery January day, at the request of Pastor Chiniquy, John Mason picked up the church mail from the post office. Since he could not find the pastor in his study, he stopped at the parsonage and left the mail with Euphemie. There were two thick letters, both from Canada: one from Quebec City and one from Montreal. When Pastor Chiniquy came home for his noon meal, he eagerly opened the letters. Euphemie, watching his face for clues as to what they were about, saw first incredulity, and then doubt followed by joy pass across his expressive face. The first letter contained nearly 500 names of well-known persons from Quebec City and the second held signatures of over 100 French Canadian Roman Catholics from Montreal. They were friendly invitations to go to those cities and expose his motives for leaving the Church of Rome.

He ate his food, totally preoccupied with the letters. Before he left the table, he said, "I have often thought it my duty to go to Canada to attack Rome in its own fortress, but I put off this work because of the difficulties and dangers attending it. One probably cannot find in the entire world two other places where the clergy is so strong as in Quebec City and Montreal."

"Oh, Father, I mean Pastor, please don't go. You must not go."

"That was my decision until the moment I received these two letters .Now I have changed my mind. How can I shut my ears to the cries of the souls in danger who ask me so ardently to go to give them the bread of life?"

"But your life. Must you endanger it for them?"

Neither her pleas nor those of his parishioners could dissuade him. With tears, they begged him not to expose himself to the danger so evident in Canada. He assured them that he felt it was the will of God that he make the journey. He asked them to pray for him during his absence he thought would be a month or longer. He promised to return to Ste. Anne full of renewed vigor after having spread the good seeds in their dear Canada. He arranged for Martin Demers and John Gauthier, capable laymen, to replace him in the pulpit on Sundays during his absence.

It was a journey fraught with danger. Before the first Sunday of his visit, the Bishop of Montreal issued a mandate to be read in all churches and published in all French newspapers prohibiting all Catholics from having anything to do with Chiniquy. Despite the mandate, crowds gathered in Montreal, Quebec City, Toronto, and Napierville to cheer him. Other crowds gathered in those same cities to jeer him. He was often attacked with rocks and barely escaped death three times.

Euphemie heard nothing of these adventures from Pastor Chiniquy. Neither did he mention the interdits and defenses against him by the priests of Saint Pie, Sainte Marie and Saint Greguire nor of the attempt on his life when he stopped on his way back to Ste. Anne in Muskegon, Michigan. He told her only of the thousands of converts in all those places and the particular joy he felt when he addressed zealous Baptist missionaries from the mission of Grand Ligne. These converts, as well as their pastor, were among a number of such Protestants he had insulted and persecuted when he was a priest of Rome. How happy he was to have an opportunity to obtain their pardon and have them unite with him in prayer!

He said, "I know you worried about me, and I am grateful for your prayers. I was not alone. No, I was under the protection of my God during all that time."

It was not until years later as she pored over the pages of his book manuscript that she learned of his perilous times and marveled he lived to write about them

Chapter XXII
Added Duties

The Ste. Anne Catholics did not move to Ste. Mary's or L'Erable although all their records of births, marriages and deaths were recorded at Ste. Mary's Church. The priest from that church was persuaded to travel to Ste. Anne and say mass at the home of Desire Fortier. French families from Canada, Belgium and France continued to arrive. Hundreds stayed only a few weeks or a few months before they pushed on to new homesteads farther west. They were glad to take a break in their journey in an area where French was the language spoken. Of those who remained, some became converted, but many continued to practice Catholicism. The Fortier home became too small to hold the Catholic worshippers so they erected a small frame chapel within calling distance of the Presbyterian Church.

Euphemie knew many families torn and embittered by religious differences. Her heart ached for them because she knew how strong family ties are for French people. How she wished they had all turned Protestant! At times, she regretted that they had not all stayed Catholic under the beautiful priesthood of Father Chiniquy the way it was during the first few years of the colony. She knew Pastor Chiniquy well enough to know hers was a futile dream. Still, she often felt like a Catholic clad in Protestant garb.

It was a time of great turmoil and animosity. The winds of war were blowing nationally, but the slavery problem did not affect the French

Canadian immigrants nearly so much as the religious schism. Hatred among brothers, sisters, cousins and neighbors caused mischief of serious nature to take place. Dr. Legris was called to a country home on a fake illness report, his carriage was waylaid and he was tarred and feathered. Rocks were thrown through windows, homes were invaded and Bibles destroyed. Retaliatory attacks were made by the Protestants. There were many fires, and arson was often suspected. Boys, young and old, engaged in name-calling and egg and rock throwing.

In the midst of the turmoil, Euphemie became more and more efficient at managing the parsonage. She learned to go for groceries in spite of the danger of being spat upon or hit with a rock by boys or tongue-lashed by some of the bolder women. Many wayfarers, either on their way through or not yet established in the town, made the parsonage their headquarters. Some stayed in the parsonage, especially during the cold weather if they had babies and small children. Most of the families made their wagon beds their home and used the parsonage well and outhouse. More often than not, the newcomers had relatives in Ste. Anne with whom they stayed.

Euphemie learned much from the women who crossed her threshold. French women are very frugal. They are wise in the ways of cooking. They taught Euphemie many things, one of which did more to improve her meals than any other. That was --better to throw away some bad butter than ruin an entire meal. Euphemie thought this strange advice from the frugal French.

"Can't it be used some way?" she asked.

Her advisor shook her head. "With bad butter, you turn from your dreadful slice of bread to your beefsteak which you have fried in the same butter; you think to find relief in a vegetable diet, and find the butter spoiling the string beans, polluting the peas, and ruining the corn. Even succotash and squash as well as beets and onions taste bad because of it. You hope to satisfy your hunger with dessert, but you find the pastry and cake cursed by the same bad butter."

Pastor Chiniquy overheard the discussion and said with a smile, "There ought to be some way I could incorporate that idea in a sermon. I like it better than the theory that one bad apple spoils the barrel."

If the French cook throws out bad butter, she does not waste any meat. Even tough animal cartilages and sinews are specially treated and come out in savory soups or stews. Euphemie's mother could do good things with soup, but the traveling cooks introduced the young cook to the French soup kettle with a double bottom that prevents burning. For them the soup kettle always stood ready waiting for bones, thin fibrous flaps of skin, sinewy and gristly portions that are otherwise wasted. The secret, the cooks from France said, was applying the heat slowly and steadily, never letting the liquid reach the boiling point but let it simmer quietly for hours. Euphemie became expert at that kind of cooking. Her delicious soup often helped stretch a meal to accommodate another family arriving unexpectedly.

Pastor Chiniquy seldom complained about her cooking even when she was in the learning stage because he knew how hard she was trying. He did mention one night after a visit from some ministers from Chicago that he wished she could do something different about coffee. He recommended that she purchase new equipment if necessary. Euphemie had to admit her coffee tasted terrible. She learned that a Mrs. Chayer, who camped in the parsonage yard that winter, made delicious coffee. She sought her out to learn her secret.

Mrs. Chayer said, "I roast my own coffee beans in this little coffee roaster."

"And then do you use this grinder?" Euphemie asked.

"Yes. I grind only as much as I need for a potful. I also use a linen filter. I put the freshly ground roasted coffee in this linen filter and place it in the top part of the pot. Then I pour boiling water over it. The liquid percolates down to the bottom of the pot. The spout should be stopped with a wad of cloth to keep the essence from escaping."

Pastor Chiniquy bought a roaster and grinder for Euphemie. She made some filters from linen scraps. She soon became known for her fine coffee. The dark liquid was called *café noir*. She prepared *café au lait* by adding a tablespoon of the dark, flavorful liquid to a cup of hot milk that had been boiled, not merely warmed, and simmered until thick and creamy. Sparkling beet sugar was added to suit the drinker's taste. She collected and experimented with recipes, many of which caused her despair and anxiety because they directed, "add flour" or "cook until thick." How she longed for explicit directions!

Letters from Mina came often at first with scribbled hurried notes from Evaloe. He wrote that Marie was responding to the treatments and they had wonderful hope for full recovery although it would take a long time. Evaloe had a job in a wagon shop, the children were content, but Mina often talked about Euphemie and missed her very much, always remembering her in her bedtime prayers.

The mail was carried to and from Ste. Anne to the trains in Kankakee City. Townspeople as well as farmers in Ste. Anne went to the post office for their mail. Whenever Pastor Chiniquy brought home a letter for Euphemie from Evaloe, he noticed how her face lighted with pleasure and anticipation. His heart ached that she was wasting herself on such a hopeless romance. He often attempted to interest her in this or that handsome young minister who came to study the reform movement. If any would-be suitor seemed her preference, he noted, it was the young teacher, Francis Bechard, whose devotion to Euphemie was noticeable to everyone.

With this in mind, Pastor Chiniquy requested Euphemie to be young Bechard's assistant in teaching adults to read. The converts' schooling had been little or none, and they were longing to know how to read so they could read their Bibles for themselves. It was his plan to encourage the children taught during the day to tutor their parents after school. Classes for children were in session all year round. The bigger boys and some of the girls stayed home from school during the planting or harvest to help on the farm or to help care of a new baby

"I have a request," Pastor Chiniquy said as he sat in the kitchen eating a hurried meal before going to the Spenard home to make funeral arrangements for the eighty-year old Adrian Spenard.

"More pie or coffee?"

"No, not that kind of request. I need your help on a little project I have in mind."

"My help?"

"Yes, your help. As you know, I have received a large shipment of New Testaments. Our people long to read for themselves the good news. Some are doing it already. Some are not. Can you guess why?"

"They can't read."

"Precisely. They want to learn to read. That is where you come in."

"But I am not a teacher."

"No, but you are an educated young woman with superior intelligence."

"You cannot be talking about me."

"Yes, I can and I am. Now, stop protesting and listen to my plan."

He explained what he had in mind. It sounded like hours of time and work to her although the idea intrigued her.

"I don't see how I can find the time," she hedged. "We have so much company. I have a big garden. The canning, the washing and ironing as well as the shopping and cooking leave me hardly any time for my sewing, my English lessons and a little practice on my fiddle. I don't see how I can do it all."

"I don't intend for you to do it all. I want you to instruct some of the young girls of our parish to take over the manual chores of the parsonage. I will pay them for their work."

"But...this may sound conceited, but I would be afraid they would not do the jobs right."

"My dear, do you have your Bible near at hand?"

"Right around the corner on my bureau."

"Get it for me, will you please? I want to read you a scripture about Moses and his father-in-law, Jethro."

She obediently went for the Bible, somewhat bewildered as to what Moses and his father-in-law had to do with hiring young girls for household chores. He instructed her to turn to Exodus 18 and find verse 18. He read to her how 3,200 years ago, Jethro, an Arabian priest, gave his son-in-law advice in statecraft efficiency and thus helped avert the nervous breakdown of the great leader. In the wilderness, Moses was trying to make all the decisions of the tribes. The burden of the myriad decisions was wearying him to the point of collapse and he could barely think straight. Jethro said, "Thou shalt surely wear away for this thing is too heavy for thee; you are not able to perform it thyself alone." He advised Moses to instruct men to be rulers of thousands, hundreds, fifties and tens in order to judge all small matters thus freeing himself, the leader, for concentration on the difficult big decisions and tasks

"But a Moses I am not."

"Not a Moses, perhaps, but a well-trained mind. The first business of a good housekeeper is that of a teacher. It requires tact, patience and clarity of directions. Good servants do not often come to us. They must be trained. You will have to bear patiently with their faults; teach them how to improve; and trust them and treat them in such a way to lead them to respect themselves and feel proud of the job they are doing. By doing this, you will be released from your household duties to take on the duties of assisting our already over-worked teacher, Francis Bechard."

With a boldness she would not have imagined herself possessing six months earlier, Euphemie asked coyly, "Could you, perchance, have arranged such a plan to foster a greater friendship between Francis and me?" It had suddenly flashed across her mind the memory of his fraying the cords on the statues of Ste. Anne and Ste. Mary.

"Ridiculous!" he sputtered. "You hardly need help to foster friendship with young men."

"My mother does not seem to think that way."

"How's that?"

"Well, I just happen to know she made a novena, back when we were still with the other church, that I would find some nice young man to marry. I am certain she is still praying lest I be an old maid."

"I am not praying about it…although I am delighted to see that you are accepting the attention of several young men. And since you brought it up, that young Bechard is a fine young man. Well, I must hurry to the Spenards. Tell me at the evening meal that you want to help those thirsting and crying for knowledge of the Gospel."

He made it seem she had a choice, but Euphemie knew very well that there was no way she could refuse his request. In fact, she was flattered to be asked and looked forward to the association with Francis, whom she considered a good friend. She cheerfully took on the new duties of training household help and teaching the converts to read.

Chapter XXIII
Treachery at Home

Life at the parsonage went along rather smoothly in spite of the new help and the fact that Euphemie spent so much time at her new assignment. She found herself enjoying the reading class as well as the good company of Francis, who praised her highly for how proficient she became at teaching adults to read.

One October day, Pastor Chiniquy met her at the door as she came home from class. "Would you pack my bags again? I have another speaking engagement."

"Of course. How long will you be gone?"

"Six months."

"Six months?"

"Yes," he said, taking an envelope from his pocket. "Your old pastor has the honor of being invited to attend the 300th anniversary of the Protestant Reformation in Edinburgh, Scotland. Sir John Lawrence, Viceroy of India and one of the greatest heroes of our time, is the president of the meeting. Prominent ministers and laymen throughout the world are invited. They want to hear about our work here."

"How wonderful!'

"They have requested that I speak to the assembly two times."

"No one could be more deserving. Will the conference last six months?"

He laughed. "No, We ministers are long-winded but not that bad. I have been asked to speak at several churches in Glasgow, Scotland. There I will be a guest of John Henderson, a Glasgow merchant. I have been told he has a beautiful mansion. Perhaps I can bring back some ideas to improve my house. At any rate, from there I plan to fulfill a dream of mine to lecture in London, Liverpool and perhaps Sheffield and Oxford in England. Fortunately, my English has improved considerably since that first horrid day in Philadelphia."

"Who will be in charge of our church"|?"

"I have written to the Chicago Presbytery to send a minister to fill my pulpit during my absence. Young Henry Morrell, who helps me out during my short trips, will be valuable help to him. I am counting on you and Francis to make him welcome here."

"I will do what I can," she said. "I must go now and check your wardrobe." She hesitated.

"Yes, Miss Allard, what is it?"

"Well, this is rather bold of me to suggest, but you could use some new underwear and stockings."

"You are absolutely right. I will attend to that immediately."

Theodore Monod arrived from the Chicago Presbytery three days before Pastor Chiniquy's departure and in time to be introduced at the Sunday service to the congregations he was to serve. Euphemie, like the other women, was immediately taken with Reverend Monod. He was not tall, but he seemed it standing by the short, thickening figure of Pastor Chiniquy. He was in his mid-twenties, brunette with dark brown eyes. Angular and erect, he walked and moved with a quickness that suggested a superabundance of energy. He displayed a friendliness and calm poise unusual in one so young. Born in Paris, he had received his bachelor's and master's degrees at the University of Paris and studied law three years before receiving a degree in theology from Western Theological Seminary. He was not yet ordained, but Pastor Chiniquy requested that he be called "Reverend."

Euphemie served a noon meal to the new minister, Pastor Chiniquy, Henry Morrell and Francis Bechard. During the meal, which Euphemie served but did not eat, she noticed a certain arrogance, almost an air of condescension, of the Frenchman toward the French Canadians—more toward Henry and Francis, but to a degree toward Pastor Chiniquy. Although he was charmingly polite to her, she knew from the moment he entered the house and she took his hat he thought of her as merely a lowly servant..

He was well educated, the son of a famous minister in Paris. He had read widely on the subjects of philosophy and theology and was well versed in church government. He seemed to be interrogating Pastor Chiniquy about his knowledge of Presbyterian tenets rather than letting the pastor examine him. Euphemie had a strange sense of foreboding that she tried to shake off, attributing it to her reaction to his manner toward her.

Her fears seemed ill founded during the first six weeks. The congregation was at first somewhat in awe of him and did not fully comprehend his sermons. He soon learned to simplify his message to meet their level of understanding. It was not apparent until the end of the first three months that he was sowing seeds of discord. Francis noticed it and mentioned it to Euphemie. They wished Pastor Chiniquy would shorten his European tour and send the young troublemaker back to Chicago or Paris or anywhere to get him away from Ste. Anne.

Reverend Monod completed his studies and received his final degree from the seminary. He gathered around him and Henry Morrell a number of younger families and a few older men and women and instructed them in Presbyterian law and tenets. He pointed out that Pastor Chiniquy was not truly operating a Presbyterian church, that his method of conducting affairs was patterned after the totalitarian church system he had left. He emphasized that Presbyterianism calls for decisions to come from the group and not from the top down.

Pastor Chiniquy was, of course, unaware of young Monod's treachery. In Edinburgh, he met the young man's father, Felix Monod, who was president of the Synod of the Free Presbyterian Church of France. The Rev. Monod invited Pastor Chiniquy to address the church of France in St. Etienne when the Synod met there. After his months of lectures in English speaking countries, Pastor Chiniquy was delighted to be among French people whom he could address so much more easily in his beloved French tongue.

From Paris, he wrote Euphemie to tell her he would soon be home. He expressed anxiety about the state of the union because rumors of civil war in the United States were circulating rapidly in Europe, especially in England where sympathies for the most part were for the southern states. He closed his letter by telling how much he was enjoying the company of the father of Theodore Monod and hoped the son would become as fine a minister as his father. He said how grateful he was to have such a fine young man tending his flock while he was gone.

He ended his letter with a description of his trip to the opera in Paris with the elder Rev. Monod. "He took me to the opera last night. Opera in Paris is a magnificent affair. We dined at a delightful sidewalk café and lingered overlong drinking *café au lait.* We missed the overture. Ordinarily, no one is seated except between acts, but because we were to occupy the private loge loaned us by one of France's great statesmen, we were permitted late entry. The attendant unlocked the loge door with a key from his heavy key ring. We walked from the bright lobby into the darkened outer loge furnished with lounges and small tables for between-acts entertaining. The loge proper, where six upholstered chairs sat waiting our occupancy, was separated from the outer loge by a red velvet drape. Rev. Monod pulled aside the drape and motioned for me to enter and take a front seat next to the balustrade. The loge extended over the orchestra pit and looked almost directly down on the stage. The performance that night was a new opera, *Faust,* by the French composer, Charles Gounod, and was based on Part I of Goethe's *Faust.* It was performed for the first time two years ago in Paris. As you probably recall…"

Euphemie knew nothing at all about Faust, opera or Goethe, but she was flattered that he thought she did.

"As you probably recall, Faust was a German magician and charlatan of the 16th century, famed in legend and literature as the man who sold his soul to the devil in exchange for power and knowledge. Although Humanist scholars scoffed at his magical feats as petty and fraudulent, he was taken seriously by Luther and Melanchthon. Mephistopheles was the name of the fiend with whom he made his pact.

"As we entered through the drape, Faust was crouched on the dimly lit stage. In just a moment, a flash of powder would ignite and give off a cloud of pink smoke out of which the devil, Mephistopheles, a tall handsomely built man, would appear in a bright red suit. At that very time, I, not noticing there was a step down to the front two chairs, missed my footing. But for my firm grasp on the balustrade and a quick grip from behind on my black cloak by Rev. Monod, I would have catapulted over the railing with my black cloak flaring out behind me to the darkened stage to make a simultaneous entrance with Mephistopheles. I can well imagine how the newspapers with Catholic editors would have handled that headline, 'Devil Chiniquy and Mephistopheles Make Pact with Faust on Opera Stage.'"

Ephemie read the letter aloud to Francis before their students arrived for English class that night. They chuckled over the spectrum of Pastor Chiniquy, clothed in a black cloak, soaring through the air to land on the stage in a puff of pink smoke

They wondered how to break the news to him of the treachery of Theodore Monod and Henry Morrell because by the end of April, the dissident group had purchased some land on the west side of Main Street about a block west of the church and erected a building in which they held their first service on Easter Sunday. The group applied to the Chicago Presbytery for membership as the Second Presbyterian Church of Ste. Anne. The Reverend Monod tirelessly conducted classes for Sunday School teachers and officers instructing them in the disciplines of Presbyterianism Anger and antagonism were almost as strong between the old and new church as between Protestants and Catholics. The elders of the First Presbyterian Church did not appeal for another replacement. They held the services with laymen doing the preaching until Pastor Chiniquy returned. Weddings, funerals and baptisms were performed in Ste Anne by the Presbyterian minister from Kankakee City.

It was into this situation that Pastor Chiniquy returned from Europe. The exact date of his return had not been determined so no one met him at the train station in Kankakee City. He hired a driver and buggy at the livery stable and made the trip to Ste. Anne alone, remembering the times he had returned in the midst of a caravan of shouting, admiring parishioners. He smiled to himself at the surprise his arrival would bring. He looked forward to showing the gifts he had brought for the church, the parsonage, Achille, Lucy and his housekeeper.

Euphemie was putting the finishing handwork on a dress she was making for her mother when the strange buggy swept up the driveway. She was delighted to see him. At the same time, she was upset because she had nothing special to serve for supper. Achille and Lucy had seen him go by their home, and they soon arrived to greet the traveler. They stayed for supper, which was not sumptuous but adequate. Pastor Chiniquy said the good home cooking tasted like pure ambrosia. It was nothing but bowls of hearty vegetable soup, slabs of homemade bread and butter, apple butter, and Euphemie's special *café au lait.*

They listened with pride when he told how he had been received by the people of Europe who were eager to hear about the reform in Ste. Anne. He told of the general meeting in Edinburgh to celebrate the tercentenary of Scotland's reformation There, he mingled among great religious leaders and was privileged to address that august group two times. During his lecture tour through Great Britain, France and Switzerland, he was given over $15,000 for the preparatory college he planned to establish in Ste. Anne. The crowning event of his six months' stay was his being given the privilege of addressing the Synod of the Free Protestant Church of France.

After the meal, during which no mention was made of the Reverend Monod and his treachery, Pastor Chiniquy opened his small trunk and took out gifts—a lovely silver thimble for Lucy, a pocketknife with a blade of Sheffield steel for Achille, and for Euphemie a bright red velvet pin cushion surrounded with hundreds of bright pins standing in circular rows in perforated metal. She was delighted.

"Now," he said, pleased that she liked his gift, "you won't have to use weighted bricks to hold the patterns when you sew." She did not know he ever noticed things like that.

He told them of the works of art he had purchased in Paris to add to the collection on the mezzanine floor of the parsonage. He said he also ordered a new organ for the church. The gifts brought cries of delight from the women and a smile of pleasure from Achille as he gently ran his finger over the edge of the sharp blade.

"Now, if I were superstitious," Pastor Chiniquy said with a laugh, "I'd insist that you, Achille, and you, Miss Allard, pay me a penny for these gifts or else our friendship will be cut by the giving and accepting of these sharp items. There's no greater blow than a severed friendship."

Suddenly, no one was laughing except Pastor Chiniquy

"What is the matter? Why are you all so suddenly solemn?"

Euphemie said, "I must see if the dishwater is heating," and she went to the kitchen.

Lucy jumped up. "I'll help you clean the table, Euphemie,"

They left Achille to tell the story. Pastor Chiniquy was stunned by the report. His faith in the two young men had been misplaced. That they would betray the trust he had placed in them was devastating, but even more devastating was the departure of what he had believed to be his faithful followers. Achille tried to comfort him by pointing out that most them were newcomers to the village and not those who had weathered the dramatic break with the Church of Rome

By the time the Sabbath came, the wound had begun to heal. For his sermon, he chose the scripture from Matthew 21 in which Jesus tells the parable of the vineyard. "I know you have been wondering what I would say when I returned to find trouble in our spiritual vineyard. I would be wrong to tell you I had no ill feelings when I heard the news. I was devastated. I was angry. I was crushed with despair. I spent many hours praying and studying the Gospel. I have come through the despair with the gift of forgiveness and tolerance for our brethren who worship the same God but from different pews. Let us not widen the breach between us. Let us walk along together toward our houses of worship."

The extent of the treachery had not yet been revealed. The next week, Pastor Chiniquy was called before the Chicago Presbytery to answer charges that he had fraudulently collected money on his speaking tour for a non-existent Presbyterian seminary in Ste. Anne.

He cried out in disbelief, "They say my school is nothing more than a grammar school. What do they expect? I have to prepare my poor ignorant French Canadians for higher education. It will be a seminary, a fine one. They must give me time."

Euphemie had never seen him so despondent. He was unusually non-communicative during the trial. She learned about the trial by putting together bits and pieces of what she heard in the parsonage and what her father told her. The charges against him were extravagances in the use of the church funds and misrepresentation in obtaining means of support for the church. The Chicago Presbytery did not convict him, but they passed an implied censure on him. He appealed to the Synod that was to meet in mid-summer. That was four months away.

Chapter XXIV
Whitehouse Visited

Euphemie worried about Pastor Chiniquy because he seemed so unlike himself during those weeks he waited for the Synod's decision. She was glad to hear of his plans to go by train to Washington City although she was completely taken back by his mission.

Early one morning, he said, "I will be leaving for a few weeks sometime tomorrow. Would you get my things packed, please? I am going to Washington City."

"Washington City? The Capital?"

"Yes. Perhaps you don't know that President Lincoln is my friend. Years ago, when he was a circuit lawyer in Illinois, he defended me in a trial that saved my career and my good name."

"Yes, I know that Mr. Lincoln was your lawyer. When the trial was moved from Kankakee City to Urbana, Papa went down with a big group of men and they camped near the courthouse. Wasn't the suit brought by a man named Spink?"

"That's the rascal. Mr. Lincoln did me a great service then. I hope to help him now by warning him of a conspiracy against him. I heard about it while I was in Europe."

"A conspiracy? To remove him from office?"

"In a manner of speaking. It would remove him permanently. There is a plot brewing among his enemies to kill him."

"Kill President Lincoln? How awful! Who would want to do that?"

"I am sorry, Miss Allard. I can tell you no more right now."

He left for Washington City the next day. The President's secretary was reluctant to give him any time with his busy employer, but Pastor Chiniquy persuaded him to allow him a ten-minute interview. Lincoln was not surprised at the news his friend from Illinois brought. Samuel Morse, inventor of the telegraph, had returned from Europe with the same news.

"I might very well be headed for assassination," he said sadly. "Man must not care where and when he will die, provided he dies at his post of duty. If God calls me through the hand of an assassin, I will say, 'Let Thy will be done.' My dear Chiniquy, I wish we could talk longer, but I have many pressing duties today. Could you possibly stay over and attend a dinner I am giving tonight? The guest of honor is a Frenchman like you. He is Prince Napoleon Jerome Bonaparte from France. Although he is known to speak English, I am certain we will be able to communicate better if you could be there as an interpreter."

Pastor Chiniquy was flattered and delighted to be invited, and he was eager to meet the young prince from France. He said, "My grandfather, Martin et Chiniquia, was a fearless sailor from French Biscay in the service of the king of France."

"Is that a fact?"

"Yes. His ship, like many of the ships of those days, was half military and half merchant and was well known by English warships with which it had several encounters. Wolfe, on his way to capture Quebec in 1759, seized the ship and forced my grandfather with other pilots to navigate the fleet through the dangerous St. Lawrence River. He did so well his new masters, after the conquest of Quebec, put him in as the head of the harbor of that city. He sent for my grandmother, and that is why we come from Canada rather than France."

After the banquet, President Lincoln, impressed with Chiniquy's charm and knowledge of international affairs, asked him to become a secretary to the ambassador of France. He suggested, "Once on the staff of my ambassador, might you not soon yourself become ambassador? I am in need of Christian men in every department of the public service. What do you think?"

"My dear President," he answered. "I am overwhelmed by your kindness. Surely nothing could be more pleasant to me than to grant your request. The honor you want to confer on me is much above my merit, but my conscience tells me that I cannot give up preaching the Gospel to my poor French Canadian countrymen. I appeal to your own Christian and honorable feelings to know if I can forsake one for the other."

President Lincoln became very solemn and said, " You are right. You are right. There is nothing so great under Heaven as to be the ambassador of Christ." Then he added in a joking manner. "Yes, yes, you are an ambassador of a greater Prince than I am, but He does not pay you with as good cash as I would."

While waiting for his train at the Washington City depot, Pastor Chiniquy purchased two copies of a magazine at the depot newsstand, one for Lucy and one for Euphemie. The magazine dealt with the newest dress styles and home furnishings and other items of feminine interest. It was called *Godey's Lady's Book*, and was edited by Sarah Hale. Lucy and Euphemie had questioned him after his return from Europe about the fashions for ladies there and had been disappointed at how little attention he had paid except that he thought the ladies looked lovely.

He glanced through the magazine en route from Washington City to Chicago, where he was to change trains. He was intrigued by an article about Elizabeth Cady Stanton. A picture showed her clad in a costume of loose pantaloons bound at the ankles and topped by a three-quarter length coat. The name affixed to this Turkish garb was "bloomers" because Mrs. Amelia Bloomer, editor of *The Lily*, a temperance magazine, was the first to wear such an ensemble. Mrs. Stanton, according to the article, believed that women are partners in the family and should have the privilege of sharing the family purse. A congressman's wife went to Mrs. Stanton in tears because whenever her husband returned from Washington City, he chided her about her cooking and miserable meals. Mrs. Stanton advised her to go out and buy a new stove. The woman was horrified. She said her husband would be enraged because he always bought everything, even her clothing. Mrs. Stanton advised her to buy the stove, and if he flew into a rage, she should go sit in a corner and weep. That would soften him. Then when he tasted the good food cooked on the new stove, he would know she did the wise thing. She also predicted that when he saw how much fresher, happier and prettier she was in the kitchen, he would be delighted and would not mind paying the bill.

It never occurred to Pastor Chiniquy that this magazine with its revolutionary ideas would change Euphemie's attitude about the rights of women. Rather than worrying about that, he found himself thinking how nice a new stove would be for the parsonage.

He delayed his departure from Chicago long enough to buy such a cook stove to be sent out by freight the following week. He was fascinated with the model he chose, and he was certain Euphemie would be delighted and would be the envy of all the women in the parish. She deserved a good cook stove. So many guests passed through his doors and sat at his table, it was only proper to have a stove that made serving big groups easier. "Surely," he thought, "the Chicago Presbytery cannot begrudge a minister a decent cook stove, one that conserves fuel and easily converts raw groceries into tasteful, health-giving victuals."

News of Marie's death circulated rapidly in the village. More than a dozen women commented to Euphemie that it was a blessing for all concerned. She could not agree. They did not know how Marie's parents had struggled to make their daughter's recovery possible; they did not know what pulling up his roots and moving his small family to Canada meant to Evaloe; they did not know the hopes the family had entertained for a complete recovery and a return to the life Marie and Evaloe had planned for themselves in the new colony.

Francis was morose when he heard the news. He feared that any progress made in his courtship of Euphemie was all for naught. With Evaloe freed from his obligation to Marie, he would be claiming Euphemie.

Euphemie wondered if she and Evaloe would ever get together. She had schooled herself to think of him only as a friend who needed her prayers. Not a night passed that she did not remember the Morais children, their papa and their mama in her prayers. Francis was the only man whose company she truly enjoyed. She was unaware of the restraint he exercised to keep the relationship on a friendly basis. .

It was not until Pastor Chiniquy's return that they learned Marie's tragic story. She had responded with remarkable improvement to the treatments, so much so she was promised release after one more month of confinement. Two weeks before that date, she came down with influenza and carried a raging fever for three days. She recovered but the fever caused a setback, and her release date was postponed. She suffered deep depression. When the nurses were not watching, she left the hospital in her robe and slippers and started walking, supposedly for home. Montreal was experiencing a late spring snowstorm. The drifting snow covered her tracks so even when her absence was discovered, it was several hours before she was found. By the time they found her lying in a snowdrift, she had died from exposure.

Evaloe's cry of despair he repeated again and again, according to Pastor Chiniquy, was, "She was trying to get home. How much she wanted to be home!" His pastor comforted him by telling him she was truly home at last, safe in the arms of Jesus where she would wait for her loved ones to join her.

When Pastor Chiniquy told Euphemie about it, he said, "I assured Evaloe that he, Marie's parents and the children would some day no longer grieve; that the memory of Marie, instead of an agony, would be a sad, sweet feeling in their hearts—a purer, holier sort than they had ever known before."

"Oh, what a comforting thing to say! I am so glad you were able to be with Evaloe. What is he going to do now?"

"He plans to come to Ste. Anne for a few days. He is going to enlist in the Union forces by joining the Illinois cavalry."

"Evaloe in the army? But why? He is a father. What about Mina and Stephen? First their mama and now their papa."

"The children will be happy with their grandparents who need them in their time of loss. At least, I know Stephen will be happy. Mina is a sober, quiet child who may be happy in her own way, but she is never overtly so. Her grandmother says her brightest times are when she receives a letter from you. You must continue to write to her."

"Oh, I will. I will."

"Marie's father questioned me at length about our colony. I think they may pull up stakes and come here soon."

"Oh, I hope so. I love that little Mina. Perhaps I could teach her to laugh."

"If your kind of laughter can be taught, you should open a string of schools," he said sincerely for her laughter filled him with happiness.

It took longer than Evaloe had expected to get his affairs in order. The sanitarium was cited for negligence by the coroner. The courts awarded Evaloe $1,000 which he set up in a trust fund for his children, naming Marie's parents as their guardians in the event he should not return from the war. After years of struggle to keep his family together during his wife's frightening illness and the months of litigation following her death, the war fever was on him. He was eager to enlist. Like many others who enlisted in the summer of 1862, he thought the war would soon be over. Neither side anticipated the magnitude nor the duration of the conflict. Each side looked for an early triumph.

Euphemie wondered what her relationship with him would be. She worried about their first meeting. She need not have worried. Pastor Chiniquy brought him to the kitchen door with a hearty, "Look who has heard about your famous coffee all the way to Montreal!"

Evaloe had gone to the pastor's study at the church, and the two of them walked across the lawn to her kitchen. Evaloe looked thinner and older and his hairline had receded a little. He commented on it. Pastor Chiniquy said, "Don't complain. Look at the forehead I have to wash each day. That's why I grew a beard. As Achille says, 'If you cannot have hair on top of your head, have it on the front.'"

On Evaloe's arm was a black mourning band, a grim reminder of his recent loss. She touched the band gently and said, "I am sorry." He covered her hand with his and looked down at her upturned face. Her heart beat rapidly. She was glad she was wearing a high neck dress so he could not see her rapid pulse in her throat. It was not right to thrill to the touch of her dead cousin's husband, especially while he still wore his badge of grief.

"Would you like *café noir* or *café au lait*?" she asked.

"*Café au lait*, please."

"My favorite, too," said Pastor Chiniquy, "Although for the sake of my vanishing figure, or should I say my appearing figure, I should avoid *café au lait* and take my coffee black. But this is cause for celebration, so make mine *au lait*, too. Set out a cup for yourself. Miss Allard."

Evaloe returned to the parsonage on each of the three days he spent in Ste. Anne, always with his father or one of his brothers or when he was certain Pastor Chiniquy was home. On the last evening, when she showed him to the door, he pulled her gently out the door into the shadow of the porch and said, "I know I haven't the right to ask, Euphemie, but would you wait for me? When this war is over in a few months, I'll be back and give you a proper courting."

She slipped into his arms and their lips met. She was 28 years old and unused to giving herself. It was an awkward kiss, quick and almost furtive.

"Of course I will wait, Evaloe."

"I am so glad. I was afraid there might be some other man."

"No one special."

"Good! I need a woman like you, Euphemie, to be a mother to my Mina and Stephen."

She stiffened. She loved his children, but she did not want to use them as a pawn to get him.

"I need you, too," he added. He kissed her again, this time like a man searching for a mate not a governess. She eagerly sought his mouth and thrilled to the pressure of his lean body against hers. He let her go abruptly and hurried down the wooden walk, whistling a happy tune. At the end of the walk, he stopped whistling, turned, waved and disappeared into the darkness. Her whole being vibrated with the intimacy. Evaloe wanted her. He loved her.

With her heart beating so loudly she was afraid Pastor Chiniquy would hear, she tiptoed to her room and dropped to her knees by her bureau. She felt around under the pile of underwear until her fingers touched her crucifix. "Thank you, Jesus. Thank you Mary, Mother of Jesus."

She rose, and taking her fiddle from its case, cradled it against her shoulder and played as she often did in times of stress or excitement. The tender melodies filtered out past the kitchen and into the study where Pastor Chiniquy was preparing his Sunday sermon. He did not need to be told of the promise she made Evaloe. Euphemie was playing the love poems Pastor Chiniquy introduced to her, playing them in a manner more touching and beautiful than she had ever played when she played for him alone. She was playing them because her heart was filled with love for her young man. He knew he should be happy for Euphemie, and, yes, for Evaloe, but he was filled with a peculiar sadness he could only analyze as envy. He put down his pen, shut his Bible and quietly left the house to roam aimlessly in the dark, away from the house filled with the music of a woman in love.

Evaloe left the next day. Francis left town, too. He had obtained a teaching job in Galena, Illinois on the Mississippi River. He sent word to Euphemie by Pastor Chiniquy that he was leaving. He said if she ever needed a recommendation for a teacher's assistant, he would gladly oblige. She was hurt because he didn't come by to say goodbye personally.

She discovered she missed him even more than she missed Evaloe. She had no really close female friends except Lucy. She had become very fond of Francis. They shared many common interests. She admired his quick mind that in all their studies together singled out values she had missed. He had an acute sense of differences and relations and a flashing memory of related matter that made any study with him a stimulating, exciting experience. She missed saving up things to share with him at their next meeting. She had a premonition they would never meet again. That her dear friend would suddenly depart without even so much as a hint he was searching a job elsewhere devastated her. Even her euphoria about Evaloe's proposal was not powerful enough to ease the pain.

Chapter XXVI
Lovers

Euphemie experienced days and days of extreme loneliness that she tried to erase by immersing herself in the wartime projects of the Ladies Aid at the church. In addition to rolling bandages made from old sheets and blankets, the church women knitted socks and packed boxes of food and goodies. Euphemie missed her jolly companion, Francis. She no longer did any teaching because the new teacher took on four young women for assistants, leaving her out completely.

On June 11, 1863, the Presbyterian Church of Ste. and its pastor were officially welcomed into the Presbytery of Chatham of the Canadian Presbyterian Church. The issue of the Savior College seemed inconsequential in the light of the Civil War. Every day, more boys volunteered for the Union Army until the new college had but four students left.

War stories were the main topics of conversation when the women gathered to roll bandages. Euphemie learned at the bandage table about Pastor Chiniquy's part in exposing a large cache of ammunition and other supplies hidden in the nearby swamp of Indiana by Confederate sympathizers.

"But I thought Indiana went Union," she said, disbelieving

"It did. It is furnishing many boys to the Union Army, but there are a great number of secret organizations aiding the Confederacy cause," explained Mrs. Lambert, whose husband helped recruit Union soldiers.

Mrs. Morais said, "My husband and Pastor Chiniquy were hunting wild geese in that marshland about 12 miles east of here. They found the cache of ammunition and supplies. They reported it. My mister said men at the courthouse had heard rumors that Confederate General John Morgan was planning to sweep down the Kankakee Valley with the aid of Southern sympathizers in Indiana and lay waste to Momence, Ste. Anne, Kankakee City and Wilmington."

Mrs. Goudreau, whose son had recently enlisted, said, "A regiment of U.S. Infantry was sent to the swamp area to get the stuff. My Maurice was one of the soldiers."

"It's hard to believe all these things are happening," Mrs. LaGesse said as she vigorously tore an old sheet into strips. "I heard there is a local way station for the Underground Railroad and that some Ste. Anne people are suspected of hiding slaves." She looked around at the women rolling bandages as if to spy any in their midst who might be guilty. Euphemie shivered. The war had seemed so far away. Somehow it was so much more real knowing that Ste. Anne boys and Ste. Anne itself were in the midst of danger and intrigue.

Letters arrived occasionally from Evaloe. Euphemie was pained that his spelling and poor sentence structure embarrassed her so much. She showed his letters to no one. Pastor Chiniquy, noticing this desire for privacy, assumed the letters were filled with words of love. Actually, they were reports of life in camp that could have been written to anybody's sister.

The first letter told of the gathering place at Camp Worcester where Evaloe enjoyed camp, even drilling in the hot sun. Then they were sent south. His letter from that camp was written on a dirty piece of paper, which he had turned sidewise and written across what he had already written because he had so little paper. He told of the unsanitary conditions and of the men dying from lack of food and from disease. A later letter told of the terrible winter when Burnsides was besieged by Confederate General Longstreet and was shut up in Knoxville, Tennessee The hardships suffered by his regiment were terrible. They were cut off from supplies and they had a hard struggle to keep from dying of hunger and cold. For a time, they had but one ear of corn a day, no tents and not enough clothing to keep them warm. Many were barefoot or nearly so.

Evaloe wrote of his close call with death. His regiment was dispatched to build temporary fortifications with tombstones from a nearby cemetery. One of the stones handed him was engraved "Wife and Mother." He vomited as he put it in place in the fortification. About midnight, his regiment was surprised by the sudden arrival of the Confederate cavalry who opened fire on the building where the men were sleeping. As the gunfire started, Evaloe caught up his clothes, mounted his horse and galloped down the hill. The horse stumbled over some rocks and threw him to the ground, scattering his clothes. There was no time to stop. He got hold of his horse, ran beside it, remounted and went on. Fortunately, the next morning he recovered the clothes. They were all he had to wear. Euphemie packed Evaloe a box filled with socks, underwear, and hand knit sweaters She tucked in tins of cookies and maple sugar patties. She prayed they would reach him.

One day, she received quite a different letter. It was from Francis, who had enlisted and was with the 53rd Illinois Volunteers. He had left his teaching job at the urgent suggestion of the school board; in fact, he was forced to hand in his resignation. One of his 16-year old pupils named him the father of the baby she was to deliver in May.

Euphemie could hardly believe what she was reading. Francis and a 16-year old pupil! In all the time she worked beside him, she observed not one word or look of impropriety between Francis and his female students. They all adored and respected him. She read on that the girl, Julia, from a poor, uneducated family, was a bright girl and Francis thought he could train her to become a teacher. He tutored her every night after school. Sometimes, during the winter months, he walked her home if the sun had already set when they closed up the school. An alcoholic uncle, who lived next door with a tribe of children, often pestered her if he happened to find her out alone after dark. One night the uncle forced his attentions on her. She did not tell anyone about it until she discovered she was going to have his baby. In desperation, she turned to Francis.

"Where was she to turn, Euphemie?" he wrote. "I offered to marry her and say the child was mine. God knows what the child will be like being fathered by an uncle, but I felt at least I could provide a home for it and Julia away from that environment. My thanks for that charitable act was losing my job and the respect and trust I had built up in the community.

I enlisted and sent Julia home to my parents in Three Rivers. There she and the child will be away from that family and safe from the gossipy tongues of Galena.

"Oh, Euphemie, how different it all could have been! If ever I run into that Evaloe, I'll shoot him for coming back and claiming you. I was hoping you would learn to love me as I love you and would some day consent to be my wife. Even though Evaloe's uniform is the same color as mine, I hate him. Hate comes easily to me now, fostered by my wartime activities as a lieutenant in this dreadful war."

She was astonished at his confession of love for her. It was a romantic notion she had never given a thought. At last she understood his sudden departure and it eased the pain she had felt all those long, lonely months. How like him to take on the responsibility of the unwed mother-to-be and her child by an incestuous uncle! She loved Francis in a very special way. Perhaps she could have learned to be his lover had she not been blinded by her love for Evaloe. She sighed. Life with Francis would have been comfortable and secure. Life with Evaloe would be, no doubt, a constant struggle burdened immediately with a young family, little money and the constant memory of his first love, his dead wife Marie.

There was more to Francis' letter. The last page made Euphemie realize that he would never again be the jolly young man he once was. He wrote, "We send out raiding parties here and there and instruct men coolly to burn, kill and destroy. The invariable instruction, as against the guerillas who infect this country, is to take no prisoners but to shoot them down in their tracks. I find myself talking as flippantly about killing men as I would have done at home on any trivial subject. Yet it does not astonish me. We easily fall into regular channels of habit. When a man goes to war as a soldier, he soon finds the duties of war come upon him easily. Our army is rapidly approaching a fight. I want to try my hand at battle. I do like a good fight. There is something in it that seems to thrill and charm me."

Euphemie seldom laughed those days. It was sad to think of Evaloe, cold and hungry, building ramifications with tombstones stolen from the grave of "wife and mother." It was equally sad to think of Francis, embittered and hardened, looking forward to combat and killing with the danger of being killed himself. And if not killed, then he must return to his child bride and her baby that could very well be mentally afflicted. Euphemie's world was filled with sorrow and hatred; the nation was divided on the slavery issue, her village was divided on the religious issue, her church was divided on the issue of doctrine. Family against family in both nation and village created bitterness and gloom almost impossible to bear.

Evaloe's furlough was finally granted. He sent word he would be home only a short time because he felt he must make a trip to Montreal to see his children and arrange for a tombstone for Marie's grave. His experience on the cemetery battlefield had given him an urgency to provide his wife and mother of his children a suitable grave marker. Euphemie understood full well his obligation to his children and his duty toward his dead wife's grave, but she begrudged every day he spent away from her.

He returned from Canada, eager to be with Euphemie. He had installed Marie's tombstone, and observed that his children were well cared for and content with his in-laws, who seemed inclined to move to Ste. Anne after the war ended. He looked forward to a peaceful life in the colonies with Euphemie as his bride and second mother to his children.

Euphemie's father offered to take Evaloe in as an assistant in his harness shop after the war with the hope he would soon become a full time partner and would later pass the business down to Stephen and any sons Euphemie and Evaloe might have.

The thought of sons belonging to her and looking like Evaloe thrilled Euphemie. She had great plans for Evaloe. She would teach him to speak English and help him shed his country ways. He would learn to love books and good conversation around beautifully appointed tables. They would build a home and fill it with lovely things and bright, beautiful children. She realized she was a little old to be planning a big family, but they would have Mina and Stephen to start with. Like Evaloe, Euphemie thought the war would soon be over. She was confident Evaloe would return to her safe and sound.

As it turned out, their few days together were shared by many others. Because Evaloe had so little time to spend in Ste. Anne, much of it was spent in his parents' home so all could share his homecoming. Euphemie had almost forgotten how it was to live in such poor circumstances. The luxury of the parsonage and its convenience for cooking, laundry and entertaining had spoiled her. Her own parents had things much better than the Morais, whose little house, even with Evaloe's addition, was crowded with children, hunting equipment, beaver skins and dirty laundry. She was filled with disgust and assured herself that life with Evaloe would never be like that.

It was Pastor Chiniquy who arranged for Evaloe and Euphemie to go on a private picnic. "Why don't you take my buggy after church Sunday and drive out to Willow Slough to see the sand cranes? That is quite a sight. They are migrating south and now, and they have a resting place there. Euphemie, you could pack a basket of food and take your fiddle along. Evaloe has not heard you play since he came home. Take my new roan, Evaloe. She is quite a sprited mare."

They left the parsonage soon after the morning service. It was a hot, beautiful October day with a high bright sky. Evaloe drove the roan with delight and almost splendid fury. Bare-headed, sleeves rolled up and eyes sparkling with *joie de vivre*, he masterfully manipulated the roan into so fast a canter the light weight buggy seemed to skim the surface like a low-flying bird.

Euphemie could not take her eyes from him. He looked as she imagined Phaethon looked as he furiously drove his father's sun chariot so near the earth he scorched its surface. She was about to shout that to him when she remembered with regret he would know nothing of the Greek mythology Francis had introduced her to. Some day he would. Someday she would share her new learning with him. As the pace grew faster and faster, the brisk breeze whipped up by the wild ride tugged at her hair loosing it from the large chignon and throwing celluloid pins in all directions.

"Evaloe, slow down. Look what you are doing to my hair."

"It's beautiful," he cried. Gathering the reins in one hand, he reached out and freed the last two pins. Her hair streamed out on the wind, the sun threading the auburn locks with golden strands. Her heart leapt up, as if it, too, were freed from all bonds.. "This," she told herself, "is what a woman in love feels."

She could have ridden on forever, but Evaloe pulled in on the reins, slowed the horse to a walk and turned up a little used lane to select a grassy spot in the grove of maple trees for their picnic. Euphemie tried to gather up her hair into a knot that she was going to secure with a few pins she found in the buggy.

Evaloe ran quickly to help her from the buggy. He insisted, "Leave your hair loose, Euphemie." He lifted her in his strong arms and held her close as she slid to the ground. They stood locked in an embrace. He covered her hair and her cheeks with kisses. Their lips met in a passionate, lingering kiss. It was a delicious feeling. Euphemie responded with an abandoned passion she never dreamed she was capable of. No matter that Evaloe knew no Greek mythology, no matter he was so unlearned in many of the things she had come to love, no matter he was still in mourning for Marie...

Marie! How often her name arose when they were together. It was as if her presence was felt now even more than when she was sick in the next room. Euphemie pulled away. Taking the sash from her skirt, she tied her hair in a ponytail. "Oh, Evaloe, we mustn't"

'Why not? Don't you love me?"

Love him. With all her heart. With a love so wild it could make her forget all scruples and morals.

He persisted, "You know you like to kiss me. What a tigress you are!"

So she compared favorably with the other girls he had kissed. How, she wondered, did she compare with Marie? There she was again—always Marie.

"Of course, I love you, Evaloe. Didn't I promise to wait for you? I want to be your wife." She turned toward the buggy, "Come, let's get the picnic basket. You'll see what a good cook you are getting."

"Good cooks come and go, but lovers come forever," he muttered.

She couldn't get the basket from between the seats. "What did you say?" she called over her shoulder.

"Oh, just some barracks saying. Here, let me do that." He easily freed the basket and carried it to a grassy spot. She followed with an old quilt that they spread over the thick prairie grass. They laughed like children as they ate the fried chicken, boiled eggs and warm, spicy potato salad.

"Here are some tomatoes," she said. "Probably the last of the season, kind of little but still good."

"Know what we used to call them? Love apples."

"Oh you have love on the brain."

"Aren't you having any cake?" he said eyeing the piece left on the plate.

"No, you eat it. I'm full." She started tidying up.

"Oh, don't be so neat If you must keep busy, why don't you get your fiddle and play for me. Pastor Chiniquy says you are really good."

When she returned from the buggy with the fiddle, he was stretched out beside the quilt, his eyes closed, one arm under his head and the other brushing away a fly trying to lick the speck of sticky white frosting clinging to the corner of his mouth. She played tunes she knew were his favorites and laid the fiddle aside.

"I did not know you could play like that. Play some more."

"It's your fiddle, Evaloe. Anyone could play it. Such a beautiful, fine instrument! When this war is over, and God grant it is soon, you must make many more like this." She picked up the instrument and played again, this time the tunes she played to relax Pastor Chiniquy after a difficult day. Evaloe closed his eyes again and was soon gently snoring. The trip to Canada and the excitement of being home again had tired him more than he realized. Although he was in excellent condition, his healthy body needed sleep. With a full stomach, a grassy place to lie and his love playing the fiddle he made for her, it was only natural that he drift off to sleep. Euphemie did not resent it. It pleased her to watch him—as handsome in repose as he was awake and active.

She laid the fiddle in its case and packed the picnic scraps in the basket. On the edge of the quilt she sat down beside Evaloe and drew his head on to her lap. When she gently kissed his brow as she smoothed back his hair, he stirred and smiled slightly but did not waken.

About five o'clock, the air was rent by the harsh, penetrating call of the sand cranes returning from the feeding fields to their resting place. Evaloe awoke. "There they come," he said. He did not seem a bit surprised to find his head cradled in Euphemie's arms. "I hope we get to see them dance."

"Dance?"

"Yes. They do a lively dance, especially if they mate. Male and female face each other and dance about, sometimes jumping up eight or ten feet.

Look at them come. There must be thousands of them." The sky was filled with birds.

"You should have seen the passenger pigeons going south right before I left Kentucky. The noonday sun was hardly visible, almost like an eclipse. The droppings were like snow in the air and on the ground."

"Oh, I never thought about the droppings." She covered her hair with her hands.

He laughed. "They wouldn't dare let go their droppings on your beautiful hair. I'd wring their necks with my bare hands."

"That would take some doing," she said. "I never dreamed the birds would be so big. They must be three feet tall or taller. I tried wringing a rooster's neck and Papa had to finish the job. These birds are five times as big as a rooster."

'Oh, I could do it if I had to," he boasted. "The big problem would be their windpipes. A little crane chick has a simple tube, but the adult birds have a windpipe about five feet long all curled up like those fancy French horns. That's how they can make that noise."

The flocks of greenish brown cranes landed in an arena of the slough they had already trod down. It was as if they had their roles assigned. Many hunched down in a large circle. The dancers, whether appointed by the leader or a volunteer group, Euphemie did not know, stood in the center in pairs facing each other. Their harsh cries grew in intensity as the dancers sprang about like boxers, coming in close together and jumping apart. The voyeurs on the edge stepped up the beat of their call, and the dance grew more and more frenzied with both the male and female at the peak of their excitement jumping ten or more feet straight up, touching together, landing on their feet to prepare for another jump.

Euphemie and Evaloe watched the ritual, hypnotized by the sound and fury. It was contagious. Evaloe pulled loose the sash that held Euphemie's ponytail, and her hair fell about his face as he rolled her over on his outstretched body.

"Oh, Evaloe, we mustn't." But she did not mean it. She was deeply, hopelessly in love and at the mercy of her desires. She had thought herself immune to such passion, but all of a sudden, midst the croaking cavorting cranes, she felt nature would approve her passion. Even as she clutched for a shred of modesty and proper decorum, she was desperately wanting

Evaloe to pursue. She found the new passion almost unbearably exalting and wanted to cry out like the mating cranes. Instead she said, "What if someone comes down the lane and sees us?"

"They'll never see us now." He hugged her with his arms and wrapped his legs around hers. Over and over he rolled, managing somehow in the turn to keep his body from pressing down on hers. They rolled into the nearby tall prairie grass which provided a delightful hideaway. Although hidden from the ring of voyeur birds, they loved to the rhythm of the calling fowl. "How strange." she thought, "to feel beyond evil." The birds, the war, all things together made her feel no damage would follow her complete abandonment to passion. .

It was over. She wanted it to last and last. He was going to go back to the battlefields the next day. This would be all until his return. What if he didn't come back? Men and boys were being killed by the hundreds and thousands. What if Evaloe was shot down?

"I love you so much, Evaloe. Promise me you will not get killed." Tears came to her eyes. Running his finger down her cheek to trace the path of a spilled tear, he said, "No bullet could stop me now. The war will soon be over and so will my mourning period for Marie…"

Marie! There she was again.

Suddenly the birds stopped their calling. In the silence of the gloaming, Euphemie was overwhelmed with guilt. She gathered her clothing and ran deeper into the tall grass where Evaloe could not see her dress. Like Eve in the garden, she covered herself. She wondered if Eve had, amongst all her guilt, felt one little precious memory of pleasure.

She finished dressing, tied up her hair and stepped out of the tall grass to find Evaloe dressed, the quilt and picnic supplies packed away. He was closing her fiddle in its case. He said reverently, "I didn't know you could perform like that."

What did he mean? What performance was he surprised about?

The ride home into the sunset was quiet and dreamy. Evaloe, apparently experiencing no guilt feeling nor aware that Euphemie was, talked of their future together, dreaming out loud. "We'll have a beautiful house, not as fine as Pastor Chiniquy's, but nicer even than the one I built for Marie."

Why must he always mention Marie?

"It will be a nice place for you and Mina and Stephen. When Stephen gets old enough, your father and I will teach him the harness business, and you will teach him and Mina all the fine things you know. I want my son and daughter to be educated."

"How about our son?" She asked. "Perhaps we will have a little Evaloe and maybe a little Euphemie to grow up with Mina and Stephen."

She was amazed at his reaction.

"No. No babies. Absolutely not! I would never put another woman through what Marie suffered."

"But I am not Marie," she almost shouted in defiance.

"I know that, Euphemie, but don't you see, I cannot take a chance on losing you now that I have found you."

She had to content herself with that for the time being. She was certain she would be able to change his mind. For now, she was caught up in ambivalent feelings of elation and guilt. How she longed for the absolution of confession to free herself from guilt so she could enjoy the elation!

Pastor Chiniquy was nowhere about when they first arrived at the parsonage, but he appeared at the stable when Evaloe turned the roan and buggy over to John Mason.

"Did the birds dance for you?"

"Did they ever!" said Evaloe. Euphemie blushed.

Pastor Chiniquy's face was composed and noncommittal, but his eyes seemed to pierce her very soul. She wanted to run to him, drop to her knees and cry, "Father, forgive me, for I have sinned."

Her parting with Evaloe was formal. He promised to write more often and to come home unscathed. He bid them both goodbye and left Pastor Chiniquy comforting Euphemie.

"Take good care of her, Pastor. Better get yourself a new housekeeper lined up because I am going to take Euphemie away from you."

"I believe it, Evaloe. God bless you both and Godspeed to you, my son."

Chapter XXVII
Casualties

The national war did not cease in a few months as Evaloe and many others prophesied. It went on and on. One day Euphemie, arriving late for the Ladies Aid bandage rolling, found the room buzzing with news. Emilie Soucie Hubert's voice could be heard above the others, "They say he was wounded by a shot to his knee at the same time the captain was killed. He took command, and at that critical moment when the men were faltering, he pulled his sword and holding it high cried, 'Men, stand firm. We must not lose our ground.'"

"Who?" asked Euphemie. "Who are you talking about?"

"About Francis Bechard. Haven't you heard, Euphemie? He's a hero!"

Beatrice Pelletier spoke up, " Remember when he led the cheer the day the bishop was here and we sent him packing? I'll never forget how Francis raised his arms high over his head and cried, 'People of Ste. Anne, you have just gained a most glorious victory. Hurrah for the Village of Ste. Anne.'"

Emilie continued, full of importance at knowing the details, "The regiment was saved but not before a canister shot hit Francis in the chest."

"Francis is wounded?" Euphemie's knees buckled and she sank into a nearby chair.

"Not wounded! Killed!" Emilie cried dramatically.

Euphemie wanted to go back to the parsonage where she could cry, but she did not trust her legs to hold her. She took great care to speak and relate to the women at her table. She was in a daze. Francis dead! She remembered how they roared with amusement when they read Pastor Chiniquy's letter from Paris telling how he came near appearing on the opera stage in a puff of pink smoke with Mephistopheles. She remembered how patient Francis was teaching her English and introducing her to the classics. She recalled how he shared her pleasure over the new cook stove. She felt a desperate loss as one might feel at the passing of a dear brother. She prided herself on behaving bravely, outwardly not revealing how shattered she was that she would never see Francis again.

In about an hour, Pastor Chiniquy appeared at the door and beckoned to her. She went to him. She failed to close the door behind her.

He asked, "Did you hear about Francis?"

Her bravery collapsed at the sound of his kind voice, and she began to tremble all over. Her shoulders shook with quiet sobs. He put his arm around her and they walked out of the church together, sharing a common loss for he had loved Francis as a son. It was well neither of them saw the knowing looks that passed among some of the members of the Ladies Aid.

Francis was buried in Three Rivers, Canada, in the cemetery plot of his family. Pastor Chiniquy, unable to attend the funeral, sent his condolences. Three weeks later, he received a letter from Francis' mother. He found Euphemie kneading bread dough in the pantry.

"I have a letter from Mrs. Bechard in Three Rivers."

"Mrs. Bechard? Francis' wife?"

"No. His mother. I wrote to express my deepest sorrow at the loss of a wonderful young friend who had touched so many lives with his inspired teaching. I congratulated her on his heroic action and opined that their pride would offset part of their grief. I extended my sympathy to his bride and baby-to-be."

Euphemie sprinkled more flour on the bread board. "I know they will treasure your letter for surely Francis has told them of you."

"Yes, his mother mentions that he had a great love for me. I am humbly grateful. To tell of his praise seems boastful, but his love and friendship are among my greatest treasures."

"For me, too. He was a dear, dear friend."

"Because I know that, I hesitate to tell you of the other paragraphs in the letter."

"What could possibly be worse than the fact that Francis was killed?"

"He was betrayed by one he befriended."

"Certainly not me."

"No. By the girl he married. I believe her name is Julia, yes, here it is, Julia. His mother writes, 'You waste your sympathy in extending it to the ingrate Julia. When Francis married her and brought her here, he said she was with child and we assumed it was his. We were heart-broken that our boy, who had always been such a good Christian, would have broken God's laws and caused a young girl, a pupil who had been entrusted to his care, to become with child. We felt he made the right decision in marrying her and were dismayed that his school board took such harsh measures as to discharge him. We tried to dissuade him from enlisting, but he was determined to go.'"

"I wish he had not gone," said Euphemie, lifting the mound of bread dough and slapping it hard on the floured board. "Will his family keep the girl and the baby?"

"There is no baby. It was all a lie. She confessed her uncle had never touched her. She made up the story of the baby so Francis would feel sorry for her and marry her and take her away from the home she hated. She could not say she was carrying Francis' child because he would have known that was a lie so she implicated the uncle."

"That horrid girl! Did Francis know?" She divided the dough into loaves and deposited the sections in the buttered pans.

"His mother is not certain. She said that after three months when she could see no change in the girl's waistline, she questioned her about it and asked if she would like to see a doctor. Julia said, 'The women in my family birth their babies with the help of a midwife called after the pains start.' A month ago, when Julia's time should have been but three months away, Mrs. Bechard confronted her and she confessed. She ran away that night. They tried to find her, but finally they had to write the sad news to Francis. They received the telegram about his death a week later. They do not know if he received the letter."

"I hope he did not," said Euphemie. "Better that he should die thinking he did a good deed, and it truly was a wonderful, unselfish act, so like Francis." She tenderly draped a tea towel over the loaves and left them to rise.

"That's what I have been thinking. Of such noble stuff are heroes made."

Evaloe's in-laws and his children moved to Ste. Anne that winter. Mina stopped in to see Euphemie every afternoon after school. Often there were children in the parsonage yard searching in the snow for the metal disks Pastor Chiniquy floated out the drain. Either he or Euphemie redeemed the disks with coins whenever a youngster appeared at the parsonage door with the disk and recited the Bible verse cited on it. Mina was shy around the children and preferred Euphemie's company.

Evaloe's letters after his furlough took on an entirely different tone. He wrote little of his battle activities. His letters were filled with dreams and ambitions for making her father's harness shop the best in Illinois. Apparently, he had given up all thoughts of making a living designing fiddles. He hoped Mr. Allard would agree to a plan he had for making buggies, a skill he had learned in a wagon shop in Montreal. He spent all his spare time in the barracks drawing designs for a new style buggy, a little beauty, that could be managed easily by a woman driver. He asked Euphemie to send him paper and a rule because such supplies were short. He said they would not be able to build a house right away after the war because he wanted to put his small savings into an addition to the harness shop to make room to construct the buggies.

She was pleased and displeased. She was happy he had dreams to help him through the weary war, but she would have liked him to dream of building a pretty cottage and perhaps a stable for horses and a fancy buggy. Instead, he dreamed of a buggy shop where he could create fancy buggies for fancy ladies while she lived goodness knows where…certainly not in that crowded little Morais house.

She just happened to be visiting Evaloe's parents the day a soldier appeared at their door. His name was John Benson. He was back in Kankakee City on furlough from Evaloe's regiment. He said he brought good news and bad news.

"The good news is that Evaloe is a hero," he said proudly. "He always could make things do even though we had very little to work with. Whenever we need him, Frenchie, that's what the guys called him, Frenchie..."

Euphemie was insulted by the name. She knew they must have thought Evaloe uneducated and ignorant because he spoke very little English and that with a strong French accent. She was surprised that John Benson could speak such good French, which he had probably learned in school. That was probably why he was chosen to take the news to the Morais family. She wanted to interrupt to find out about the bad news, but the proud look on the faces of Evaloe's parents made her hold her tongue. They loved hearing about his cleverness.

The soldier continued, "Well, as I said, Frenchie always could figure a way to get a job done. One night, our regiment was ordered across the Clinch River in east Tennessee to guard a narrow passage. We were camping in a bend called Bean's Station. We had crossed the river in pouring rain. It kept on raining, and that stream rose a foot and was running fast. Our officers learned that three brigades of rebels were between us and the gap we hoped to cross. We had to retreat, but to cross a mountain river in such circumstances would have been suicide. Knowing Frenchie's woodsman skills, our officers called him out of the sick bed...he had a terrible chest cold...to figure out a way we could get back across the river."

"I'll wager he did it, too," said Evaloe's father proudly.

"He surely did. He and I bailed out an old canoe we found and managed to cross the swift stream. He handles a canoe like an old French trapper. We went to General Henson's headquarters and requisitioned some cannon rope and we made a cable across the river. In the meantime, six men followed Frenchie's instructions to raise an abandoned half-sunk barge. It carried twelve men or one horse a trip. We propelled the barge by pulling the cable from one side to the other. Your son was thrown into the water twice and continued to work all night in his wet clothing. By daybreak, the entire regiment, horses and supplies were out of the reach of the enemy. Evaloe's sure to get a medal for saving the regiment."

Mr. and Mrs. Morais beamed. "That's my boy," said his father.

"And what is the bad news?" his mother asked fearfully. Euphemie's heart beat rapidly.

"Just that he's in the field hospital."

"He was shot?" asked Euphemie.

"Oh, no, ma'am. We did not get fired on. You know I told you they got him up out of a sick bed. Well, all that exposure did not help him. They say he has pneumonia."

Two days later, a telegram arrived stating that Evaloe Morais had died from pneumonia resulting from exposure in a heroic, successful attempt to save his regiment. It was Evaloe's mother who rode her horse into town to tell Euphemie about the telegram. His father was too grief-stricken. Each of his seven children was precious to that kind-hearted father, but his eldest son was his favorite. Mrs. Morais' eyes were red and swollen, but she no longer wept. She had spent an agonizing two days, fearing her boy would not make it through his fight with the dreadful pneumonia. Now that his battle was over, she went stolidly about the chores needed to arrange for a proper burial of the body that was to be sent by train to Kankakee City. She did not linger long at the parsonage.

Euphemie, like Evaloe's mother, had feared the worst when she heard about the pneumonia and thought she was prepared for the news. She spent hours on her knees praying Jesus would look after her man and bring him back to health and back to her. She was alone in the house after Mrs. Morais left. She went to her room and flung herself across her bed and wept—wept tears of bitterness as well as sorrow. Jesus had not heard her prayers. How could He notice her petitions when He had so many to watch over in these perilous times? She should have appealed to Him through His mother, Mary. Euphemie had read the scripture verses Pastor Chiniquy recommended, and in times of peace and happiness, she agreed with him, but with her world tumbling down around her, she longed for her childhood faith in Mary. She got up from her bed and searched through her bureau drawer until she found the charred crucifix carefully wrapped in soft linen. She knelt down by the bed and prayed to Mary to help her through the days and years of emptiness ahead. A strange peace came over her. She fell asleep there on her knees with her crucifix held to her heart. Her last thought was regret that the consummation of her love for Evaloe had not resulted in a child. After Evaloe returned to battle, she had spent an agonizing ten days fearing she might be pregnant. Now she wished she was carrying his baby.

It was dark when she was awakened by a knock on her door. Pastor Chiniquy called, "Are you there? Could I speak with you for a moment? It's about Mina."

Mina! How could she have forgotten her? She loved her papa so much. Such a little girl to bear so much sorrow! She would need a great amount of loving attention. Euphemie rose from her knees, laid the crucifix in the open drawer, closed the drawer quietly, squared her shoulders and went to the door ready to assume the responsibilities that were hers, ready to shake off her personal grief in order to help Mina. She would endeavor to give her little friend a measure of the peace she, herself, had received from her old friend, Ste. Mary.

"Yes, Pastor," she said, opening the bedroom door. "I must go to Mina. Could you manage your own supper? There is cold roast chicken in the pantry, and the coffee pot is on the back of the range. Just pull it over so it will heat. May I bring Mina home with me if she will come?"

"Certainly. I was about to suggest it. It will be good for her to get away from the house while the coffin is there. Bring Stephen, too, if he wants to come." And so Mina moved in. Stephen preferred to stay with his grandmother.

The army sent home Evaloe's personal things. A roll of papers, tied with a piece of leather that must have been part of the reins for his horse, had her name on it. Sheet after sheet of papers she had sent him were covered with sketches—front, side, rear, wheels, top—of the most handsome little buggy anyone could imagine. It was a four-wheeled carriage with or without a top. It had a light seat for two resting on top of two large springs. The graceful design omitted the clumsy sidepieces in front of the seat. The full view sketch showed a high-stepping Arabian horse prancing along ahead of the buggy. Printed across the buggy in each of the back view sketches was the name THE EUPHEMIE. A note, in Evaloe's handwriting, said, "I showed these drawings to my captain and he said Euphemie is a good name for my new buggy. It comes from the Greek, he says, and means praise or good omen."

The drawings were extremely neat and precise. The handwritten note, in contrast, was smudged with crossed out words and some untouched misspelled words.

She showed the drawings to her father whose eyes lighted up with appreciation.

"It's a beautiful buggy. Beautiful! What a shame Evaloe did not live to build it! Maybe someday I could do it. I'll see what Bernice thinks."

"Oh, Papa, you couldn't."

"What's the matter? Do you think I'm too old to start something like that? I'm a month younger than Pastor Chiniquy and look what he does."

Yes, they were the same age, but somehow Pastor Chiniquy seemed much younger. He had the power and ability to accomplish things far beyond what any ordinary person could be expected to accomplish. He did what younger men might have wished to do or if they tried would have done badly or indifferently. But he achieved. He was a special person and her father was just an ordinary one. She loved her father with a tender devotion and would not have hurt his feelings for the world.

"Of course not, Papa. I just meant your business is harness making, and you are the best harness maker around. You couldn't possibly be a buggy builder, too."

"Oh, couldn't I?" he asked, touching her nose gently with the tip of his index finger. "Just you watch your old papa." He left the house with the roll of drawings tucked under his arm. She had never seen him walk with such a jaunty step. Perhaps the Euphemie buggy would become a reality, after all. The old pioneer blood that stirred her father to set out for the Illinois wild prairie leaving behind a comfortable job and home in Canada was still coursing through his veins.

Chapter XXVIII
The Proposal

Euphemie tearfully packed the fiddle Evaloe had made for her in its case and vowed never to play it again. She was grateful Pastor Chiniquy did not question her about it or request that she play for him.

Not all men were willing to go to war. Those affected by the draft could purchase a substitute for $300. Achille Chiniquy, who could easily have afforded a substitute, enlisted as an officer in the Illinois Voluntary Infantry. His eldest son, 17-year old Charlie, enlisted with him in the same regiment. The Chiniquy Committee felt Achille's absence, and Pastor Chiniquy found it expedient to spend more time in Ste. Anne than had been his habit. Since travel was curtailed and often dangerous, Euphemie was relieved he was not exposing himself to such danger.

Mina asked to stay on at the parsonage for a few weeks after Evaloe's funeral. Her grandmother granted her permission, grateful to be free of worry about the child with whom she had never been close. Mina was not a naughty child for her grandmother. She was simply withdrawn.

Christmas was a quiet, prayerful time with so many young men away, some on the battlefields, some in army hospitals, and others, like Francis and Evaloe, in their graves. The Christmas celebration for French Canadians does not include the giving of gifts and the spreading of sumptuous feasts. Those activities take place on New Year's Day with the family gathering in the home of grandparents, or, if no grandparents live nearby, in the home of an old aunt and uncle.

Pastor Chiniquy announced to Euphemie and Lucy the day after Christmas, "Enough mourning has taken place. For the sake of the children, let's have a big family party at the parsonage on New Year's Day."

Achille and Charlie, of course, would not be there, but Lucy was invited to bring the rest of her family. Euphemie's parents, her aunt and uncle, Evaloe's children and the entire Morais family were invited. It was a busy, exciting week of preparation. The big day finally arrived.

The great hall of the parsonage was decorated with pine branches and streamers made from strips of cloth made into circlets and strung together. The rope for the children's socks was stretched across the great hall. Socks of different shapes and sizes were hung there the day before by the children. Pastor Chiniquy filled them before he went to bed New Year's Eve with little gifts he had collected on his trips and a tiny book containing the entire scriptures from the Book of John for each child. Euphemie and Lucy, with Mina's help, dressed clothespin dolls for the girls. The boys each received a hank of string wrapped around a clothespin. A boy could always find uses for string, and to have a hank of it was a real treat.

The women prepared the meal—roast goose, baked chicken and dressing, canned vegetables, parsnips and carrots from the cellar, pumpkin pies, mince pies, cakes and a big basket of gaufres. Gaufres were rich butter cookies made on a special iron and sometimes called Belgian waffles. Each cook prided herself on having the most special secret combination of the ingredients of butter, flour, sugar, eggs, milk and spices. The gaufres were usually made in October and stored between layers of linen in big baskets in a cool place until New Year's Day. A few may have been stolen from the basket from time to time, but the big day of openly enjoying gaufres was New Year's Day.

The pantry shelves at the parsonage were lined with goodies—many were gifts from Pastor Chiniquy's admiring parishioners. There were fruit cakes, cans of mince meat, pickles of all kinds including, beet, cucumber, sweet and sour dill, green tomato, bean, chou-chou made of cabbage and green peppers, as well as blood sausage and head cheese and trays of gaufres.

The men sat around the great hall talking about the war, politics and farming while the women prepared the meal. The little children played with their stocking gifts while the older boys and girls played games of dominoes, chess and checkers.

Ordinarily, the children at family parties sat at the "second table" in the kitchen and were served after the grown-ups. They did not mind because they could giggle and tease each other and eat as much or as little as they liked with no grown-up admonitions to spoil the fun. Pastor Chiniquy insisted they all eat in the grand hall. The adults sat at the regular tables, pulled out from the walls and lashed together at the north end of the room. The children's table at the south end was made of boards laid on sawhorses. Chairs from the church were hauled in for extra seating.

After the meal, the children entertained the group with little plays, songs and memory work from the scriptures. Then came the game time with everyone participating in charades, button-button, hide the thimble and blind man's bluff. Pastor Chiniquy got down on all fours and gave each of the little children a camel ride. They sat astride his broad back, put their little arms around his neck and hung on to his long beard as he took them around the room while everyone watched and laughed. It was a joyous day. Euphemie was glad to observe that Mina was enjoying herself—in her quiet way—but nonetheless having a good time and mixing with the other children.

Euphemie found, to her dismay, that in the midst of all the busy, happy preparations and at the party she experienced sharp pangs of loneliness A word, a smell, or the sound of certain laughter could spark a memory and, once it was gone, there was left only a hollow emptiness. There didn't seem to be any escape from it or any defense against it. The feeling flashed in and out at will no matter when or where. Evaloe and Francis seemed to haunt her, filling her heart with fresh regret.

She slept fitfully every night and often worried that she was disturbing Mina, who shared her bed. Her dreams were mixed-up nightmares of Evaloe and Francis—one man made up of two. Sometimes he would be standing at a window with his back turned or he would be lying close to her in warm intimacy. Sometimes Evaloe's mouth would talk like Francis'. Other times, Francis' mouth would kiss like Evaloe's.

The night following the big New Year's party was an especially restless night. She tossed and turned and finally put on her robe and slippers and tiptoed out to the kitchen to drink a cup of warm milk in the hope it would help her sleep. She knew Pastor Chiniquy was leaving for Washington City the next day, and she wanted to be up early to prepare a good breakfast for him,

She sat a long time at the table with the lamp turned low. She rested her head on her arms in weariness. Her hair, prepared for the night in long thick braids, was topped with a white, lacy nightcap. Her feet were covered with crocheted footlets. She felt warm and sleepy. She hesitated to go back to her room lest she break the spell of drowsiness. She dozed off and had another dream. She was, in her dream, waiting in her own lovely cottage for her husband to come home. She saw him coming up the drive. His face and most of his body were hidden because he was bearing a huge, fancy cook stove—the kind that took six strong boys to carry into the parsonage. She did not know if the dream man would have a face like Evaloe or Francis. She only knew she awaited his homecoming with eagerness. When he set the stove down, the man was neither Evaloe nor Francis. He was Pastor Chiniquy and she rushed into his outstretched arms.

A noise startled her. She awoke to find Pastor Chiniquy, fully clothed, trying to shake quietly the bedding ashes from the coals of the cook stove. He was to catch an early train from Kankakee City to Chicago and then go on to Washington City. He had noticed Euphemie at the table. When he saw the milk cup beside her sleeping head, he guessed what happened.

She jumped up, embarrassed, and ran to her room, calling over shoulder. "Oh, Pastor, I'll do that. It will take me only a minute to get dressed. I'm sorry I overslept."

He thought she looked like a little girl in her long flannel wrapper and her auburn pigtails hanging from that ridiculous little nightcap that had been pushed to a jaunty angle during her nap.

Mina, exhausted from the excitement of the New Year's party, was sleeping soundly. Euphemie hurriedly changed into her red print dress and pinned her long braids around her head in a coronet. In her haste, she could not find the buttonhook for her shoes so she padded out to the kitchen in her crocheted carpet slippers. She stood near Pastor Chiniquy at the stove. He was surprised how short she was. Never before had he seen her without shoes. He felt a new protectiveness for her as they worked side by side preparing the breakfast of salt pork, fried mush, eggs and coffee. He insisted that she sit down and eat with him,

She complied with his request, but she was uneasy. The dream was fresh in her mind, and she was, for the first time, ill at ease in his presence. She chattered on and on as if compelled to fill every moment with conversation. She talked about the affairs of the house she would see to during his absence; she talked about the church activities for the coming week; she talked about the New Year's party

He said very little. He was thinking all the time what she had meant to him these past seven years; how she had blossomed into a mature, capable woman who, at times like this morning, still seemed to be a charming little girl. He remembered the long talks they had—the first time, in his study at the church when she told him of her love for her cousin's husband; another time, after the vicar had come to the parsonage to woo him back to the Church of Rome; another, when she sewed a button on his new suit and confessed to having hidden the charred crucifix; another, while he was recovering from a serious illness and he told her about his vision of Ste. Anne and Ste. Philomene; and still another, after the death of Francis, the young teacher who was their mutual friend. He had not talked privately with her about Evaloe's death. Somehow he could not find the words. He never really analyzed his feelings about it, but this day sitting across from her in the early morning gloom, it occurred to him jealousy and a sinful relief that Evaloe would not return to claim her for his wife had silenced his usually active voice. He wondered how long he had known secretly in his heart that he loved her—not as a sister in the Lord's work, not as a trustworthy servant, but as a woman—a romantic love.

At times, it may have seemed to him that she loved him in return, but a word or a gesture from her made him realize that she had never entertained romantic thoughts about him. He was simply a middle-aged friend, in the same age bracket as her father. Her very kindness, her freedom of companionship was based on the impossibility of thinking of him romantically. If she had had any inkling that he thought of her in a lustful fashion, she would have left his household, he was sure. It was the normal aspect of things. Youth and age. She had been loved by two men of her own generation and had pledged her troth to one. Now that the ravages of war had torn them both from her, she might possibly settle for an older man, like him, but he could not deceive himself enough to think she would ever have a passion for him

His reflections were interrupted by her laughter. At first, he wondered if he had been thinking aloud and, believing that she was laughing at him, he recoiled from the laughter he usually loved to hear

But she was saying, "I'll never forget the camel back rides you gave the children. Little Eugene Morais was the funniest of all. How he squealed with the danger of it, but he held on as long as the bigger children."

"He should have. He almost pulled off my beard."

"That was such a wonderful party. It was so like you to realize how much we all needed that."

He smiled, accepting the compliment. "As it says in Ecclesiastes 3, 'For everything there is a season; a time to break down and a time to build up; a time to weep, and a time to laugh; a time to mourn, and a time to dance.' To laugh and enjoy the company of our friends and children is not to desecrate the memory of loved ones who have gone on to the joys of Heaven. I am sure they would prefer such behavior to dour, glum faces that scold and rail at the children who cannot be expected to be sad very long."

"You are so good with children," she said sincerely. "What a shame you don't have some of your own!"

Precisely what he had been thinking! How much he would enjoy a son like his namesake, Achille's boy Charlie! And, he thought, looking at Euphemie and remembering her long braids and jaunty nightcap, how he would love having a little daughter who looked like Euphemie!

"Yes, I often wonder what life would have been like had I taken several different turns in the road rather than the route I chose. For example, since I have been associating with Protestant ministers, I have observed what a joy I have missed in not having taken a wife. A minister who has chosen a good wife has a real treasure not only in the parsonage but also in the church. As the sun gives light and life, so is she the focus and light and life in the church. Not only does she add moral strength to the minister, she is also a tower of strength herself. As the sacred duties of the minister of the Gospel are numerous, very often he finds it impossible to see and do everything he has to see and do. She supplies him with the zeal, will, and a success which no one can equal."

His voice was firm, calm and impersonal. She listened attentively. "Someday," she thought, "he will return from one of his trips with a wife, and then what will happen to me?"

She knew, if retained at all, she would find life much different being the housekeeper for the mistress of the house instead of enjoying the autonomy over the household Pastor Chiniquy granted her.

He said, getting up to refill his coffee cup from the pot on the stove, "I think I have been hoping all along you would fall in love with me. I must confess I was jealous when Evaloe came back to claim you, although I never thought of interfering. Now that the war has taken him from you and since Francis is no longer around to pursue his long-suffering courtship, I thought perhaps there might be just a chance you could care enough for me to consent to be my wife."

She was stunned. She stared at him blankly. He sat down at the table and reached to cover her hand with his. She did not move. She did not speak.

He said sadly, "I see now it was all a mistake. You will soon find a husband from your own generation. Good for you. Marry anyone you really love. I would be honored to have you for a wife and mother of my children, but I will maintain only a fatherly affection from now on. Never fear. I will not again mention the subject. When you find that fortunate young man, I pray you will grant this old pastor the privilege of performing the marriage ceremony for you." He started to withdraw his hand. She covered it with her other hand. A mental picture of him as she had seen him in her dream flashed through her mind—his carrying home the stove it ordinarily took six young men to lift,

"Oh, Pastor, you are not old. You are worth any half dozen younger men. But for me to become your wife...I...it's difficult for me to believe this is happening. I must be dreaming."

He took new hope. He laid his other hand on hers. It was a sacred moment as the laying on of hands in an ordination service. "A pleasant dream, I hope," he said quietly

At that moment, Mina, in her long flannel nightgown and lacy nightcap, opened the bedroom door and walked into the kitchen. The spell was broken and the two pairs of hands were quickly pulled apart. Euphemie jumped up guiltily. "Oh, Mina," she scolded. "You should not run around on these cold floors without your slippers, and put on your robe until we get the fires going."

Mina obediently returned to the bedroom. Pastor Chiniquy went upstairs to get his valise. When he came back to the kitchen, he said, "When I return from Washington City in two weeks, perhaps you will have an answer for me. Remember, I want always to remain your dear friend whatever your answer."

Euphemie was pouring milk in a cup for Mina, who was still in the bedroom. She raised her head but did not turn toward him. She said firmly, "I've thought it out, and I think it is the best thing for both of us. If you still are of that same mind when you return, I would be most proud to say yes. But you must hurry. I hear a sleigh coming up the drive. It must be Papa coming to drive you to the depot."

Mina seemingly noticed nothing unusual about their behavior so they assumed their secret had not been revealed to her. With an unexpected show of affection, she put her arms around Pastor Chiniquy's neck when he leaned over to plant a farewell kiss on her cheek. She gave him a big hug and said softly, "Thank you for letting me stay with Aunt Euphemie while you are gone." Embarrassed by her temerity, she ran to the room she shared with Euphemie and stayed there until he left with Euphemie's father.

The two men, bundled under the warm beaver robe Evaloe made when he was home, pulled their hats down around their ears and started the cold journey to Kankakee City. The cold, crisp air made their breath snow-white and steamy. The moisture quickly froze on their beards and turned them a premature white. Conversation for several miles was general about the snow, when spring would come, whether the Osage hedge would be big enough that year to permit taking down the log fences, and whether or not a railroad would ever be built through Ste. Anne.

When they were more than halfway to Kankakee City, they fell into a companionable silence as two old friends can do. Strangers sharing a sleigh or carriage feel the need to keep the conversation going no matter how inane and boring it might be. Old friends enjoy the quiet almost as much as the talk.

Reluctant to break the spell and yet encouraged by the quiet camaraderie, Pastor Chiniquy said, with far less finesse than he intended, "What would you think of my getting married?"

"Married? You? Well, I suppose that would be all right. It's an idea I'd have to kind of get used to—you having been a priest and all."

"But I am no longer a priest."

"I know that. Just yesterday Bernice and I mentioned what a shame you don't have little ones of your own. All children are so fond of you."

"And I love them. I imagine all men dream of having an extension of themselves through their children."

Euphemie's father thought about his family…two boy babies born dead and a third taken at five years old with diphtheria. Euphemie was the only child he and Bernice were able to raise. They had been afraid she would be an old maid until Evaloe announced his intentions after his mourning period for his dead wife. Then the news of his death on the battlefront cut off their dreams of having a son-in-law and some grandchildren to carry on the bloodline.

"I was wondering," Pastor Chiniquy continued, "if you thought Euphemie would have me for a husband and if she will, would you give us your blessing?"

"Euphemie?" The father was at once surprised, delighted and relieved. His old friend was suggesting a solution to the worry Bernice and he had often mentioned---what will happen to Euphemie when we are gone? She will have no family. When Pastor Chiniquy first mentioned marriage, the friend's first thoughts had been of Euphemie—not as a bride but as a housekeeper without a job. He had to readjust his thinking.. His immediate reaction was one of joy, and then, recalling the accusations hurled at his friend's moral behavior, he experienced a sudden fright.

"Euphemie's not…Euphemie's not …with…?"

"With child? You, too, Brutus? You, too, accuse me of those horrible acts of immorality dreamed up by my enemies. Let me assure you, I have not made a single advance toward your daughter. Until this very morning she had no idea she meant anything more to me than a trustworthy housekeeper and a good friend."

Euphemie's father relaxed his tight grip on the reins. "You talked with her about this?"

177

"Just briefly. I asked her to think it over. She told me we will make a decision after my return from Washington City. Until Evaloe's death, my proposal would have been a ridiculous gesture. If Francis Bechard had lived, I would never have considered interfering with her life."

"Euphemie needs someone," her father said. "But are you in love with her?"

"In love? I love her dearly. If you mean do I love her with the passion of youth—do I sigh and starve for her? I do not. I admire her, her youth, her beauty, her charm and the comfortable, happy feeling she brings to me. She knows just when to listen when I am serious and just when to laugh when I am in a jolly mood. If I thought I could never again hear her laughter, I would indeed be devastated. She makes me like myself. She boosts my ego. She will make me a good wife and a fine mother for my children. You don't think me too old to start a family, do you?"

"No, indeed. Think of Abraham! I was just wondering if it would be fair to Euphemie, and to you, too, to be hitched up like these horses here if there is no love between you."

"I did not mean there is no love. I am not at all certain about her. I feel she admires me and likes me and I hope she will grow to love me. As for me, I am looking forward with pleasure to our marriage bed and to sharing family life with her. I may not live a great many more years. My father and my grandfather died young. If I should be the exception, I hope she can tolerate the eccentricities of an old man for when she is the age I am now, I shall be fourscore years. I am not foolish enough to imagine I can arouse the great passion in her she felt for Evaloe, but if she will have me, I want her for my wife.".

At the parsonage, Mina dressed and made the bed and returned to the kitchen for breakfast. Euphemie went into the great hall to tidy up. Before departing the night before, the women guests had taken down the streamers and the sock rope. They had swept up the crumbs. The men had stacked the chairs in the corner to be taken back to the church by the big boys after the morning chores.

In the emptiness of the great hall, Euphemie stood remembering. The room brought back memories—the first time she had seen it, the time Pastor Chiniquy, then Father Chiniquy, interrupted her pattern cutting to request that she sew on a button for him, the children playing on the floor with Pastor Chiniquy on New Year's Day. What would it be like to be his wife, to see him romping with their own children, to share his bedroom as well as his great hall and his kitchen? What would she call him?

She thought, with a kind of personal detachment, marriage to him would mean a lifetime of trying to understand him. He was perhaps a mystery even to himself. But that made him attractive. From the first day she met him when he came to persuade her father and mother to leave Canada and pioneer the prairies of Illinois, she had been impressed with his power of persuasion, his fascinating personality. Seven years as his housekeeper had introduced her to the complexities of this man whom many labeled dangerous. He was always hurrying on to some new struggle He seemed to hunger for confrontation and thrive on danger. She was caught up in his dreams and defended him to others like a tigress. She knew that being married to him would be exciting. But did she love him? An inner voice seemed to say, "Remember your dream." Not Evaloe, not Francis, but Pastor Chiniquy was the one in her dream who returned home to her eager arms. In the dream, he was bearing a stove. Was that the attraction--the material things he provided, the things once considered luxuries she had come to regard as necessities?

Her tortured thoughts were interrupted by the arrival of the two big Morais boys and their friend, Jules Raymond. They had come to carry the chairs back to the church.

"That was some party yesterday," said Alphonse Morais.

"Pastor Chiniquy enjoyed it more than anyone, didn't he? " commented August Morais.

"Wish I could have been here. We didn't have any fun at my grandparents'," said Jules. "Pastor Chiniquy sure is nice."

"Our little brother, Eugene, woke up this morning and the first thing he said was, 'I want Pastor Chiniquy. I love Pastor Chiniquy.'"

Euphemie asked, "Did he like the gifts Pastor Chiniquy put in his sock?"

'Yes. Most of all, he liked playing on the floor and riding on Pastor Chiniquy's camel back."

The boys left. Euphemie leaned against the door after she closed it behind them. "You may have all the answers, little Eugene." She said to herself. "A little child shall lead them."

"The children loved him for the gifts he gave them, but most of all they loved him because he gave of himself," she mused. The fact that she enjoyed the luxuries he could provide in no way overshadowed the joy of being with him. Mrs. Hector Goyette had once told her the Goyette family would gladly have followed him to the ends of the earth. Euphemie felt that way, too. But to be his wife! What would the congregation think? What would his enemies say? What of the celibacy vows he once took?

Chapter XXXIX
Return to Washington

Euphemie's father did not ask his friend why he was going to Washington City nor did Pastor Chiniquy volunteer any information about the reason for his sudden decision to travel there in the dead of winter. The President had sent word he wanted to talk with him and included a pass to permit him to enter the war-torn capital.

The later days of 1863 were the darkest days of the war. On September 22, 1862, Lincoln had issued his Emancipation Proclamation, the gist of which was that on January 1, 1863, all slaves held in a state or a part of a state in rebellion should be then and forever free. In the summer of 1863, the Battle of Gettysburg had seemed the turning point in favor of the North. In November, Lincoln dedicated a cemetery at Gettysburg with what Pastor Chiniquy considered one of the most eloquent distillations of American ideals. However, late in 1863, reverses were met with great oppressiveness because high hopes were dashed. No good news came from the army, and confusion reigned in politics. A movement was afoot to force Lincoln to withdraw as a candidate. The death of his son Willie was a hard blow, but his sense of public duty gave him strength to carry on. His year-end message to Congress early in December ended with a document entitled "Proclamation of Amnesty and Reconstruction." Reactions to the proclamation were varied. In the North, some thought it outrageous and an example of wheedling. Others thought it sagacious and a true gesture of magnanimity. Pastor Chiniquy favored the latter. The people of the

Confederacy made it clear through their elected representatives that they solemnly and irrevocably denied, defied, spurned and scorned the terms issued by the 'imbecile and unprincipled usurper in Washington City."

It was when still another accusation was hurled Lincoln's way he sent a pass to his friend, Pastor Chiniquy. The Lincoln family was near the end of a short visit to their home away from home on the edge of the city when Pastor Chiniquy arrived. An aide ushered him into the president's study. After a kind and warm handshake, Lincoln said, "I am much pleased to see you again and grateful you answered my invitation. I am not very cheery today. My head is aching and so are my feet." He extended his right foot to show he was wearing carpet slippers. "I feel crushed under the burden of affairs which are on my shoulders."

"My dear Mr. President, we see you struggling under that burden and we pray for you."

'I need your prayers and I thank you for them. I also need your views about a thing that is exceedingly puzzling to me."

"Mr. President, I am overwhelmed you are seeking my humble counsel. I want you to know that whatever need you have of my advice, limited as my knowledge is, I shall be most delighted to minister to you."

The minister and the president moved toward the desk and took chairs facing each other. Pastor Chiniquy admired and respected his president and found him a near perfect type Christian. Professedly, he was neither a strict Presbyterian, nor a Baptist, nor a Methodist; but he was the embodiment of all that is perfect and Christian. His religion was the very essence of what God wants in man. It was from Christ himself he had learned to love God and his neighbors, as it was from Christ he learned the dignity and value of man. "Ye are all brethren, the children of God" was his great motto.

In a previous conversation, Lincoln had revealed his belief in a Divine Providence and the duty, privilege and efficacy of prayer. At that time, Pastor Chiniquy expressed a mild surprise that the president thought so much on those subjects. He stated that he was certain Lincoln's friends and general public were ignorant of the sentiments he held. The president had assured him he knew God, rested in the eternal truth of God and thought on that subject more than on any other.

The president settled himself in his chair, taking care not to bump his feet against the desk. "Oh, the bane of sore feet," he said. " My dear Chiniquy, have you ever experienced sore feet?"

"Only once that I can remember. I was trudging the streets of Philadelphia on a hot summer day in the hope of securing funds from those good eastern Christians to tide over my poor French Canadian colonists suffering from famine. I developed such blisters I fell faint to the ground and was rescued by a Good Samaritan named Miss Snowden who took me to her doctor. Are blisters your problem?"

"No, nothing so temporary. I suffer from bunions. My toes are exceptionally long even for a tall man. I was poorly fitted in shoes during my younger days and now, except for specially made boots, I cannot stand shoes. Even these boots," and he picked up a boot near his chair, "are comfortable at times and at other times I cannot stand them and resort to knitted carpet slippers. To get on with my reason for calling you to Washington City--you are the only one to whom I like to speak on the subject. I will appreciate your discreet silence about our conversation."

"My dear Mr. President, our remarks today will be forever privileged information as between a pastor and one of his flock."

"Very good. A great number of Democratic papers have been sent to me lately publishing that I was born a Roman Catholic and baptized by a priest. They call me a renegade and an apostate. On account of that they heap upon my head mountains of abuse. At first, I laughed at that for it is a lie. I have never been a Roman Catholic and no priest has ever laid his hand on my head. Why would the press present such a falsehood to their readers as the gospel truth? Please tell me briefly what you think about it."

"My dear friend, I wept when I read that story for the first time. It is a fabrication of your enemies. They want to brand you with the ignominious mark of apostasy. Do not forget that in the Church of Rome an apostate like me is an outcast with no place in society. You should immediately publish a denial."

"No, my dear Chiniquy, I shall make no denial."

"You must to protect yourself from these radicals."

"I will not dignify their campaign by participating in it. We have religious tolerance in this country, and a man's religion is his private affair. My religion is my own, and I shall make no public statement about it."

His voice was gentle but firm. Pastor Chiniquy could see nothing would change his decision. He begged, "In the name God, I beg you, then, pay more attention to the protection of your life and do not expose it as you have done until now."

"You are not the first to warn me against the dangers of assassination. I see no other safeguard but to be always ready to die, as Christ advises. As we must all die sooner or later, it makes very little difference to me whether I die from a dagger plunged through my heart or from inflammation of the lungs." He coughed a long, loose cough.

He continued, "When I read in the Bible about Moses not crossing into Jordan, the more it seems God has written about me as well as Moses. I hope we are near the end of this terrible conflict, and I pray God grants me long enough life to see the days of peace and prosperity. Yet every time I ask with such longing desire, a still small solemn voice tells me I will see these things only from a long distance and I will be among the dead when the nation crosses the Jordan and dwells in the Land of Promise where peace, industry, happiness and liberty will make everyone happy."

Never had Pastor Chiniquy seen a face so solemn and so prophet-like. He begged permission to fall on his knees and ask God that the president's life might be spared. President Lincoln knelt beside him

After the prayer, Lincoln said sadly, "So many plots have been made against my life, it is a real miracle they have all failed. Can we expect that God will make a perpetual miracle to save my life? I believe not. Just as the Lord heard no murmur from the lips of Moses, so I hope and pray He will hear no murmur from me when I fall for my nation's sake. I pray that my son, Robert, will be one of those who lift up the Flag of Liberty and carry it with honor and fidelity to the end of his life as his father did."

He pulled on his boots. "It has been good talking this out with you, my good friend. My headache is gone and my feet feel good enough to bear the pressure of these boots. Have you any plans for the rest of the day?"

"None whatsoever. Is there something I can do for you?"

"If you have nothing better to do, I would like you to take a drive with me. As you may know, I have been troubled with inflammation of the lungs from time to time. Mrs. Lincoln insists that I have some fresh air every day. She often drives with me, but she is indisposed today. Tell me, Chiniquy, have you ever regretted not taking a wife?"

"My dear friend, it is odd that you should ask. Taking a wife is exactly what I plan to do when I return to my home. That is, if the lady of my choice will have me."

"Is that a fact? And who is the lucky lady, if I may ask? Is she pretty?"

"Yes, very. She, like many young women in our land, has suffered a great loss as the result of the war. Her fiancé died a hero a few months back."

"From gunshot?"

"No, from pneumonia, but it was a war-related death."

He told the story, including the sad death of Evaloe's first wife, Marie. "Euphemie is much younger than I. In fact, her father and I are contemporaries. She has been my housekeeper for seven years, and I have felt a fatherly affection toward her. Her sunny presence in my house makes every homecoming a joy. I knew of her desire for Evaloe while he was still married to Marie, and I suppose, in a sense, I was happy for her when at the end of his mourning period, he asked her to wait for his return from the war. Like most of us, he thought the differences between the states would be settled in a few months. It wasn't until his untimely death and the death on the battlefield of another would-be suitor that I began dreaming Euphemie might consider me."

"Euphemie? What a pretty name!"

"It stems from the Greek and means 'praise' or 'good omen.'"

"Let us hope she becomes a good omen for you. Have you asked her to marry you?"

"The morning I left for Washington City I brought up the subject. I think she was dumbfounded. She is very fond of me, of that I am sure. I am just as certain she has never thought of me in a romantic sense. Do you think such a marriage can survive?"

"Real love will grow as years go by. The very experience of loving will lead to the discovery of how to love better. As in my case, love's development is like the growth of a tree, not steady but irregular. My Mary's love is at a standstill right now. I must be patient and hope and pray it will flourish again. Now, at last, I am getting to the real reason I asked you to come to Washington City. If anyone can restore my wife's mental health so cruelly affected by the death of our dear son Willie, you, my dear Chiniquy, are the one. However, she seems inclined to believe in mystics, so I don't know if she will talk to you. To win her confidence you may have to devise a clever approach."

"Although her grief will never go away completely, little by little she will return to her love of life and her living family." A wonderful idea occurred to him. "I understand she likes very much to shop. I want to buy a trousseau for my bride, and I have no idea how to go about it. Do you suppose she might accompany me on a shopping trip while I am here? It would be a big favor to me, and perhaps it would do her good to think on other matters."

"A capital idea. Shopping is her greatest delight. No doubt, it would be good for her. I rather imagine she might do it. As for her help being a favor for you, unless your pocketbook is fat, you might find it a disfavor. She has extravagant taste. Therein, do we greatly differ. I feel that differences can be nourishing if you don't waste time and energy fighting them. A good marriage made of an impossible combination is probably the strongest kind of marriage there is. I am happy for you, Chiniquy. I am looking forward to meeting Euphemie. I hope she is as pretty as her name. Now, for our drive. My carriage is here."

"I am wondering," questioned Pastor Chiniquy, 'if it is good that you be seen keeping company with an apostate. Your enemies are bound to say, 'Birds of a feather flock together.'"

"Nonsense. I told you that in this country a man's religion is his own business. I feel the same way about friends."

During the next few days, shopping trips proved to be fine therapy for Mary Lincoln and a hardship on Pastor Chiniquy's bankroll. They ordered a green taffeta gown with a full crinoline underskirt, a peach velvet dress embroidered with tiny pearls and a pale gray traveling suit with a bunch of artificial violets pinned at the waist. She selected hats and gloves to match each outfit and arranged privately for the corsets and chemises. The gowns, she said, could be altered a bit because the bridegroom-to-be was not exactly certain of the size. He pointed to a seamstress who seemed about Euphemie's size.

They chose a lovely nightgown and negligee for the wedding night—a sheer batiste, pristine in design and embroidered with tiny forget-me-nots. Shoes were a problem. He said that Mason's Shoe Store in Ste. Anne would be able to furnish appropriate shoes. The cloak he picked was of midnight blue wool fastened with matching braid trim and clasps and lined with a rich silk damask of a lighter shade of blue.

The shops, pressured by Mrs. Lincoln, gave priority to the orders, and he was able to take the boxes of beautiful clothes with him when he left Washington City a week later.

The President was back at his desk and had little time for further talks with his friend. He found ten minutes to bid him farewell and wish him marital bliss. "Thank you," he said, "for the fine counseling you gave my Mary. She plans to continue to visit the wounded in the hospitals as she did with you this week. It is my fervent hope that by submerging herself in the problems of others, she will be able to shake the deep depression haunting her since Willie died. She probably told you her two brothers, soldiers for the Confederacy, were killed in action."

"Yes, we had many long talks. She is a fine woman and deeply concerned for your welfare and for the fate of the nation. I believe you can rest assured now that she has herself firmly in hand she will be the helpmeet you need."

"God bless you, my dear Chiniquy. Have a safe journey home."

"Thank you, Mr. President. May God bless you and keep you safe."

"Just grant me one favor, Chiniquy. Don't name that first baby Abraham."

"If God grants this old man a baby, I will be the one to be called Abraham, like old Abraham in the scriptures."

When his train pulled out of the Washington City depot, his mind was filled with ambivalent thoughts. He was grateful he had been able to counsel Mrs. Lincoln and set her on the road to normalcy, if such a state could be possible in a nation torn by war. He was alarmed by the dangers the president faced daily, especially since the press accused him of apostasy and he refused to publicly deny the accusations. He was distressed and heartbroken at the plight of the many, many wounded he and Mrs. Lincoln had visited in the army hospitals.

Heavy though his heart was for the ones he left behind, he turned toward home with eagerness and a renewed youthful vitality. He was a man of vision, not content to let the vision rest but eager for action to implement the vision. He felt, with Euphemie as his helpmeet, he could truly become a second Luther as the Rev. Leprophon had once accused him of trying to be. Together, they could ignore the advice that well-meaning mentor had given the questioning young Chiniquy during his days in seminar. He had advised, "Let the small grain of sand remain still at the foot of the majestic mountain and let the humble drop of water consent to follow the irresistible currents of the boundless seas, and everything will be in order."

During the daylight hours of the trip, he studied his Bible and his grammar book. His command of the English language was improving rapidly but not rapidly enough to make him comfortably articulate in a lecture hall when questions were fired at him. He continued to think in French and translate. This hesitation made his arguments less convincing. It was his desire to become bilingual so his English delivery would be as powerful as his French.

When it was too dark to study, his thoughts turned to what it might be like should God bless him and Euphemie with children—a boy to carry on the Chiniquy name and a girl like Euphemie to add to the sunshine. Would he, like Lincoln, want his son to take up the Flag of Liberty and carry it with honor and fidelity to the end of his life like his father? The Chiniquy Flag of Liberty signified freedom from the influence of the Church of Rome. What could he and his son following in his footsteps do for the great cause of the religious reform?

He and Achille had often talked about what could make Ste. Anne the cynosure of reform in the world. Achille thought something physical like the sudden capacity to heal multitudes of the lame and the blind would bring fame to Ste. Anne of Illinois as it had to Ste. Anne of Beaupre in Canada. Pastor Chiniquy believed what was needed was an ever-expanding ministerial college to send young men, and perhaps someday young women, into the cities and the byways of the country and of the world to spread the good news of Christ for the only Savior and the Gospel as the only rule of faith. He was determined that when the war no longer drained the country of young men, his dream of a Savior's College would materialize.

He slept fitfully during the night's journey, waking to peer out into the darkness at each stop, wondering about the joys and sorrows of the inhabitants of each town. When daybreak came, he recalled a book he had been given by Mrs. Lincoln. He took it from his valise and fondled the red morocco binding. He loved beautiful books. The pages were edged in gilt and the title, was stamped in pure gold. It was written by Thomas Jefferson and published after his death as the Jefferson Bible. It was a beautiful book. Its unusual approach appealed to Pastor Chiniquy, who agreed in part with the Jefferson philosophy.

He, too, would write a book someday, but it would not be an expensive, beautifully bound book. It would be nicely and durably bound and printed on paper that permitted easy reading. His book would not be one to rest idly on the shelves of a rich man's study. It would be passed from hand to hand by readers and thinkers from all strata of life. Its influence would be felt around the world.

The train pulled into the Chicago freight yard, the lifeline of the growing city. He put away the Jefferson book, his own Bible and his grammar book and latched his valise for detraining. He wondered if Euphemie would accompany her father to Kankakee City to meet his train.

Euphemie! The thought of having her for a wife stirred his adrenalin and made him dream new dreams about a thriving Savior's College, Ste. Anne as a national center of new reform, and the publication of his widely read book. What love can do to accelerate a man's dreams! He longed to hold her in his arms He wondered what her dreams were. He desired so much to have her love him—not as a father figure, a pastor or a friend, but as a lover. For one who had always so boldly gone after what he wanted, he marveled at his apprehension and timidity.

It was not that he was unaware of his appeal to women. There were many women he could have had during his lifetime. In fact, their amorous advances had been a nuisance and downright embarrassing at times. Because he wanted so much to be loved by Euphemie, the possibility of being rejected frightened him. He hoped President Lincoln was right when he said her love would grow as the years passed, that the very experience of loving leads to the discovery of how to love better. What a dear friend was Abraham Lincoln to give such encouraging counsel and not once allude to the aspersions once cast on his character in respect to women. In 1856, at the Spink-Chiniquy trial when Lincoln successfully defended him against the testimony of Father LeBelle, he proved that testimony false. Lincoln not only defended him with the zeal and talent of an able lawyer but as a devoted and noble friend. As such a friend, he naturally would not recall such calumny when Pastor Chiniquy told him of his plans to marry

He wondered if Euphemie had ever heard the story against his character or the false rumor circulated that he was father of a dozen or more illegitimate children in Canada. Doubtless her father had heard the story at his harness shop because it was circulating like wild fire in Ste. Anne until he had a confrontation with the perpetrator of the lies and forced him to confess they were false. Until now, he had refused to let the false accusations hurt him, but if the echoes of those rumors degraded him whatsoever in the eyes of Euphemie, their perpetrators would have accomplished far greater damage than they had ever dreamed possible

Chapter XXX
Accusations

Pastor Chiniquy had been gone a week before Euphemie told her mother of his proposal. During that week, she thought hard about their relationship. He said if Evaloe or Francis had lived, he would not have interfered, and she would never have known he desired her. Being wanted by such a man was exciting in itself. Or was his desire a wish to be mothered? Or the desire to be a father? Was her feeling the compulsion to be needed? Or perhaps the determination not to be an old maid?

Her days were filled with routine tasks and teaching Mina some of the domestic tasks including tips from *Godey's Lady's Book* on how to make life easier and more pleasant. After they completed their chores, Mina often curled up with a book in the window seat of the study, sometimes wrapping herself in an afghan and pulling the curtain across to hide away in the delightful privacy with her book friends

Euphemie's mind reviewed a conversation she and Pastor Chiniquy, then called Father Chiniquy, had on the evening Vicar Mailloux called to persuade him to return to the Church of Rome. They talked about an apostate named Fluet and how Father Chiniquy had been commissioned to offer him $10,000 to care for his wife and children in order that he might leave them and return to the Church of Rome as a priest. Mrs. Fluet had said, "Go tell them there is not gold enough in Canada or the whole world to tempt me to trample under my feet the honored and blessed crowns of wife and motherhood which the great God that governs this world has given me." Surely that woman had found happiness with an ex-priest.

The rumors of his fathering illegitimate children in Canada bothered her somewhat although she was quite convinced they were but rumors. His behavior in Ste. Anne had been exemplary so far as she knew. Perhaps that was because he was getting older. Would he be too old to father children? He mentioned that was one of his desires. What would he be like in the marriage bed? He was often compared to Luther, the German sixteenth century apostate. She had read that Luther married Katherina von Bora when he was forty-two. She was a nun who had renounced the convent life. Luther fathered six children by her but insisted that his marriage was not a relationship of passion. He vowed he could have improved on God's plan for producing new beings by making them out of clay thus eliminating the need for copulation, which he considered sinful even in marriage. Euphemie wondered what Katherina Luther thought of that.

The rumors about Father Chiniquy certainly did not indicate he shared Luther's views on that subject. If, indeed, he had been as promiscuous as he was reported to have been, how would he compare her performance with that of other women he had slept with? Or was there any guarantee he would not continue to find other women attractive—even to the point of engaging in extra-marital relationships?

She ate very little and slept fitfully during that week. Finally, one day, when Mina was back in school, Euphemie's mother visited her and remarked about her pallor and observed that she seemed much thinner.

"Are you still grieving over Evaloe?" she asked with concern. "You must try to accept that his death was God's will. That same God willed you must go on living—living, that is, not walking around in a trance. There are other men, and although you are almost thirty, you are extremely attractive, but not when you look like this."

"Oh, Mama, I was devastated when I learned about Evaloe's death. I was grief-stricken by Francis being killed in action. But when Papa picked up Evaloe's plans for the Euphemie buggy and walked out of here with such a jaunty step, I resolved I come from hardy stock and I must put my grief aside. I remembered how you and Papa lost your babies and yet you made a happy life for me. Except for a now and then pang of loneliness, I have put away my crying towel and my mourning band."

"Then what is troubling you?"

"Oh, Mama, Pastor Chiniquy wants to get married."

Mrs. Allard's immediate reaction was the same her husband's was when Pastor Chiniquy broached the subject. "Would you no longer be his housekeeper?" she asked with apprehension. She was proud her daughter was chosen for such a position.

"No. I would be his wife."

"His wife? Euphemie, has he...have...that is..."

"No, Mama," Euphemie said blushing. "Nothing like that. Almost like a bolt from the blue he asked me to marry him while I was preparing his breakfast the day he left for Washington City."

"What did you say?"

"I said if he still feels of the same mind when he returns, we will decide then."

"But of course you will say yes," her mother said urgently. The French mother looks at marriage for her daughter from the point of view of establishments and children. That she, the mother, had always found the man extremely attractive was so much icing on the wedding cake. Here was an excellent chance for a fine marriage for her Euphemie, who was indeed facing the probability of becoming an old maid. War had killed or maimed so many young men, there were precious few to choose from and not many would want a woman in her late twenties. Surely this girl child of hers who had flowered into quite a woman in these past seven years could not for one minute think of refusing.

"Would it be foolish of me? Is what I feel for him love?"

"Love? What is love? In spite of all people tell us, no one truly understands. There probably is less heartbreak in a marriage where love of the passionate sort is not considered so important."

"But I do not want a marriage without love."

"Love could be described as the desire of two people to make each other happy and perhaps the facing of a life of sacrifice together for the sake of both. Don't expect life to be all happiness. It isn't. "

"Oh, Mama, if we could be as happy as you and Papa!"

"You will be," said her mother confidently. "Now I can take my wedding gown out of the mothballs. How your father fretted about my carrying that dress clear to Illinois! My mother spent hours and hours on it and my grandmother made all the lace. I wanted it for my daughter. To tell the truth, Euphemie, I was beginning to think it would lie in mothballs forever."

"Don't get it out yet. Wait until Pastor Chiniquy returns. Perhaps he has changed his mind. Perhaps he was only feeling the afterglow of that wonderful New Year's party. Mama, don't say a word to Papa. You know how men cannot keep a secret. He would tell it down at the harness shop If the news gets around and then nothing comes of it, I would never be able to face anyone again."

So the mother kept the secret and the father kept the secret as he had promised Pastor Chiniquy. They seldom had much time to talk because he put in long hours at the shop hoping to complete the first Euphemie buggy that he might give it to his daughter for a wedding gift.

The Saturday Pastor Chiniquy was to return home was also the day, according to a note Lucy Chiniquy received from her husband, Achille was to come home for a few days' furlough. Lucy invited Euphemie and Mina to go with her to Kankakee City to meet the train. They imagined what a happy surprise it would be if the brothers met at the Chicago station or on the train.

That morning about nine o'clock, Euphemie went to Pastor' Chiniquys' bedroom to put fresh linen on his bed. She placed the feather ticking on the airing balcony and returned to the room to clean the mirrors. She unhooked the side wing mirrors on the tall armoire and swung the wings forward on their hinges to form a three-way mirror with the big front panel. She stepped back and looked at herself from this angle and that. She was a little thinner, perhaps, but unlike her mother, she found it pleasing. She straightened her shoulders and threw back her head in a haughty pose. She would have to study *Godey's Lady's Book* more seriously to learn what kind of clothes to make for her trousseau. What would the bride of a well-known clergyman wear on her honeymoon? Where would they go? Would it be in June? If so, should she stay in the parsonage during their engagement period? She pushed the mirror wings back in place against the sides of the armoire and fastened their hooks.

When she stepped out on the airing balcony to get the feather ticking, she saw two women marching militantly up the front walk. Their shoe heels tapped indignantly on the wooden planks. She knew with foreboding their visit was not for any good. She could not see their faces from where she stood above them, but she recognized their hats. They were Mrs. Boucher and Mrs. Versailles, pillars of the church and self-appointed guardians of morals.

Euphemie regretted she was dressed in her work dress and her hair around her face was wrapped in rag curlers. She managed to get the curlers out as she ran downstairs. She thrust the rags in her apron pocket, smoothed the bouncy curls and opened the front door in answer to the persistent knock.

" I am sorry, Ladies," she said sweetly. "Pastor Chiniquy won't be home until late this afternoon, but won't you come in out of the cold?"

"Indeed we will." They both tried to get through the door at the same time. Euphemie wondered why people who have an ax to grind always have to come in pairs, as if to shore up each other's courage. Mrs. Boucher stepped back and let Mrs. Versailles precede her. Euphemie showed them into the pastor's study. There was no sitting room or parlor except the great hall and that did not seem an appropriate place. .

"We did not come to see Pastor Chiniquy, anyway," said Mrs. Versailles.

"No," said Mrs. Boucher. "We want to talk to you."

Euphemie's heart began to beat rapidly. Had her mother broken her promise to keep her secret? What could they want?

"I'll get right to the point, " said Mrs. Versailles.

"Please do."

"We demand that you resign this job as Pastor Chiniquy's housekeeper and move out immediately."

"Resign? Why?"

Mrs. Boucher pulled herself up righteously. "We think it very improper for you to be living here with Pastor Chiniquy."

"Why? I have lived here for seven years."

"Yes, but you were Evaloe's girlfriend then."

Mrs. Versailles said, "We all know how you carried on in Evaloe's house right under his sick wife's nose when you were their housekeeper."

"I did no such thing."

Not one of the three noticed a movement behind the drawn curtains at the window seat.

"No use denying it," said Mrs. Boucher. "Everyone says it's so. Now you are probably bedding down with our pastor or wanting to. We see you making moon eyes at him as you sit in church."

"Oh, you dreadful women. Get out of this house." To her utter dismay, Euphemie started to cry.

The curtains at the window seat parted, and Mina jumped from the seat to stand between Euphemie and her accusers. The ordinarily shy young girl cried out in a bold high-pitched voice, " How dare you make my Aunt Euphemie cry?"

Mrs. Boucher reached out to pat her, and Mina moved away. The woman said in a voice dripping with sympathy, "Oh, you poor darling. You've been living in this house and seeing what goes on. You could tell us whether your 'Auntie' has been sleeping upstairs." The way she said "upstairs" carried a sinister meaning.

"She sleeps with me right there." Mina pointed through the door to the kitchen toward the bedroom. "All she and Pastor Chiniquy do is hold hands at breakfast."

"Hold hands at breakfast? How touching! And with this child looking on!"

"It's not what you are making of it," protested Euphemie. "How dare you poison the mind of an innocent child? Get out of here and never come back."

"We are going. But don't talk to us of poisoning a child's mind. You had best get your things packed before our husbands, who as you know are presiding elders, speak to Pastor Chiniquy about this matter," threatened Mrs. Versailles

They departed as militantly as they had come. Euphemie gathered Mina to her and wept great sobs. The little girl stroked her hair gently and cooed, "Don't cry, Aunt Euphemie. They are mean old ladies. I saw the tall one kick a puppy once just because he wet on her rose bush."

Chapter XXXI
The Wedding

Pastor Chiniquy had to wait two hours in the Chicago depot between trains. As he entered the depot restaurant, he was hailed by a familiar voice calling out in the melodious French Canadian tongue, "My dear brother Charles. Is that really you?"

He turned to find Achille dressed in his captain's uniform.

"Well, well, Captain Chiniquy! What a happy surprise! I see you have not had to shave off your beard."

"And I see you now have more hair on your chin than you have on your head. Are you going toward Kankakee City or just coming from there?"

"I am on my way home from Washington City. How about you?"

"I have a two-week furlough. Unfortunately, young Charlie could not arrange a leave. You know, of course, we are in the same outfit?"

"Yes. How is my namesake doing?"

"Wonderfully. He is working under a Major Russell in stores. The major tells me he is doing a fine job. He has a real head for the work. In fact, he is talking of going into merchandising when he is mustered out. The indoor life is not for me, but he likes it. Lucy will be disappointed because he did not come home, too, but we are getting organized for a big push."

"Is that so? When and where? Or are those questions out of order?"

"Well, I should not say, and I do not really know for certain, but I am quite confident we will be joining Sherman on his push toward the sea. Should be exciting. We're all ready for action. This winter of sitting and waiting has been intolerable."

"You always did like to be where the action is. Let's find a table and have a bite to eat."

"Fine. How about over there by the window so we can watch the trains. Tell me, what about my family? How are Lucy and our children?"

His brother brought him up to date on the family news. Assured that he would find all well at home, Achille's thoughts turned elsewhere. He observed the train yards with interest

"Trains fascinate me," he said. "They tell me the North has three miles of track for every mile in the South, and that's a great advantage in moving men and supplies. May be the winning factor for the North."

"Railroads are going to make towns grow into cities," predicted Charles. "We must find a way to get a railroad to run through Ste. Anne. Without a railroad, a town not on a river will not grow. Mark my word; Kankakee City will rapidly grow bigger than Bourbonnais and Ste. Anne. Kankakee City has both river and railroad."

"What we need is two railroads running at right angles or thereabouts making Ste. Anne a junction. Junction towns grow in a hurry. Are there any plans in the making?"

"Dozens of plans for railroads, but few are beyond the talking stages. Remember the line proposed back in 1857 that was to have run from Paris, Illinois through Danville to Chicago and we hoped it would pass through Ste. Anne? Well, that line may be considered again after the war. The trouble is they have no land grant from the government and each township would have to pass a referendum to pass bonds to finance it."

"We could do that, Charles. With your power of persuasion you could easily convince the Ste. Anne people what a splendid investment that would be. But, tell me, what ax were you grinding in Washington City?"

"No ax. The president sent me a letter and asked me to call on him at my convenience. Naturally, I went immediately. It was some personal matters he wanted to discuss."

'Oh, I see. Wish I could meet him again. I get a great deal of pleasure out of telling my friends in the army that my brother is Abe Lincoln's friend. I had no idea he was calling you in for conferences. How did you get through?"

"He sent a pass."

"A personal pass from the president? You kept, it, of course. It will be a wonderful keepsake to hand down to your grandchildren...oh, I am sorry...to your nieces and nephews."

"I may very well keep it for my grandchildren."

"What do you mean?"

"What I said—I may very well keep it for my grandchildren."

"Charles, you are not going to get married?"

"Perhaps"

"To whom? Do I know her?"

"Very well, I believe. Her name is Euphemie."

"Euphemie—like Euphemie Allard, your house.... Do you mean that Euphemie?"

"That's the one. Do you think I am too old for her?"

"No, never. Oh, there are a number of years between your ages, but you are a young fifty-five and she's a mature twenty-six or seven or whatever."

"I believe she is about thirty."

"A wonderful age. You'll have children, of course. A woman any older might have trouble bearing healthy children. When is the date? Wouldn't it be wonderful if it would be while I am home?"

"There's no date set. She hasn't said yes yet. I brought up the subject the morning before I left for Washington City."

"You brought up the subject? Sounds like the agenda for a meeting of the elders. What did she do, table the subject?"

"Well, yes, in a manner of speaking. She said we will make a decision when I return if I am of the same mind."

"And are you?"

"I have spent a fortune on trousseau things that Mrs. Lincoln helped me choose while I was in Washington City."

"You are confident."

"I pray to the gracious God that it is not a false confidence. I have long felt the need for a good wife. Our great God knew well what he meant when he said, 'It is not good for man to be alone.' Marriage is not a human institution; it is a divine one. It was instituted by God himself."

"Spoken like a lover."

"Had Evaloe returned from battle to claim her or had Francis Bechard lived to pursue his suit, I, no doubt, would have never considered such a proposal."

"Charles," Achille lowered his voice and leaned over the table. "If I may question you on this very delicate matter, what of your vows of celibacy? Were they not forever?"

"The vows of celibacy," his brother said in a confidential tone, "are an insult to God. This is why we do not find a single word in the Bible in favor of celibacy. As I have mingled with other Protestant ministers, I have seen the blessed influence of the wife of the minister not only in the parsonage but in the church."

"I think you are absolutely right. Does Lucy know about you and Euphemie?"

"There is nothing to know. Until I spoke to Euphemie about ten minutes before I left, I am sure she never thought of me as anything but an old friend."

"Is that what you thought of yourself?"

"For years, yes. In the two weeks since I made the suggestion, I have come to realize how much I want her."

The announcer entered the restaurant and called out the departure of their train. They quickly paid their checks and headed for the departure gate. As if it were a subject too personal to share even with a brother, they both avoided any further talk of the marriage. They spent the train time catching up on the news and speculating on the war's end and its aftermath.

They were met at depot by Lucy, her fifteen-year old son and Mina. The other Chiniquy children were waiting at home for their father. There was a flurry of hugs and kisses and compliments. They were settled at last in the sleigh, all except Pastor Chiniquy.

"Where's Charles?" asked Lucy. "Doesn't he know he is supposed to ride with us?"

Achille looked toward the depot. "Oh, he said he had to arrange to have his baggage sent out later. Seems he bought a trousseau." Achille delighted in springing the news in such a casual manner.

"I hope he doesn't take long...he bought a what?"

"A trousseau. I think that is what you call it."

'I doubt it. A trousseau is made up of dresses and such for a honeymoon."

"That's the word then. A trousseau."

"Who's getting married?"

"He is"

"Who is?"

"Charles."

"Our son Charles?"

"No, my brother Charles."

"Your brother Charles is getting married?"

"That is what he said."

"To whom? I didn't know he was seeing anybody."

"To a young woman named Euphemie."

"From Washington City?"

"No, from Ste. Anne."

Mina had not said a word. She looked back and forth from Achille to Lucy, following their animated conversation.

Lucy was dumbfounded. "From Ste. Anne? You don't mean our Euphemie? Euphemie Allard?"

"That's the one."

"Well, I am speechless."

"Never."

"To think Euphemie never said a word. When is the wedding date?"

"No date set. In fact, I may be premature in telling it. She said she would give an answer on his return. I saw him looking all around when he stepped off the train. I think he was disappointed she did not come to meet him."

"Charles and Euphemie! That news will rock the countryside."

Charles hurried across the parking lot and stepped with a lively bounce into the sleigh. "Sorry to have delayed you," he said. "There was a bit of mix-up, but it is all straightened out now."

Lucy turned to him and said in a teasing voice, "You rascal, you. Why didn't you tell us you were courting?"

Achille said quickly, "Sorry, Charles. It slipped out. It won't be a secret now that Lucy knows."

"Look who's talking," she laughed. "You couldn't wait to tell."

"No matter," said Charles, smiling broadly. "I was going to tell you myself. I was hoping Euphemie would come with you so we could tell you together."

Mina said primly, delivering the message she had been told to give, "Aunt Euphemie would have come but she is indisposed."

"Indisposed? I have never known her to be ill."

"She's not ill. She's been crying. Her eyes were red and puffy."

"Crying?" His heart sank. When Euphemie was not at the station, he had suffered pangs of anxiety. To hear that she stayed home to cry did not make him believe she was a woman about to give an affirmative answer to a marriage proposal.

Mina said, telling more than she was supposed to, "Two mean ladies came to see her this morning and shouted naughty things at her."

"What ladies?"

"I forget their names. They go to our church. They said their husbands are elders, and if Aunt Euphemie doesn't pack up and leave right away, they are going to have their husbands speak to you."

He did not question the child any further about the nature of the naughty things the mean ladies had shouted. With a shake of his head at Lucy and Achille, he silenced them. The child had already heard too much.

"Well, well," he said. "We will dry up your Aunt Euphemie's tears when we get home. Wait until she sees what is the big boxes I brought home."

"Another new stove?"

Everyone laughed.

"No. Something even nicer."

He was relieved that Euphemie's tears were not over him. He was confident he could straighten out those two women and assure Euphemie their tongues would hurt only themselves.

The sleigh pulled into the parsonage drive in late afternoon. Lucy ran to Euphemie and hugged her. "We are so pleased with the good news about you and Charles."

Achille put his arms around both Euphemie and Lucy and planted a kiss on Euphemie's cheek, "Greetings, my new sister-to-be!"

Mina whispered in Euphemie's ear, "Now you won't have to leave."

"Whatever are you all talking about? cried Euphemie, her face pink with embarrassment.

"Your wedding, of course," said Lucy.

Euphemie glanced over Lucy's shoulder at Pastor Chiniquy, who was looking earnestly at her. A smile tugged at his lips. He asked, "There is going to be a wedding, isn't there, Miss Allard?"

Before she could answer, Achille said, "I want to know when. Is there any reason it can't be while l am home to be the best man?"

"It would be a little difficult to arrange so soon," said Lucy. "But it can be done. Oh, Charles and Euphemie, please say you will have the wedding while Achille is here."

"How long will you be here, Achille?" asked Euphemie, caught up in the planning.

"I have a two-week furlough, but that includes travel time so I should be here about ten days."

"Let's all go over to our house and make plans," said Lucy, suddenly remembering the rest of her family. "Our children will be wondering what happened to us."

"I have prepared supper here."

"Bring it along. We have much to celebrate. Victor, you run over and tell Euphemie's parents to join us."

"Oh...Papa!" Euphemie cried. "I must talk to Papa first."

"Never mind about Papa," said Charles. "I spoke to him on my way to Washington City."

"Two weeks ago? Why, Mama didn't say anything about it."

"He promised not to mention it until I returned. He said something about ladies not being able to keep secrets."

Euphemie laughed her deep throaty laugh. "How funny! I told Mama, and we agreed not to tell Papa until you returned because men can't keep secrets. But Achille," she turned contritely to him. "We cannot possibly have the wedding so soon. I need time to prepare a trousseau."

"That's no problem."

"That is what you men think. Tell them, Lucy."

Before Lucy could speak, Charles said, "I happen to have a lovely trousseau just your size selected with the loving advice of the First Lady of the Land, Mrs. Lincoln."

The engagement was announced at Achille's home in the midst of the excitement and confusion of his homecoming. Before the meal was over and almost without Euphemie's approval, Lucy and Bernice had the entire wedding planned. Bernice confessed that she had taken the wedding gown from the mothballs and hung it in the attic to air out. Except for new shoes, the trousseau was about ready.

Euphemie went to church on the Sabbath with trepidation. She heard little of the sermon, the text of which was the story of Ruth. Pastor Chiniquy extolled the virtues of a wife. He closed by saying that marriage is a divine institution, not a human one, and that God knew well what he was doing when he said, "It is not good for man to be alone."

Word had already spread through the village of the coming marriage. The parishioners were unprepared for such a short courtship. They were taken back when he said, "So it is with great pride that I announce to you my marriage on Friday of this coming week to Euphemie Allard. It is our desire to have the wedding while my brother Achille is home on leave. We extend to each and every one of you a cordial welcome to attend. Now let us kneel for the benediction."

He had talked earlier that morning to Evaloe's family and received their blessing on the union. He asked them and Achille's family to gather round Euphemie after the service to ward off any sharp-tongued comments. She left the church in the midst of friends who kept her so occupied she did not see the little knots of folks gathered to cluck over the news

Euphemie spent the remainder of the week at her parents' home so the wagging tongues of the village gossips would have less to speculate about. Mina returned to live with Stephen at their grandparents' home. Euphemie and her mother made the adjustments on the wedding gown and the trousseau items from Washington City. Never had they seen any clothes so beautiful! Luckily, Mason's Shoe Store had shoes appropriate enough for each costume.

The wedding was a beautiful candlelight service performed in the Ste. Anne church by the Presbyterian minister from Kankakee City.. Achille in his uniform and Lucy in her Sunday best were the best man and matron of honor. Mina was the flower girl and Stephen the ring bearer. Flowers from Euphemie's greenhouse and geraniums from Lucy's kitchen decorated the altar. Euphemie carried a white Testament, a gift from her bridegroom. The wedding supper was served in the church basement. To the credit of all who attended, no disparaging remarks were made about the wedding itself or its sudden announcement.

An unusual January thaw melted the snow in the streets. After the wedding supper, Euphemie's father escorted the newlyweds to a waiting buggy. It was their first glimpse of The Euphemie, designed by Evaloe and built by Mr. Allard and his assistants. Euphemie was thrilled. Tears came to her eyes. She kissed her father and mother and turned to follow her new husband. She thought no girl could have had a more glorious wedding day or a more attentive, wonderful husband. He helped her into the buggy and carefully tucked the robes around her.

"Why bother with the robes," she asked. "It is only around the block to our house." How strange that sounded--our house!

"I thought we might take a little ride in our new buggy," he said as he went around and seated himself in the driver's seat. He pulled her to his side and drove off with one arm around her. Such a clatter of noise arose. Tin pans, spoons and old shoes were tied to the buggy. Euphemie looked around and was surprised to see other carriages falling in behind theirs.

"Oh, Charles," she said, and she found it easy to call him Charles. "You knew they'd do that." She was amazed how comfortable and natural it seemed to snuggle next to him during the ride through town with the noisemakers tied to their buggy and the crowd following them.

The wedding party finally stopped in front of the parsonage where Mrs. Allard had gone ahead to open the front door and light the lamps. Euphemie could not remember having entered the front door in all the seven years she lived there. Victor Chiniquy said, "I'll take care of your horse and buggy, Uncle Charles."

Charles helped her from the buggy and up the steps. He opened the door. As she started to step in, he said with authority, "Just a moment, Madam Chiniquy."

For an instant, she thought he was going to precede her through the door in the manner of priests. Instead, he caught her up in his arms and carried her over the threshold as the departing guests cheered. They were to spend the first night of their honeymoon in Ste. Anne. Their bags were packed for an early morning departure for Kankakee City where they would catch the same train Achille was taking back to Chicago. The newlyweds planned to stay in Chicago a week. Charles promised that as soon as wartime restrictions on travel were lifted, they would go together to far off places, places where he had been before and wanted to show her as well as places he had never been.

The bridegroom stayed downstairs in his study while his bride prepared herself for bed. Her mother had turned down the bed and laid out Euphemie's gown and negligee and Charles' nightshirt. She changed from her wedding gown to the nightgown Mrs. Lincoln selected for her. She washed her face and took the pins from her hair. She brushed her hair carefully and started to braid it. "No," she thought, "tonight I will leave my hair unbraided." That was something she had not done at night since she was a little girl. She said her prayers, climbed in bed and pulled the covers up to her chin. There was a cozy fire in the bedroom fireplace, but she was shivering. She waited nervously for her husband to come to their wedding bed.

He came upstairs shortly. He left the bathroom door open and she could hear him splashing about and singing lustily. She could not suppress a nervous giggle that came at a pause between verse and chorus.

"Why are you laughing, My Pet?" he called gaily.

"I never heard you sing like that before," she called back. She always admired the way he led the church singing, and she remembered hearing him sort of half hum and half whistle a tune when he puttered around in the garden. This singing was different.

"You have heard cicadas sing in the fall, haven't you?"

"Yes."

"Well, did you ever notice they don't always sing the same?" He appeared in the bedroom doorway clad only in his trousers and a towel draped over his shoulders.

"No, I guess I never really paid attention." This seemed an odd time for a lecture about cicadas. She wondered if other women had lovers like hers—Evaloe excited by the frenzied cranes and her new husband excited about the mating songs of cicadas

He explained, "Male cicadas of each species have three different sound responses. One is a congregational song that is regulated by daily weather fluctuations and by songs produced by other males. A second is a disturbance squawk produced by an individual cicada captured or pursued by the enemy. The third, and best of all, is the courtship or mating song usually produced prior to copulation. So what you hear tonight," his brown eyes twinkled wickedly, "is my mating song." He returned to the bathroom and sang vigorously the chorus, "Work for the night is coming when day's work is done."

In a few moments, he returned to the bedroom. Ignoring his new nightshirt spread on the foot of the bed, he turned down the lamp, threw back the covers, climbed in bed and gathered her to him. She tried to remember what her mother told her in the vague discussion they had, something about letting him do what he wished and to pretend she liked it. She could only think her mother had not told her how pleasant it could be with a gentle, thoughtful man like her new husband.

"Oh, Phemie," he said, caressing her long hair. She was glad she had obeyed the impulse to leave it unbraided. "My wonderful wife. My dear Phemie." It was the first time he had ever called her anything except Miss Allard, or a few times that evening, Madam Chiniquy.

He whispered, "Solomon in all his glory had no possession to equal the treasure I have here." With soft caresses and low murmured quotes from *The Song of Solomon*, he worked his way down her body. "Your navel is a rounded bowl that never lacks mixed wine, your belly is heap of wheat encircled with lilies. Your rounded thighs are like jewels, the work of a master hand."

His was a master hand at exciting a woman. Euphemie knew instinctively she was not her husband's first lover. Celibate he was not. If he sensed that he was not her first, he did not reveal it in anyway.

Euphemie warmed by his caresses, responded with eager parted lips to his warm kisses. The gentle crackle of the logs in the fireplace of what was now her bedroom contrasted sharply with the wild cacophony of the sand cranes just as her patient husband contrasted with the eager, passionate Evaloe. Exciting as that roll in the prairie grass had been, Euphemie recalled it as a fantasy. Under her husband's expert guidance, Euphemie bloomed. She, too, remembered a verse from *The Song of Solomon*, "I am my beloved's and he belongs to me."

His joy at her response pleasured her. He may have had other lovers, but no matter, she thought; "Now he belongs to me. He's mine. Mine." Of one thing she was certain, and the certainty filled her with happiness—in the marriage bed, her Charles was no Martin Luther. Euphemie could not help feeling sorry for Katherina von Bora Luther.

The next morning, she was embarrassed to awaken and find her bridegroom still asleep but clad in his nightshirt while her pretty nightgown lay in a heap on the floor. He rolled over so his back was to her and gently snored. She clutched the sheet around her and reached down for the gown.. As soon as she smoothed it over her legs, he turned to her and said gently but formally," Good morning, Madam Chiniquy."

This was to be his attitude throughout their long marriage—a gentle joyous lover in the bedroom but elsewhere very formal. Life in the parsonage for all outward appearances was to be about the same as when she was Miss Allard. Although she was "Phemie" in their bed, he always called her Madam Chiniquy in public.

On the first morning, he climbed out of bed and went toward the fireplace. "Stay there, my dear," he said. "I will poke up this fire and add a log or two. Then I will go down and shake the cook stove grate so we can cook our breakfast, our first breakfast together as Mr. and Mrs."

She laughed merrily. He looked so funny in his nightshirt.

"What's so funny?"

"Oh, I was just thinking that you don't have to wonder if I know how to cook eggs and bacon the way you like them."

"You are right." He poked energetically at the logs. He must have risen in the night to add to the fire, but she had not heard him. "Not many bridegrooms have a bride all schooled in pampering them. I just may pamper you today and go down to get your breakfast and bring it to you here in bed."

"No, indeed. I have never had breakfast in bed unless I had the measles or something. I will be down in a few minutes."

He added another log, put on his robe and slippers and padded downstairs. She got out of bed, threw back the covers to air the bedding and started to dress. She decided to wait until after breakfast to put on the gray traveling suit. It was too elegant to wear to fry bacon. She pulled on a rose-colored challis robe. There would be time to dress before her father came in his carriage to take them to the train. He said he would use his own carriage rather than the new Euphemie. The Euphemie! What a wonderful wedding gift! She had told her father he could not build it and he had chided her saying he was not too old to try something new. Fifty-five was not truly the static age she had once thought. Her fifty-five year old husband certainly did not fit the image she used to have of men that age.

Her long auburn braids had always been so easy to arrange in the morning. However, she found her long, unbound tresses unruly and difficult to dress. Still, she was happy she had chosen to leave her hair unbraided because her bridegroom had a great deal of pleasure stroking it. She brushed and combed and finally forced the unruly hair into a coiffure that pleased her.

Euphemie had never ridden on a train or had she been to Chicago. The trip was an adventure. She was glad Achille was along to talk to Charles so she could freely look at all the sights. She felt strangely queasy and would have attributed the feeling to motion sickness had she not felt the first uneasiness as she descended the stairs in the parsonage and smelled the bacon her new husband was frying. She was happy just to sit and listen as the two brothers talked man talk.

The Chicago railroads were flourishing. When the train the Chiniquys were riding pulled through the freight yards, Euphemie was fascinated by the freight cars on the tracks adjacent to theirs. They bore names from all parts of the country and were brightly colored yellow, red, blue, green and white. At the busy depot they bade Achille goodbye, hired a porter to store their luggage in a horse drawn cab and set out in the cab for the Tremont Hotel, where they engaged a fine suite of rooms.

Chicago was an exciting place for a honeymoon. It was a marvelous week filled with adventure. Euphemie did not mind that Charles struck out every morning to meet with this or that clergyman, combining honeymoon and business in the same week. She enjoyed lying in bed until almost ten. She reveled in the luxury of breakfast in bed sent up by Charles from the dining room where he stopped to breakfast on his way to his meetings. Her stomach felt queasy when she woke up, and the breakfast in bed seemed to settle the ripples of discomfort. She attributed the feeling to the richness and novelty of the foods she was eating every night

The afternoons and evening were filled with delightful long walks or carriage rides and charming dinners in quaint restaurants of different ethnic backgrounds. One afternoon, they visited a college campus built on ten acres of land donated by Senator Stephen A. Douglas at 34th and Cottage Grove Avenue. Jones Hall, built in 1857—the year Euphemie moved into the parsonage—was an impressive four-story building with a magnificent bell tower. The college already had two hundred students. Charles was interested in every detail of its construction and development because it was so much like his dream of Savior College for Ste. Anne.

Euphemie's favorite excursion, and one she begged to repeat whenever there was any spare time, was a visit to P. Palmer's Dry Goods and Carpet Store on Lake Street. It was housed in a splendid marble-fronted business block and was five stories high. The west part was for sales rooms displaying new arrivals of real English carpets, velvet Brussels, fine silks and embroideries. The shawl and mantilla room filled Euphemie with delight. When Charles indulgently told her to select a shawl, it took her three trips to the store to make up her mind.

Charles chided her, "You can always bring it back if you don't like it. Palmer advertises a money-back guarantee if the customer wants to return a purchase for any reason. That is a very daring offer, it seems to me, when most of his customers are women." Such a store policy was an innovation.

The week ended all too soon. Euphemie packed her pretty trousseau and watched the bellboy haul the valises to the carriage.

When she returned to Ste. Anne and her own familiar cooking, she was annoyed to find her morning queasiness continued. When her menstrual period was three days overdue, she began to suspect she was "expecting."

When ten more days of queasiness elapsed, she was quite certain she was going to become Charles' wife and mother of his child all in the same year. She had hoped for an early pregnancy because Charles loved children. In fact, she was quite confident he married her to produce a family, an objective she was happy to share because she, too, loved children. Yet, she had not wanted to conceive so early in their marriage. She would have liked a few months of being a wife without the responsibilities and discomfort of pregnancy. She was nervous about telling her husband, but she need not have been afraid. He was delighted.

"Just call me Abraham," he shouted with glee as he picked her up and swung her around.

"Charles, stop. You are making me dizzy. I may vomit right here in the great hall."

He put her down gently. He treated her with tender concern throughout the pregnancy, a concern that was almost ridiculous because after the first few weeks, the morning sickness stopped and Euphemie felt wonderful. Charles thought she never looked prettier.

He arranged for Mina to stay at the parsonage so Euphemie would have company during the hours and days and sometimes weeks he found it necessary to be away. He offered to keep Stephen, too, but Marie's parents were reluctant to part with him. Stephen was content to stay with them and occasionally visit his sister at the parsonage.

Euphemie carefully laundered and packed away her mother's wedding dress, wondering if it would be used by the child in her womb or, if the child should be a boy child, would his bride want to wear the beautiful family heirloom. She slipped the crucifix her grandmother gave her as a child between the folds of the dress. Tradition and heirlooms had taken on a wonderful new importance. The trousseau dresses were packed away, too, because they were too elegant for Ste. Anne wear. By the time the wartime travel restrictions were lifted, she would be too great with child to get into the trim waistlines.

Charles received an invitation to attend the official dinner in Washington City at which Lincoln was to receive word he was nominated for a second term as President of the United States. The invitation included Euphemie. Because of her pregnancy, she thought it best not to make the trip. It was not to be the last time she made a decision to stay home when she wanted so much to accompany him.

Charles hesitated about leaving her. She encouraged him to accept. He was to be the personal guest of the president. She urged, "Think what a wonderful story that will be to tell your little one—that while he was preparing to come into this world, his illustrious father was standing on the right hand of the President of the United States when he accepted the Republican nomination for a second term."

Chapter XXXII
Years of Sorrow and Joy

One day while Charles was in Washington City, Euphemie and Mina rode out to Mina's grandparents' farm. Mina stayed outside to play with her father's young brother and sister. Mrs. Morais was entertaining three friends who greeted Euphemie coolly.

"How have you been feeling, Euphemie?" Mrs. Morais asked solicitously.

"Just wonderful since I no longer have morning sickness."

"When are you expecting your baby?" asked Mrs. Deleon.

"Dr. Legris thinks it will be sometime in October, probably the third or fourth week."

"Oh, October? So soon?" Mrs. Mason asked archly.

Euphemie could tell they were silently counting the months from the January wedding to the October date. She was glad she said the third or fourth week. Dr. Legris suggested it could be sooner.

"My Evaloe was born within a year after our wedding," Mrs. Morais said quickly. "I was only sixteen and the youngest in my family so I did not know much about taking care of babies. I learned in a hurry, and I have had plenty of experience since," she laughed ruefully, thinking of her seven children. "If you have any problems, Euphemie, you can call on me."

"Thank you, Mrs. Morais. I'll surely remember that."

"Sixteen is a better age to have your first, I've always said," commented Mrs. DeLeon. "Many complications can come from a late-in-life confinement."

"Euphemie's still young," Mrs. Morais protested. "I had Louis when I was forty."

"Yes," commented Mrs. Coderre, 'but he was your seventh and not your first."

Euphemie had entertained doubts about the health of her child because of her age. This open discussion made her uneasy. How dare they say those frightening things!

"Oh, Mrs. Morais, I am so pleased to have Mina staying with me," she said to change the subject. "She said it is all right with her two grandmothers if she stays on after the baby comes."

"She seems so happy with you, poor little orphan. She has always loved you ever since the first day you went to take care of the children when Marie was so sick."

"Sort of like her papa," Mrs. Coderre said pointedly.

Her two friends tittered. Euphemie colored at the insinuation.

Mrs. Morais hastened to say, "In so many ways. She not only looks like him, she acts like him and has so many of his dear, quiet ways."

"No wonder you are so fond of her then," Mrs. Mason said to Euphemie. "We all thought you and Evaloe..."

Mrs. Morais interrupted her friend, "Louise!"

""No, let her go on," Euphemie insisted. She got up from her chair, straightened her dress over her protruding stomach and faced the women defiantly. "You thought what about Evaloe and me?"

Mrs. Mason glanced at her friends and said, "Oh, nothing."

Mrs. Deleon, somewhat sorry for the way things were going, hastened to say, "We just hoped you and Evaloe would get married someday, but, of course, along came the war. But then, I guess you were always a little sweet on Pastor Chiniquy." She made the situation worse.

Euphemie felt warm and sweaty. She wondered if she was going to faint. "There was nothing between Evaloe and me while Marie was alive. We did plan later to marry after the war. As for Pastor Chiniquy, I was fond of him as my employer and my pastor. Not until months after Evaloe died in the service of his country, did Charles and I think of each other in a romantic way."

She turned to Mrs. Morais. "I am sorry to be so rude, but I am leaving, and I will never come back when these spiteful women are here."

Her hostess followed her to the door, apologizing for her friends. Euphemie took Mina with her and drove home at such a fast, reckless pace, Mina was alarmed. A rabbit dashed in front of the buggy, causing the horse to rear. The buggy tipped into a grassy ditch spilling out Euphemie and Mina. The horse regained its composure and waited patiently while Euphemie and Mina righted the lightweight buggy. Neither Mina nor Euphemie seemed to be hurt

When Euphemie got home, she discovered she was spotting. She sent Mina for her mother. Mrs. Allard immediately put Euphemie to bed. A week's rest reassured them that all was well. By the time Charles returned, she was up and about. He became even more solicitous—so much so she was actually relieved when the labor pains started, albeit six weeks early. Her relief was short-lived when she realized the baby would be born less than nine months after the wedding giving credence to the insinuations made by Mrs. Morais' mean friends.

She had a difficult difficult birth. The doctor warned Charles that the baby's lungs were underdeveloped and he might not live. Diphtheria was prevalent in the community and several families lost little ones from the dread disease. Charles delegated his visits to those families to an assistant. He was afraid he might bring the disease home to his sickly baby boy whom he idolized. If there was talk about the baby's being born less than nine months after the wedding, Euphemie did not hear of it. She went nowhere. Only the help and Lucy were permitted in the house. Mina went to stay with her grandmother. Charles forbade any company for fear they might infect the baby.

After six weeks of increasingly poor health, the infant Charles died. His father was inconsolable. Euphemie reconciled herself to the baby's death, preferring it to his having to go through life so handicapped. She consulted the doctor about the possibility of her having healthy children. He assured her she was perfectly capable of bearing a healthy baby.

She finally persuaded Charles to turn from his deep mourning and boldly reminded him of the story of King David after his son died. She suggested that she, like David's Bathsheba, should become pregnant again. Within a year, Rebecca was born—a bouncing, healthy baby. Euphemie feared Charles would be disappointed the baby was not another boy. He was so relieved to have a healthy child, he quickly hid any disappointment he may have felt. Rebecca soon charmed him completely.

Near the end of Euphemie's pregnancy for Rebecca, the Civil War ended. Hard on the heels of that joyous announcement came the horrible news of President Lincoln's assassination. The news threw the Chiniquy household into a furor. Charles was determined to prove an international conspiracy. Much to Euphemie's alarm, he launched an investigation into a Jesuit connection, a determined search that was to preoccupy him for many years

When Rebecca was two years old, her sister Emma was born. The birth was so difficult the doctor told Charles that Euphemie should have no more children. She grieved because her husband would not have the son he longed for. If he was disappointed, he concealed it and never indicated to the two girls he wished they were sons. From infancy, his two daughters, each very different in appearance and temperament, were loved in a special way by their father. Each of them adored him.

In 1874, Charles spent six months in Europe, where he was greeted as "The Luther of Illinois." Euphemie longed to accompany him. Both she and Charles felt she was needed at home to take care of Rebecca and Emma and to supervise the running of the parsonage and to answer the volumes of mail coming from all parts of the world. Charles lectured in England, Scotland and Ireland.

When he returned home, he found in his mail an invitation to leave Ste. Anne to preach in and around Montreal to the growing number of French Protestants in that area of Canada.

"Let's go, Charles," Euphemie urged. "The girls need a change of schools. I feel they are not getting a proper basic education here." She did not explain that they were often insulted and slighted, that they sometimes came home with tales of how the school children giggled about their mother as if she were a naughty lady.

They closed their Ste. Anne home, leaving the church sexton to watch over it and the treasures Charles had collected on his lecture tours. An assistant took over the pastoral duties. Euphemie and the girls were glad to be again with Mina, who had married and moved with her minister husband to Montreal. Years before, Charles had offered the little orphan Mina his home, but not really his love. Although she lived under his roof and he was always kind and generous to her, he was not the warm, loving tease with her that he was with his own girls. He hated to admit to himself that he was prejudiced against her because she looked so much like her father, Euphemie's young love.

Charles' first lecture in Montreal was in a French Protestant church on Craig Street. He was determined to let the French Protestants hear the Gospel and secure for themselves the right of free speech. It was rough, dangerous work and required police protection. It was almost impossible to find a church willing to risk having him.

Euphemie regretted leaving Ste. Anne. The basement of the old Erskine Church was used for a while. Then the Free Church Cote offered its facilities. Much against Euphemie's better judgment, Charles published the booklet, *The Priest, The Woman and The Confessional,* condemning the behavior of priests. She thought he was exposing himself to too much antagonism. She feared for his life.

Not only his life was endangered by the publication. Their home was stoned, threatening letters against him and his family and his parishioners arrived so often it was thought wise to maintain a guard around their home at all times. They hired a tutor to come to the house to teach Rebecca and Emma rather than expose them to attack en route to school as well as on the playground.

Unpopular as the booklet was with Roman Catholics, it sold in the thousands to Protestants, and went on to be printed in 15 editions. In Europe, it was translated in Italian, French, Spanish, Danish and Swedish. Euphemie was at once proud and afraid. Fortunately, she was unaware that he was also pursuing his investigation of a Jesuit connection with the conspiracy to assassinate President Lincoln.

In March of their third year in Montreal, Charles received a letter from Achille. Euphemie was alarmed at his reaction. He was seated at his desk. He picked up a pile of papers, threw them across the room, broke two pencils in pieces and tossed them toward the wastebasket, and pounded on his desk with his fist.

"Charles, what is it?"

"I cannot believe it. I just cannot believe it."

"Believe what?"

"Here, read it yourself." He stomped out of the room after dropping the letter in her lap.

Achille wrote that Lucy had never felt comfortable about leaving the Roman Catholic Church. Shortly after the first permanent priest was established in Ste. Anne, Lucy began to long to return to the church of her childhood. Father Letellier often visited the family and, through Lucy's influence, persuaded Achille to accompany her in a return to Roman Catholicism. The priest enlisted Achille to go with him on tours throughout the United States to collect money for the church. They were also working on a plan to obtain a relic of Sainte Anne in order to establish a shrine where pilgrims could make novenas as they do at the shrine of Sainte Anne de Beaupre in Canada

Euphemie was concerned about Charles' reaction. She could sympathize with Lucy because had she herself not such a strong love for Charles, she, too, could have found it easy to slip back into the old mores so firmly established in childhood. She secretly felt that Achille was attracted more to the excitement than to the religion. With Charles in Canada, the Protestant movement in Ste. Anne had doubtless slowed down. The new priest, bursting with fervor, no doubt appealed to Achilles' sense of adventure.

She followed Charles to their bedroom where he was angrily throwing clothes in his valise.

"Where are you going?"

""To Ste. Anne to talk some sense into Achille. I can see Lucy doing that, but Achille?"

"Charles, for my sake, won't you pray about this before you dash off?"

She was amazed at her temerity to confront him in one of his angry moods. Surprisingly enough, he followed her suggestion and retired to his study. She heard him pacing back and forth. At last, he came to the door and quietly asked her to unpack his valise.

He returned to his study and penned several pages to Achille, wadding up some and throwing them away. When he left to mail the letter, Euphemie dared uncrumple the sheets she found in the wastebasket. She was pleased to see that Charles forgave Achille and encouraged him to seek God in the Church of Rome if that was indeed where he felt he must worship. He said he felt when first converted that his act might alienate him from his brothers, and he was grateful to have had Achille by his side during the past fruitful years.

Chapter XXXIII
Separation

Four years in Montreal, Quebec City and Nova Scotia took their toll on Charles' health. During that time, he persuaded seven thousand French Canadian Roman Catholics and immigrants from France to publicly announce their conversion and their intent to follow the Gospel of Christ. The rigorous winters and the relentless schedule of lecture tours caused increasingly frequent attacks of bronchitis until at last his doctor recommended he leave that climate and take a voyage on the Pacific Ocean.

"This time, Madam Chiniquy," he insisted, "you must go with me."

Before their marriage, he had promised to show her the world, but three pregnancies and the responsibilities of motherhood and pastor's wife kept her home while he answered calls from Canada, England, France, Germany, Ireland and Scotland   She longed to accompany him on the trip West. Achille had entertained them many evenings with glowing tales of Colorado and California where he searched for gold before migrating to Ste. Anne. She was delighted when Mina and her husband offered to take care of Rebecca and Emma. Charles asked to be excused from his clerical duties of the Presbyterian Church of Montreal. He was granted a year's leave of absence.

Another letter arrived in the same post as the letter granting his leave. It was from Euphemie's father telling that her mother had had a stroke and was paralyzed in both legs and her left arm. She could not speak, but she could hear and seemed to understand. "Mama needs you," her father wrote. "Can you come?"

Euphemie was torn between desire and duty. She retired to their bedroom where she knelt in prayer and soul-searching. Charles let her seek her own answers. He knew what they would be. When she told him she felt she must go to her mother, he said, "Although, I, too, am sickly and I need you and want you to go with me, I know what a dutiful, loving daughter you are. After all, I can manage by myself. After a few weeks of rest and warm sunshine, I will feel as good as new. We can have many trips together later. Go to your mother. She needs you. Your father needs you, too."

And so it was decided. Euphemie closed up the Montreal house. She and the girls returned to Ste. Anne. Charles arranged for his replacement to continue to fill the pulpit in the Ste. Anne church. He went by train to the West coast. Euphemie moved her parents into the Chiniquy home and found a young couple to rent the Allard place. She gallantly faced a year of loneliness without a husband.

Twelve year-old Rebecca was delighted to return to Ste. Anne to her favorite old tree house, the cozy library window seat, and the open spaces of the countryside. Emma hated it. Had it not been for the horse her father bought her and the new figure skates Mina gave her as a parting gift, she would not have been able to stand it.

Rebecca was gentle and generous with her time devoted to her invalid grandmother. Emma served only when she had to and then not too graciously. One task she enjoyed was reading to the old lady. Emma loved to read aloud. Since her fifth birthday, she like her father as a little boy, had recited great sections of the Bible at prayer meetings and Sunday School programs. Her father trained her to raise or lower her voice to portray the boldest or the most timid characters of the Bible. She was a born performer. She read to her grandmother the adventurous reports in her father's letters, wishing all the time she were traveling with him. She especially liked the part about the train ride across the Rocky Mountains.

He wrote, "No words will ever give the idea of the magnificent spectacle of the mountains, whose tops are constantly covered with ice and snow. The perfect peace and calm which surround them, the millions of glittering diamonds which cover their white robes, give more the idea of an angel from Heaven."

Emma's' grandmother shed a few tears. Emma read on, her voice becoming more and more dramatic because she felt she was thrilling her grandmother.

"But suddenly, dark clouds rose behind the mountains and quicker than I can say it, the magnificent vision disappeared. The earth trembled under us; our ears were deafened by peals of thunder such as we had never heard before. Our eyes were blinded by terrible lightning. It seemed the doors of Hell opened and all its armies were hurled against the world. For more than a half hour, we were witness to a battle for the mountain. From the closed windows of the cars, we watched the sublime and terrible conflict. Suddenly, the noble mountain appeared again, its gigantic head above the clouds. It had conquered. The storm clouds were torn and broken into fragments; they rolled at the feet of the conqueror to disappear on the plains below. The white robes looked whiter than ever and the rays of the sun came as messengers of God."

Always eager to offer a sermon, he added, "And if your soul has to pass through great tribulations, if you see dark clouds at your horizon, even if you find yourself struck by a hurricane, my Christian loved ones, you will surely hear a sweet voice whispering in your ear, 'Fear not, I am with thee. In the world ye shall have tribulations; but I have overcome the world. Abide in Me and I will abide in you to be your strength, your joy and your life eternal.'"

"Oh, doesn't Papa write beautifully? I wish, oh, I wish I could have gone, too." She leaned over and gave her grandmother a rare kiss. The old woman reached for the girl's hand with her good arm. For a moment, a beautiful understanding passed between them stimulated by their mutual admiration of the man whose thoughts could fly back over the mountains into their hearts.

Chapter XXXIV
Oregon

The next letter from Charles brought back old memories. He wrote to Euphemie, "You remember Hector Goyette and how he refused the gift of a Bible on the eve of his departure to Oregon? That was back when you first came to manage my household. Do you remember taking his good wife a Bible the next day as a farewell gift from me? We later heard how their wagon train was attacked by Indians. His horses, wagons, and furniture were stolen by Indians. About 12 years later, and I may not have mentioned this to you because little did I ever dream of coming here, I received a letter from Mrs. Goyette telling me that they often read the Bible I had given them . She managed to save it from the savages. In spite of great trouble, they arrived in Oregon and later accepted the Gospel of Jesus as their only rule and guide of their lives. In her letter, she said a great number of French Canadian neighbors would also see the light if I would but carry the message to them I deeply regretted at the time I was unable to answer her call for help.

"When I was in San Francisco, I learned I had to go only 800 miles to reach the Oregon settlement of the Goyette family. I also learned that five or six days' navigation on one of those splendid steamers of the Pacific would take me there. Such a voyage was just what the doctor ordered. You will never know their joy, as well as mine, when I entered their happy home and knelt with them to thank and bless God."

Euphemie stopped reading and said to her mother, "I never dreamed such a thing could happen. You remember, Mama, I told you Mr. Goyette told Charles before he left, 'Those you think most loyal are going to wake up to the mistake they have made and that includes you, young lady, and your mama and papa.' He shook his hat under my nose and stomped out of the parsonage. I guess he was the one who did the waking up."

She read on, "I spent 13 days among those dear countrymen going day after day from door to door carrying the good tidings of salvation. Walking through those forests of giant trees, measuring wider in diameter than our great hall, is the most pleasant thing you can imagine. Several times the road took me along the shores of the Cowlitz River. I had only to throw my line in for a moment to catch some excellent trout that were a welcome offering to families I visited

"My dear Euphemie, I can hear your lovely laughter as you visualize me, like a true apostle of old, when at the setting sun I knock at the door of a dear countryman bearing a Bible in one hand and a dozen fishes in the other."

The description made Euphemie laugh, something she seldom did those days. How she longed for his return and hoped the next news of his trip would come from his mouth and not his pen.

That was not to be. He wrote he had received a request from his old friend, George Sutherland, who had helped him in his great time of need with contributions for his starving colonists. Sutherland had gone as a missionary to Australia. He asked Charles to join him there to preach the message of salvation. He was so certain Charles would respond to his call to make the 10,00-mile trip, he sent money for his passage aboard the steamer called the City of Sydney. Charles hoped Euphemie could understand his obligation to go. He said they would probably exchange few letters because of the difficulty of sending mail 10,000 miles across the Pacific to Ste. Anne. He would be gone a year or so.

She was overwhelmed with anger and frustration. She could not imagine why a 70-year old man subject to severe attacks of bronchitis would want to undertake such a trip. She resented George Sutherland's asking him. She was about to tear the letter into bits when she noticed some more writing on the back of the last sheet. There he expressed concern for her invalid mother and sent his greetings to her father and to the beloved parishioners of Ste. Anne. He sent kisses for Rebecca and Emma. To her, he said, "The cicadas will be singing a special tune when I return." It was a reference to their wedding night. How could she be angry with such a dear man?

He had already sailed from San Francisco when she received the letter. She faced another midwestern winter with an invalid mother, two children, her father and a stable boy. In the village she was labeled by her enemies as the "apostate's woman." She was not really the wife of the pastor in her own church because her husband was no longer the active pastor. That position was being filled by The Rev. Mr. Paradis. His spouse took up the role of pastor's wife. She was pleasant to Euphemie, but she made it quiet clear that she, not Euphemie, was the pastor's wife

The cicadas were in good voice that autumn. Their songs, rising and falling in intensity in the late afternoon and early evenings, filled Euphemie with an inconsolable longing that broke down her discipline. She was cross with the girls, short with her mother, and she could no longer concentrate on her reading that had always been her solace. She spent the entire month of September after she received the letter in a daze and yet terribly awake, filled with a longing that was akin to pain.

She had a terrible sense of foreboding that she would never see her husband again. Going to their bed that seemed wide and empty without him, with no arms to embrace her, no voice to sing the mating song, was torture. She had been lonely before, but always comforted herself by knowing that her husband would return and that his first embrace would erase all the wretched lonely weeks.

"Storybooks," she thought, "always leave the impression that love and passion are reserved for the young. The real love story is lived by those who have shared the years and learned to lean on each other." She, at least, had learned to lean on Charles.

Her distress was so great she wondered if she might be going through "the change." She longed to ask her mother about it. Something like this required a different kind of communication than she was able to carry on with her invalid mother. She had no close women friends. Mina was really the best friend she had, but she was more like a daughter and she was far away in Montreal. Lucy, although pleasant and sociable, was no longer the close friend she was when Achille and Charles were on better terms.

She was so concerned about herself she made up her mind to consult Dr. Legris. Before, that however, something happened to break the spell. On the last Sunday night in September, she joined in the singing at the evening church service   It was a hymn with which she was not familiar so she had to pay close attention to the words:

" Ho, my comrades, see the signal waving in the sky;
Reinforcements, now appearing, victory is nigh,
Hold the fort, for I am coming,
Jesus signals still.
Wave the answer back to Heaven—
By Thy grace we will."

Before the hymn was over, she felt a strange surge of power, a sudden lifting of the despondency She threw back her head and sang with lusty enthusiasm. It was not until two months later when she received a letter brought to San Francisco by a returning missionary and sent to her by pony express that she could assign any reason for her return to her cheery, reconciled self.

The first part of the letter revealed no indication of the extreme danger her Charles had survived. He described the ocean voyage and his fellow passengers. He said, "Even when crossing the tropics and equator, we met with nothing but pleasant weather. When we reached the 34th degree latitude south, the skies began to cloud. Torrents of rain fell on us and we were told to prepare for an equinox gale."

Emma was reading aloud and she was thrilled by the narrative. Euphemie shivered and goose pimples came up on her arms. " On the 28th day of September about 3 p.m., the ship began to go up to the top of the waves and plunge into the profound abyss dug before her by the receding seas. It was impossible for anyone to stand on his feet without being thrown down with tremendous violence .At about four p.m., one of those waves struck me in the breast and rolled me more than 30 feet from the leeward side toward the windward side without more ceremony than if I had been a straw."

Euphemie had been standing near the foot of her mother's bed. She sank to the edge of mattress near those motionless feet and clutched the iron bedpost.

Emma loved the tale.

"We hoped the hurricane would subside at sunset, but it increased in its fury. The captain ordered the crew to have the lifeboats ready at a moment's notice. Oh, what pages I could write if I could describe the six hours that passed over us until the next morning! The greater part of the fervent Christians on board gathered with me in a corner of the upper salon. I heard such prayers as I have never heard before.

"There was a struggle that night on that little corner of the raging Pacific in which love and mercy were again to win the day against the justice and wrath of God. By four o'clock, the threatening voice of thunder was silenced and the hurricane had visibly lost more than half its strength. We were chilly and exhausted. We left each other to take some rest."

"What an experience!" commented Euphemie's father. "That convinces me. I am never going to go on an ocean voyage."

"Oh, Grandfather," cried Emma. "It makes me want to go."

"Not me," said the less adventuresome Rebecca.

Mr. Allard started to leave the room.

"Wait. There's more,"

"Not another storm, I hope," said Rebecca.

"We dropped anchor in the port of Sydney but the sanitary laws prevented our landing immediately. I asked the captain if the ship had sustained damage. He said, 'Not much But so sudden a cessation of that hurricane is one of the most extraordinary things I have seen in my life. Those equinoctial storms usually last three days and they very often keep us a whole week suspended by a thread between life and death.' I told him he had on board some of the children of those fishermen who caused Christ to stop the storm on the Sea of Galilee. He said, 'I wish I would always have on board some of those Galilean fishermen's children.'"

Euphemie said softly, "Oh, the power of prayer!"

Emma continued. " I organized a prayer meeting for our last Sabbath evening together. Jews, Christians, Romanists and Protestants, atheists and infidels joined in praising and thanking God. At half past ten, I had retired to my room when I heard distant sounds of singing. As it grew closer and closer, I heard the words,

'Ho, my comrades, see the signal waving in the sky
Reinforcements now appearing, Victory is night."

Euphemie snatched the letter from the surprised Emma. Those were the very words she sang that night when the mantle of despondency fell from her shoulders. It was on the last Sunday in September. She read aloud, not as dramatically as Emma, but her soft contralto voice was filled with wonder.

"It was George Sutherland and his friends. He said 'We have seen you. That is all we wanted. Tomorrow we will be on the wharf to give you another Australian welcome. Go and take rest. Goodnight and God bless you.'"

Euphemie folded the letter and tucked it in her apron pocket. There was still another paragraph. She did not want to share it with the others—not just yet. In the privacy of her room, she read, "I would not have had you endure the storm for any price, my dearest, but how I wish you were with me now. I know our marriage has been stormy at times, but, you, like that great steamer, the City of Sydney, have plowed on through, enduring all manner of troubles. I am eternally grateful to God for giving me a wife whose stalwart faith has caused our marriage to survive all gales even though sometimes it had to plunge blindly into a profound abyss. When a marriage survives all vicissitudes and pushes on, that is the most sublime happiness this side of Heaven! I pray that my work here will soon be completed and I am safely back in the haven of your loving arms."

It was the closest thing to a love letter she ever received. It never occurred to her that he searched in vain her chatty, newsy letters for words of passion but found there only the reports of a dutiful wife left at home to keep the home fires burning and to supervise the growth of his two daughters

Chapter XXXV
Bastard

Emma was bored and lonely for her father. When the weather turned cold enough to freeze ice on the pond back of the schoolhouse a block from her home, she spent hours skating there. She had taken skating lessons in Montreal and was an excellent figure skater. Her latest project was to write her name on the ice with her skates. One afternoon, she spelled out her entire name. The Emma part was easy and the Chini was not too bad, but the letters q, u, and y presented a problem. She pulled off her skates and ran home to get her mother. Euphemie tied on her bonnet, put on her galoshes, coat and mittens and went to see the writing. It felt good to get out of the house. She never complained about the care of her mother, neither aloud nor to herself, but sometimes the confinement was almost unbearable, especially in the winter months.

When they arrived at the pond, several boys with sticks in their hands were slipping and sliding there. They ran away when they saw Euphemie and Emma. Emma ran ahead to the spot where she had written her name with her skates. She found the Emma part still clear and beautiful, but the Chiniquy name had been smoothed off by sliding feet. Scratched by stick were the letters "B-A_S_T_A_R_D."

"Look what they did to my beautiful Chiniquy! Oh, those horrid boys!"

Euphemie's heart sank when she made out the word.

Emma spelled, "B-a-s-t-a-r-d. Bastard. What does that mean, Mama?"

Euphemie hedged. "It is probably Bachand. Do you know anyone named Emma Bachand?"

"No, Mama. It's not Bachand. That is spelled B-a-c-h-a-n-d. This is B-a-s-t-a-r-d. It's a naughty word. George Regnier called me that at recess the other day and everyone snickered."

Euphemie looked at her sadly. How she longed to protect her from the slings and arrows of nasty insinuations! She decided to be candid with her.

"Sit down on this log a minute, Emma, and I will explain."

"Just a minute, Mama. I want to do something first." She sat down and strapped on her skates. She skated furiously up to the naughty word and executed a beautiful stop, spraying ice from the sharp blades. She did that again and again until the hated word was entirely obliterated. The action was her way of venting her anger and hurt. Emma was not a crier.

Euphemie had a few minutes to plan her explanation. She wished Charles were there to do it. She learned long ago that discipline and explanations could not wait weeks for his wiser counsel but must be dealt with at once. Emma skated slowly to the log and, leaving her skates on, sat close to her mother and slipped her mittened hand into her mother's.

Euphemie squeezed the slender hand and said, "I wish your papa were here to talk to you about this."

"When is Papa coming home?"

"Soon, I hope. Now about that word. There are some people who say that your father and I are not really married—that because he once was a priest and took the vows never to marry, he cannot really have a wife."

"But he is not a priest anymore."

"You are right. And so his vows no longer bind him."

"But what about that word?"

"It is a nasty word used to insult a person. It implies that a person's father and mother are not really husband and wife. Now, you and I both know that your father and I are truly married. I will show you the marriage license and the wedding certificate signed by the minister who married us."

"Oh, Mama, you don' have to do that."

"I want you to see it. And Rebecca, too. So long as we all know we are right, no dirty words by thoughtless little boys can hurt us, can they?"

Emma seemed reassured. Euphemie wondered how deeply wounded she was. She was just a child. Euphemie knew that even adults can be deeply hurt by dirty words of thoughtless and cruel people. She knew that only too well.

She said, "I have a few more minutes before I am absolutely frozen stiff. Why don't you skate out there and do a beautiful Chiniquy on ice for me? I wager you can even dot the i's."

That night, Euphemie took out the precious marriage license and wedding certificate. She went to the girls' room where they were waiting for her goodnight kiss. She tucked them in tenderly and stood a moment uncertain how to broach the subject. Perhaps she was making too much of the issue. Rebecca reached up, pulled he mother's face close to hers and whispered, "Don't worry about that word, Mama. Emma told me about it."

Euphemie remembered reading someplace that the older child of a family is a great keeper of secrets, but the younger one cannot wait to share any new knowledge.

"She knew about it already," said Emma, almost jealously.

"How?"

"Oh, it was a long time ago when we were still in Montreal. Some boys called me that."

"In Montreal?" Montreal, too? Was there no place free of the torture?

"It was in the schoolyard before we started having a tutor. I knew it was a dirty word because of the way they laughed and because I had seen it written on the outhouse wall at school along with those other dirty words like 'whore' and 'son-of-a-bitch' and..."

"Rebecca!" Euphemie stopped her before she could finish. The words sounded so foreign on the lips of the sweet, innocent girl who, as far as Euphemie knew, had never used a naughty word in her life.

Rebecca continued, "I didn't say anything about it at the time. I remembered the word and one day when I was reading a biography of Alexander Hamilton, I came on the word and learned its meaning. It puzzled me why I should be called that. I went to Papa's study in the church and asked him to explain. We had a long talk. Then he read a passage from the Bible. Here it is. I have it marked." She reached for her Bible on the nightstand. As she read, her mother recalled the Psalm. It was the one Charles read to her and Evaloe Morais that day so many yeas ago when Marie attempted suicide and Evaloe had descended to the depths of despair

Rebecca's voice, so low and vibrant like her mother's, read, "Oh, how great is Thy goodness. Thou shalt hide me in the secret of Thy presence from the pride of man. Thou shalt keep me secretly in a pavilion from the strife of tongues. Thou heardest the voice of my supplications when I cried unto Thee."

"Oh, my darlings, you have such a wonderful papa. He always knows just what to say and do."

"We think he knew just what to do when he picked you for our mother, don't we Rebecca?" Emma said, getting out of bed and running around to hug Euphemie.

"Oh, yes. Papa told me you are the perfect wife and that Emma and I should pattern ourselves after you so we will be good wives for pastors someday."

"No pastor for me, thank you," Emma said positively. She hopped back in bed and settled herself comfortably under the heavy quilts. "I'm going to marry a millionaire and travel, travel, travel."

Euphemie blew them each a kiss as she took the lamp and left the room. Travel, travel, travel! Such had been her dream as she started her married life. Somehow it had not happened. Oh, well, maybe some day.

Chapter XXXVI
Temptation

All through the dreadful winter, Euphemie envied Charles in the down-under land where the seasons were reversed. She imagined him basking in the warm sunshine with balmy breezes blowing through his long white beard. She had no conception of what he was actually experiencing because no letters came after that first one brought by the missionary. She was faithful about making daily entries in her diary. She encouraged Rebecca and Emma to keep daily records, too, to show their father on his return. She was certain her diary would make dull reading compared with the one her husband was keeping. There was one episode in her otherwise dull life she did not record. It was one she never wanted Charles to learn about.

It happened when she and a young doctor were nursing her mother through a severe bout of pneumonia. The rigors of winter were hard on the entire family. When her mother contracted pneumonia, the additional care and vigilance exhausted everyone. Dr. Legris, himself, came down with the dreaded disease and sent his young assistant to care for Bernice. Euphemie's father tried to stay by his wife's side, but his own weariness forced him to retire early the night her fever broke. Dr. Lafond gave him a sedative and assured him he would stay on with the patient through the night. He was a man two or three younger than Euphemie, a Civil War veteran, unmarried and devoted to the pursuit of his medical career. He was tall, lean and muscular with exceptionally strong forearms and wrists that could wring out sponging cloths dipped in cool water, extracting a half cup more water from a cloth Euphemie thought she had wrung dry as possible.

From the first time she met him, she felt at home with Dr. Lafond. His openness made her feel at ease with him. That night she decided he really was quite handsome, something she had not been aware of before. As he bent over his patient, she could see flecks of gray in his curly brown hair. His ears were well shaped and snug to his head. He turned from his patient and looked squarely at Euphemie who was standing by his side. She found his eyes startling. Blue eyes were rare among the Frenchmen she knew, but that isn't what made them so unusual. Strange flecks of flinty color seemed to be layered on the iris layer after layer giving a depth to the eyes. They were knowing eyes, aware, alert, and most of all, understanding and quick to respond either in compassion or humor.

"The fever has broken," he whispered. "She's going to be all right."

Having shared the worry, they shared the relief. It seemed only natural to hug each other in their triumph over the dreadful pneumonia. The pressure of his lithe, spare body against hers aroused Euphemie's erotic emotions. She could no longer hold in check her desire for love and caresses so long unanswered during her husband's extended absence. She pressed close to the doctor, reveling in the tall leanness of his body so different from the rounded, cushiony comfort of Charles' embrace. Of a sudden, she was reminded of Evaloe. She had not thought of him in years. Was she a romantic, falling in love with any man she found herself working beside? No, there had been many young men who stayed at the parsonage for days and even weeks studying her husband's reformation, and even some older ones, too, who sought a flirtatious interlude with her. She had not been the least bit interested. Their approaches were insulting and disgusting. They all seemed so callow and unexciting compared with her brilliant, bombastic husband.

Dr. Lafond, no longer her non-threatening helpmeet at the sick bed, whispered passionately, "Only an old fool would run off to Australia and leave such a woman."

She broke from his embrace and ran from the sick room. He followed her quickly and forcibly took her in his arms again.

"You're too young to waste all these months waiting at home, and what will return? An old man, old enough to be your father. I am leaving next week for Kankakee City where I will have my own practice, but I have a little cabin on the Iroquois River, only three miles from here. Promise me you will meet me there. I must see you again. Alone."

She clung to him. She wanted him. Yes, she would meet him there. To be desired, to love, to be possessed with passion were things her heart cried out for. Sensing her desperate, pent-up longing, the doctor abandoned his caution and pressed closer covering her body with caresses. Euphemie sense of duty and loyalty brought her to her senses. A tryst in a cabin by the river, perhaps, but not here in her husband's home with her sick mother lying in the next room. She came out of her whirl of fantasies with a start and a shudder.

"I must be out of my mind," she said, pushing him away. "How could I have forgotten my mother, my children and my husband?"

"Euphemie, my darling, think of yourself for once. You're a person no longer. You're a woman no longer. You are nothing but an exhausted sense of responsibility."

The flight of fantasy had lasted only a few minutes, yet she returned from it as from a long journey. She was astonished to find the doctor still there pressed against her and to feel his hands on her body and to hear his passionate breathing in her ear.

She broke away and hurried back to the sick room, consumed with guilt. Memories of her confession of her first love to Father Chiniquy came flooding back, and she remembered his tender understanding, his extension of a release from guilt by suggesting the feelings she and Evaloe had were simply those often felt by persons sharing a vigil over a sick relative or friend. Would he be as forgiving if he were ever to learn of her yielding to temptation right under his own roof?

Her mother was awake and reaching feebly with her good arm for the water glass on the nightstand. Euphemie smoothed her pillow, kissed her blessedly cool brow and took the empty glass. "Mama, dear, I'll get you some fresh water. Would you like something to eat?"

Her mother assented with her eyes. Euphemie felt comfortable and safe again in her role of responsibility. Perhaps she was no longer a woman in the passionate sense Dr. Lafond meant, but she was a woman of integrity and loyalty. Thank God she had not let her passionate self destroy all that was good and clean and decent in her.

Dr. Lafond, shaken by her sudden turn, left the house quickly, so frustrated and angry he neglected to check on his patient. No matter. His patient was in Euphemie's capable hands. If he didn't know his duty, she, indeed, knew hers.

Chapter XXXVII
Charles in Australia

Charles was enchanted during the first month of his visit to the land down-under by the climate so contrary to the laws of the northern hemisphere. In October, which is a spring month, he was invigorated by the pure air and the exuberance of life coming from the evergreen forest and the many flowers and the balmy breezes. It was his delight to sit in a reclining chair soaking up the sunshine on the back porch of George Sunderland's home on the outskirts of Sydney. He stayed in Sydney for four months . He gave eighty-two lectures and preached fifty sermons. He loved the Sydney-siders, the boisterous and animated Sydney-siders. The male drinkers mostly shut themselves off from the sunny streets in large saloons, like banks, with nowhere to sit down. Barmaids served the masculine throng. Jam-packed and raucous, the clients swilling down enormous quantities of beer, the places were filled with animation and enjoyment.

Charles tried to approach the men by offering them his booklet, *The Manual of Temperance*. He had two thousand copies with him. The men were good natured and tolerant of him, but they paid no attention to the manual. He found his best way to get the manual into the homes was through the women who attended the services where he lectured and preached. As much as one-third of the family income was spent in many families for alcoholic beverages, mostly beer. The women desperately clung to any means to win their men away from the vice. Charles received ovations from the clergy of Sydney when they saw how his efforts redeemed thousands of drunkards. The mothers and wives to whom temperance gave back a loving husband crowded around him wherever he went to thank him and press his hand to their lips.

Although he felt he was needed in Sydney, he was eager to go for the remainder of the Australian summer to some cooler climate of the new continent. He responded to invitations to visit Melbourne, Ballarat, Geelong and Adelaide in the southern part of Victoria. These regions are some 800 miles nearer the South Pole and their southern breezes are very healthful. He spent three weeks in Ballarat, one of the thriving cities of New South Wales. It is situated in a very rich and beautiful plain where in 1851 enormous amounts of gold had been found. As in most mining towns, there were in addition to the respectable citizens a great number of drunkards, thieves and murderers. Some Roman Catholics determined to keep him from addressing the people. He had difficulty finding a place to live because a rumor had spread that the house where he stayed would be destroyed. At last he found a room in a boarding house.

His experiences in Tasmania were even less peaceful. Tasmania, called the "Island State," is about 150 miles across Bass Strait from Australia. Its inhabitants do not wish to be called Australians and they refer somewhat disdainfully to Australia as the "mainland."

When Charles arrived on Saturday, June 21, 1879, Hobart Town contained about 30,000 people and the place was well supplied with schools, newspapers and churches. He was received by a number of clergymen. He preached on the Sabbath at the Chalmers Presbyterian Church in the morning and in the Melville Wesleyan Church in the afternoon. He spoke on the duties, responsibilities, privileges and glories of the Christian. He gave a series of lectures each night the following week in the town hall located in the principal square called the Queen's Domain.

There were disturbances around the hall every night. By the last night, there was a near riot. A number of rough-looking characters armed with sticks entered the hall as soon as it was opened. They stood at the back and maintained a deceitful calm. The audience entered and sat down as quietly as a Sunday congregation. The topic of the lecture was "Liberty of Conscience." When Charles rose to speak, there was a great noise: yells, groans, loud expletives, hisses and fierce shouts accompanied by the clatter of boot heels and sticks. The sturdy Irish rowdies cried, "Turn him out." "Three groans for the apostate priest." "Three cheers for the kicked-out priest." Finally they had their way. The meeting could not go on and the audience dispersed.

On Saturday, the clergy met to protest the prevention of Pastor Chiniquy's using the town hall. They testified that during his visit and under extraordinary irritations and excitement he had uniformly behaved both in private and public with a spirit of moderation and Christian charity toward those from whose communion he had severed himself. They bade him a fond farewell, commending him and his noble mission to the grace of God.

With a heart filled with love and gratitude for their good wishes, Charles returned to Sydney for the remainder of the two years he spent in the down-under country except for a visit to New Zealand to escape the summer heat of Sydney. He delivered seven hundred addresses, lectures and sermons. He was given $40,000 as a token of appreciation. George Sunderland requested that he either send him great quantities of *The Manual of Temperance* or give him permission to have it printed in Sydney. He urged Charles to write a book telling of his life in the Church of Rome and his break with it. He saw Charles safely on board the ship for his return to San Francisco.

The voyage was calm and uneventful. He spent many hours recalling his life story. He jotted down voluminous notes that might later be incorporated into a book—a book his friend George suggested he write.

He was filled with a desperate homesickness and prayed for the days to hurry by so he would soon be home with his wife and family. He wondered what kind of news they would have for him. He reckoned the girls would have grown a great deal. He hoped they would enjoy the gifts he had brought and the stories he had to tell. He resolved not to tell of his narrow escapes because he was aware of how much Euphemie worried about him. Better that she not know. Charles, the family man, was headed home.

His return from Australia was a joyous occasion for the Chiniquy household. His tales of the land down-under fascinated Emma and Rebecca. Euphemie's mother rallied from her listlessness and seemed to enjoy the stories although she could not speak or smile. Euphemie was happy to have Charles home. It was several nights before she asked in a low whisper as she lay in their bed in the circle of his arm, "What are the Australian women like?"

He misunderstood her concern and launched into a discussion of the secluded but hard-working life the Australian wife and mother leads in a land so dominated by adventuresome, bold men.

"But didn't you get to know any of the women personally?"

He raised up on his left elbow and stared down at her face. The curtains were open. The moonlight fell across the bed so he could see her serious expression.

"Yes, quite a few. Like women everywhere, they are concerned about their husbands and their children. I wish you could have met them, Phemie. You would have liked them and they would have loved you. Maybe someday we can go there together."

"Maybe we can," she said and she patted his cheek. He was in his seventies and not likely to make such a rigorous trip again. In his seventies! She had been silly, perhaps, to entertain jealous, suspicious thoughts of other women. To her he seemed very appealing and desirable. It was easy to think other women felt that same attraction.

Her mother slipped away in her sleep three weeks after Charles' return. It was as if she had been holding on by sheer determination until he got back. Euphemie missed her but not nearly so much as her father did. He had spent many hours reading to his wife and talking with her. Although her response was minimal, he seemed to love her more and more. In his loneliness after her death, he turned to his shop and spent long hours building The Euphemie buggies that were proving to be so popular with the ladies.

Chapter XXXVIII
Rebecca's Wedding

Writing the book took up much of the next five yeas. Rebecca and Emma in their teens, along with their mother, were the scribes. Euphemie fully realized at last the great danger Charles had endured. She told herself she understood his reasons for shielding her from the knowledge over the years. Yet she felt sadness akin to pain because he had not permitted her to share that part of his life. She was grateful he lived to write about it.

One day she commented to the girls, "I am amazed how your father seems to think in English."

"Think in English? Don't you, Mama?" asked Emma.

"No, I don't. When I was your age, I knew very few English words. It took me a long time to know enough English to carry on a conversation. Even now, I think in French and translate into English before speaking."

"That's what I do, only from English to French, when I talk to Grandfather Allard," Rebecca admitted.

"Me, too," said Emma. "Do you believe Papa thinks in English?

"I am sure of it. " She glanced down at the manuscript she was editing. "I wish he would not be so outspoken in his criticism of the Roman Catholic clergy. I am sure this section will antagonize them even more than the other parts."

"Do you think Papa wlll be in danger?" Emma asked, almost hopefully. She loved excitement.

"I hope not," said Rebecca. "Mama, can't you persuade him to leave out some parts? The book is going to be awfully long anyway. I estimate there will be well over 800 pages."

"I am afraid not. I tried so hard to talk him out of publishing a little booklet that criticized the priests a few years ago, but he absolutely ignored my pleas."

"You mean that one named *The Priest, The Woman and the Confessional*?" asked Emma.

Euphemie was surprised and displeased that she knew about the booklet because there were no copies of it in their home.

"Rebecca wouldn't read it, but I did. We found some copies when we helped Papa clean his study at the church," explained Emma.

Rebecca, sensing her mother's embarrassment and displeasure, changed the subject. "Do you think the publishing company in Montreal will do Papa's book?"

"He feels confident they will. They have asked to see the manuscript."

William Drysdale and Company did publish the book. It was extremely successful and extremely controversial. It was banned in Catholic parishes. Copies of it were stolen from bookstores and burned. Two times the electrotype plates were burned by vandals. At a great expense Charles had them replaced. Each attack on the book by the Catholic clergy seemed to increase its popularity among others.

Charles' dream of producing an inexpensive book that could be easily understood came true. The foreign rights were sold. The book was printed in seven different languages. It was not a book that lay on the library table because often such carelessly left copies were taken and destroyed by Catholics, who, on rare occasions, visited their Protestant relatives.

Charles spent less and less time in the Ste. Anne pulpit.

One day he said, "Madam Chiniquy, our book (he always called it that) has become so popular in England, they want me to go back over there and address the meeting of the British and Foreign Bible Study. Do you think you could go along?"

"I would love to go, but I cannot. Have you forgotten Rebecca is to be married in three months? We have the trousseau and the house to get ready."

"How is it that Rebecca needs three months to get ready and you did it in a week?"

"That was different. You know what a big guest list we have. Rebecca is going to live in Montreal. As the wife of a minister in a big city she will need many new clothes."

"And your bridegroom's congregation was just in a little old village of Ste. Anne. No need to impress anyone!"

"Don't be silly. Joe's church is nothing compared to yours. He influences one part of one city. Your influence is felt throughout the world. Besides, I impressed someone! Have you forgotten the furor our marriage made? Anyway, Rebecca does not have the wife of the President of the United States to furnish her trousseau."

"You were some beauty. I wish Mrs. Lincoln could have seen how her choices suited you."

"I still have those gowns wonderfully preserved. Perhaps we will do something with them for part of Rebecca's trousseau. Charles, promise me you will be back in time for the wedding. Please don't take any extra lecture tours no matter how much they want you."

"Wouldn't miss it for the world," he promised.

Once again, he went without her because her sense of duty kept her home.

Unpacking her wedding dress, which Rebecca had asked to wear, brought back many memories for Euphemie. She remembered her mother, much to her father's chagrin, carried the dress from Canada to Illinois. It had been made for her mother by Euphemie's grandmother. It was her mother's hope that Euphemie would wear it someday. Euphemie smiled to herself as she recalled her mother's worry that the dress would never be worn again—a worry so real she made a novena asking that Euphemie not be an old maid. It took more than eight years for the prayers to bear fruit. When Evaloe died during the war and Francis was killed, her mother gave up hope. How delighted and relieved she was when Charles proposed to her daughter!

Euphemie was sorry her mother did not live to see Rebecca in her wedding gown. Her father, too, was no longer with them. He dropped dead at work one day. His assistants found him slumped over a drawing board where he was making minor changes in the drawings for a new buggy he planned to call The Bernice. They laid him to rest beside his wife, Bernice. The men at the shop hoped to complete the first Bernice buggy in time for Rebecca's honeymoon just as The Euphemie had made its debut when Charles and Euphemie were married.

True to his promise, Charles returned in plenty of time for the wedding. While he was in England, the British and Foreign Bible Study organization elected him one of the governors of that society. Thousands of copies of his book as well as 100,000 printed copies of his lectures were distributed in Great Britain.

Charles was pleased with Rebecca's choice for a husband. The bridegroom was his favorite student, Joseph Morin, who had come from Lowell, Massachusetts to study the Chiniquy revolt. Joe became a fine minister. In addition to filling a pulpit in Montreal, he taught classes in religion at McGill University in that city. It was while he was studying under Charles in Ste. Anne that he met the Chinquy girls. He enjoyed the company of both girls--Emma, so lively and clever, Rebecca, so sweet and gentle. Rebecca was his choice for a mate—a perfect minister's wife. Unknown to him, Emma, as well as Rebecca, fell in love with him. Emma graciously accepted his decision. She hoped no one suspected her heartbreak. She was so close to her father, she instinctively felt he had guessed her secret although he never mentioned it. She comforted herself by thinking she had always said when she was growing up she would never marry a minister.

The wedding day was sunny and warm. The bridegroom and his friends went directly to the church. The bride and her family and four attendants dressed at the parsonage and crossed the lawn to the church preceded by a band playing the wedding march. Rebecca had asked her father to perform the ceremony so her uncle Achille escorted her down the aisle. Euphemie shed a few tears as she looked at her two lovely daughters—one clad in her grandmother's wedding gown brought from Canada and the other in the latest fashion, a pale green silk dress ordered by mail from Macy's in New York City.

Euphemie's pride was equaled or surpassed by the exhilaration Charles displayed. It was his custom at weddings to make a few remarks in addition to the formal wedding ceremony. He often showed her his notes and asked her opinion. She had been so busy with the reception preparations, there had been no time to discuss what he had in mind for their daughter's ceremony. Had she known, she would doubtless have begged him to reconsider. In a way, she was proud and grateful for his public response to the many taunts and accusations their family had experienced throughout the years. He had never seemed to notice and she had tried to keep him from knowing how much she was hurt by the taunts. Apparently he knew all along.

After the opening prayer, Charles looked around at the congregation. In his most benevolent manner he said, "We are happy to welcome our many Roman Catholic and Protestant friends to the wedding of our daughter."

Euphemie could count only a dozen or so Roman Catholics there and they were mostly Achille's family. Charles' brother Louis and his wife Edna had sent word they would be at the reception on the parsonage lawn. Although ordinarily somewhat distant, they always rallied round for family ceremonies. Euphemie knew it was against Edna's principles to enter a non-Catholic church even for weddings, christenings or funerals.

Charles continued, "The marriage of our dear child is a remarkable thing. She is the first daughter of an ex-priest of Rome to be publicly and solemnly offered on the Christian altar of marriage by her father in the great Republic of the United States of America. This shows the world is moving on."

Euphemie did not know how his remarks were affecting Rebecca and Emma. She dared not look up. She carefully studied the pattern in her lace mitts.

"I feel I have a duty to answer a question which is no doubt present in the mind of everyone," he continued. "You ask, 'Are you not ashamed of having broken your sacred vows never to marry that you took before you were ordained a priest of Rome back in 1833?' It may surprise you that the Church of Rome herself is an irrefutable witness that the vow of celibacy does not come from God but from man. All her historians acknowledge that her priests were allowed to be married during one thousand years.

Even today, those of her priests who live in Greece and Asia may marry. It wasn't until the eighth and ninth centuries when the Church of Rome began to forbid her priests to marry that she began punishing those who refused to obey the law.

"I broke my vows of celibacy as Luther, Knox and thousands of holy men did before me, only when I saw that they were not ordinances of God but of man. I know some people say I left the Church of Rome to get a wife. Those who think and say that will see their mistake when they know I left the Church of Rome in 1858 and I got married only in 1864."

Euphemie looked up him. He smiled down at her and said, "A minister who has chosen a good wife has a real treasure not only in the parsonage but in the church."

She blushed and held her head high. Then Charles, moving nearer the wedding party, shattered her euphoria when he said, "The glorious blessing of marriage is the pleasure of having children—a man's extension of himself through his children and their children's children."

That, then, was his real joy. Later, at the reception on the parsonage lawn, she saw Charles hugging the toddling son of one of the guests. Rebecca and Joe stood nearby. Charles said, "Rebecca, I would love to have a half dozen young ones like this delightful little fellow." He handed the child back to its mother as he said, "How fortunate you are to have a son!"

A son! Their only son died in infancy, probably as a result of the spill she took in her buggy during her pregnancy, although Dr. Legris had assured her that was not the case. Had Charles felt cheated all these years?

"What a silly woman I am," she chided herself as she went for another pitcher of tea. "I have a wonderful husband, two beautiful loving daughters, and now a very special son-in-law. Why am I feeling so blue? It must be because this is our first child to leave the nest."

Chapter XXXIX
Return to Canada

Charles spent more time each year in Montreal. Both Mina and Rebecca lived there with their minister husbands. He decided to move the rest of his family there.

With Charles so often away from the pulpit of the First Presbyterian Church of Ste. Anne, the two Presbyterian churches became very co-operative. The young Reverend Monod stayed only two years before returning to Paris to take over his father's pastorate. The First and Second Presbyterian Churches of Ste. Anne agreed to unite. Charles made the first subscription to a building fund for a church to house the united group. He also made a donation of five acres of land for a new cemetery at the edge of town to replace the one behind the church.

The Catholic Church prospered at that time, too. The litigation over church property between the bishop and Pastor Chiniquy ended after many years with a verdict in favor of the Protestants with the stipulation that Pastor Chiniquy deed a parcel of ground in another part of town to the bishop. On that land the Catholic parishioners built a large stone church. Through the office of a cardinal in Quebec, a relic of Sainte Anne was acquired for the parish. As Achille had predicted years before, Ste. Anne became well- known for its shrine and was soon frequented by hundreds of worshippers from nearby towns and Chicago. Many cripples, after experiencing miraculous cures, left their crutches and wheelchairs at the railway station on their way home.

Charles preached his last sermon in the old Presbyterian Church before it was torn down. The sanctuary was filled to overflowing. Everyone in attendance had felt his love, concern and generosity. Euphemie was touched as she looked around the church and saw many parishioners sobbing. At his closing prayers, he folded his hands, looked up to God, and his lovely white beard shook as if he, too, were sobbing as he gave the benediction. It was a day to remember.

He left the united church in the capable hands of one of his earlier students, the Reverend Placide Boudreau, who had served as pastor of the Second Presbyterian Church.

Charles, Euphemie, and Emma packed their treasures as well as their clothing and shipped them by rail from Ste. Anne, which by that time was at the junction of two railroads. Their furniture was to be auctioned off after they left for Montreal. He had already made arrangements for a new home and had hired a decorator to furnish it.

There was little time for sentimental leave taking. The Chiniquys were due in Montreal where Charles was to receive a new kind of honor. The Presbyterian College of Montreal conferred on him the Doctorate of Theology Honoris Causa, which allowed him to put the initials D.D. after his name and call himself "Doctor Chiniquy."

At the reception ceremony in Montreal, Charles tore himself away from his distinguished guests long enough to approach his wife seated with the other wives. He pulled her to her feet and raised a glass of grape juice, saying, "This night has been the happiest time of my life save this night thirty years ago when this charming lady became Madam Chiniquy and later presented me with our loving daughters, Rebecca and Emma."

Euphemie blushed and drank the anniversary toast. She wondered if there might be a bitter grape or two in the juice. Fond as she was of her daughters and happy as she was that the family was so precious to her illustrious husband, she resented somewhat the fact that his tribute had not been for her alone. It was a silly, selfish thought. She tried to dismiss it from her mind. She had grown to love Charles with such an all-encompassing love she regretted sharing him with the very things and people that made him so special.

Little did his family know, as they sat proudly observing the college ceremony, that their Ste. Anne home was burning to the ground. Arson was suspected and the flames took such hold before the firemen arrived, nothing was saved. Euphemie marveled that she felt so little loss. She was grateful their treasures, especially her large collection of cookbooks brought to her one or two at a time by her husband from the foreign lands he traveled, were safely en route to Montreal at the time of the fire. She fervently hoped the charge of arson would be proven false. It hurt to think anyone could hate the Chiniquys so much they would burn their home. Her last stay in Ste. Anne had been lonely. Her parents were no longer living, of course, and both Achille and Lucy were dead. She had few other real friends.

Rebecca, who had lived in Montreal for six yeas, was more upset than Emma by the destruction of their old home. Rebecca especially rued the fact that the big maple tree where she had a tree house burned, too. She could not understand Emma's callous acceptance.

Emma said of the fire, "Maybe it's a good thing. Now Papa will never be tempted to go back there to live."

She was right. Charles did not return to Ste. Anne except for a week of special services in 1895. In Montreal, he established a Presbyterian Church on St. Catherine's Street and put Rebecca's husband in charge as its first minister.

Chapter XL
Reconciliation Offered

Charles, in his eighties, continued to be active in mind and body. He worked diligently on a sequel to his book, *Fifty Years in The Church of Rome*, and planned to call it *Thirty Years in The Church of Christ*. He had no regular pastorate. He was often invited for weeks at a time for revivals in Iowa, Indiana, New York and New England.

After hard missionary labor in New England in the early spring of his eighty-seventh year, he caught cold and returned to Montreal exhausted and very sick. Euphemie and Emma put him to bed and called the doctor. They sent for Rebecca and Joe, who helped enforce the doctor's orders for complete bed rest for at least a month.

Because Charles refused to be shut away upstairs, his study was converted to a sick room. He would not settle down until Euphemie promised to follow his strict orders not to let any priests or their agents into his room during his illness. He suspected the Roman Catholic clergy would make special efforts to get to his bedside in order to have some pretext to announce to the public that he, on his deathbed, had become reconciled to the Church of Rome.

The malady lingered on and although he did not succumb to it, he was slow in regaining his strength. Several priests called. In accordance with Euphemie's instructions, the maid refused to admit them.. He fretted at the inactivity and insisted on spending an hour or more each day on the manuscript of his book.

One warm July day, he felt well enough to sit up and dictate parts of his new book to Emma. Euphemie hovered nearby, ever watchful lest he overdo. About three o'clock, a good looking young woman appeared at the front door and asked the maid to present a note to Father Chiniquy—a note begging for a short audience with the sick man. He was feeling exceptionally strong that day so he agreed to see her. Rebecca, Emma and Euphemie were in his room when the visitor entered and asked if she might see him alone.

"Madam," he said politely and as firmly as his weak, hoarse voice could sound. "I do not wish to hear anything that you cannot tell me in the presence of my wife and daughters."

Euphemie was uneasy. "May I serve you a cup of tea?" she asked.

"That would be lovely," the visitor said quickly, seizing the opportunity to have Euphemie leave the room.

Charles raised his hand and instructed, "Sit still, Madam Chiniquy. The tea can wait. I want you to hear what this nice young lady wants to tell me. I think I know. Let us see if I am right."

Euphemie sat down near the head of the bed. The visitor squirmed in her chair and glanced surreptitiously at the door as if expecting someone. When the doorbell rang she relaxed visibly and began chatting about how much the flowers needed rain. Emma and Rebecca politely agreed and expressed the hope that there would not be another drought that year. Euphemie leaned toward the door in order to hear who was calling.

A well-modulated authoritative voice asked, "Did a young woman named Mrs. Denoyer just come in here? It is very important I see her at once. It is an emergency. Please take me to her at once."

"I am sorry, Sir," said the maid. "I must find out if Dr. Chiniquy is receiving visitors."

"Did I mention Chiniquy? I am in search of Mrs Denoyer."

Euphemie got up quickly. She said in a low voice to Rebecca, "Go get Joe." She left the sick room and hurried to the front hall.

"I am Mrs. Chiniquy," she said formally, introducing herself to the tall dark priest who was trying to push past the maid. "May I help you?"

"Ah, Madam," he said. She noticed he did not say Mrs. Chiniquy. The Catholic clergy refused to acknowledge her marital status. At least, he had the grace not to pretend to her, as he had to the maid, the purpose of his visit.

He said, "I am Abbe Marre of Notre Dame Church of Chicago. I have heard Father Chiniquy is very sick. I made a special trip to see him for we do not forget he is a priest and as such he is considered to belong to our parish."

"We appreciate your concern, but I am sorry to have to refuse your request. My husband, Dr. Chiniquy, left explicit orders not to allow any priest in his room. He asked me to extend a welcome to anyone who called. He asks that you return when he is well and he will be most happy to talk with you." She placed herself squarely in front of the priest. Out of the corner of her eye, she saw Rebecca slip away to look for Joe. Through the open door of the sick room she could hear the young woman entreating Charles to pray to the Virgin Mary and be reconciled to the Holy Church and to accept the ministry of a priest who was waiting in the hallway.

Euphemie turned swiftly to the sick room and advanced toward the visitor. The priest was at her heels. When she stopped at the doorway, he almost bumped into her.

"Of all the nerve," she cried to the woman. "Get out of this house at once."

The tall priest tried to go around her to enter the sick room. She braced her arm on the doorsill and blocked his entry. Charles raised up from his pillow and in a weak but forbearing voice said, "Just a moment, my dear. Let me explain to this concerned woman that Christ is sufficient for me. He is my only Savior and my only Mediator. I need no intervention of any priest."

On hearing this, the woman rushed from the room, ducking under Euphemie's outstretched arm. Joe and Rebecca arrived in time to hear her cry out to her accomplice, "Oh, Father, do not go to see him. He does not want to see you."

"I am sure he will see me," he said confidently. He shook off the woman's grip on his arm and smiled benevolently at Euphemie.

"Indeed he will not," she said in a firm, angry voice.

She took the priest and the woman each by the elbow and hurried them past the shocked Rebecca and Joe to the front door. Emma had not moved from her father's bedside.

Euphemie released the woman's arm long enough to open the screen door and then she pushed them out—first the woman and then the priest.

"And don't ever come back. Don't ever send another of your agents. Never! Never!" She reached over to the umbrella stand, plucked out Charles' big black umbrella and shook it after the retreating couple. She was suddenly reminded of how amazed she was years ago at the boldness of Emilie Soucie, who poked the retreating bishop with her parasol the day he announced Father Chiniquy's excommunication. Her legs began to tremble and she would have fallen had not Joe rushed to her side. Rebecca gently took the umbrella from her. Joe helped her to Charles' bedside. They were all nonplussed. Never had they seen Euphemie so vehement and so forceful!

Tears came to her eyes. "I've just excommunicated myself," she announced.

"You've what?" asked Charles.

"Excommunicated myself. Until ten minutes ago, I was a Catholic in Protestant clothing. Oh, Charles, forgive me. I have backslid many times. I still almost choke when I try to eat meat on Friday. I have all these years treasured the crucifix my grandmother gave me. Why, when Achille and Lucy returned to the Church of Rome, but for you, I could so easily have joined them. But no more! I have endured the insults to our daughters and me. I worried myself sick about the danger of your being killed. I didn't like it, but I understood why someone would destroy the electro-plates for your book. I lived through the burning of our beautiful home. But this trickery! Charles, never fear, unless you request it, I will see to it that you never, never have to listen to any of their pleas."

"Phemie! Phemie!" Tears rolled down Charles' cheeks. He reached for her and she fell across the bed in his arms. Their tears mixed. Their grown-up daughters and their minister son-in-law tiptoed away in awe.

Emma whispered, " I have never heard him call her 'Phemie'! That must be his secret name for her. I love it!".

Chapter XLI
Singing Cicadas

Euphemie sat up and dried her tears on the corner of the sheet. Charles continued to pat her arm

"Long ago," he said, "when you promised to marry me, I promised you when wartime travel restrictions were lifted, we would travel together. Circumstances have kept you home. You have often remarked how nice it is that Rebecca can accompany Joe on his missions. I want to make up to you what you have missed."

"Charles, you are in no condition to go anyplace. Don't worry about me. As for Rebecca, she would trade the opportunity to travel for the privilege of having children of her own. Charles, you have never heard me complain about staying home with my family."

"No. A feminist like Sarah Josepha Hale you are not. Nor have you have ever heard me complain how lonely I was without you—all those long months away. How I would have enjoyed having you beside me!"

"Charles, you didn't miss me. You were glad to go."

"I went because I felt the great responsibility to go and I was glad to do it. You stayed home because you felt the great responsibility to stay and you were glad to do it. Had things been different, we could have shared so much more."

"Charles, not ever did I suspect you truly considered it a hardship to go without me. I think of your life as one with many facets with me as but one of the facets. I try to sparkle back at you when you are turned my way. I must confess that without you here to behold me, my sparkle dulls considerably. My life is more like an opal than the sparkling many-faceted diamond. You are my world. When you are happy, I, like the opal reflecting the mood of its wearer, am happy, too. When you are dispirited, I am dispirited and dull."

"Phemie, that cannot be. You have always been my rock, my tower of strength, the one earthly person I could always count on to cheer me."

"I am glad you think that of me. Actually, I have built my world so much around you, I fear for my soul. I find you coming between me and my God."

"Phemie, what are you saying?"

"That I worship you. You are my idol." Seeing his shocked face, she laughed. "A bit tarnished here and there, perhaps, but nevertheless my idol. I recall the day, and I have never told you about this, I came upon you in the old Ste. Anne church fraying the cords holding the statues of Ste. Mary and Ste. Anne. I could not imagine what you were doing. When they fell on Sunday, I had a real revelation. While others were laughing, I was grieving because a bit of tarnish had shown up to mar my idol--you."

He smiled and patted his round stomach. "As the years went by, you must have worried that your little fat idol was a Buddha."

"I know you regret your short stature, but I have always thought of you as a giant killer. Do you remember your telling me about the day your father expelled the priest from your boyhood home. Afterwards, you jumped on the table and recited the Biblical story of David and Goliath. In your mind you likened your father unto David. You, Charles, are my David, as tall and as magnificent as Michangelo's David."

"Never have I had such a compliment," he said, visibly moved. "Would that I had known that through the years! Things might have been different. This last dreadful sickness has given me time to reflect about my life. Do you remember years ago when you laid out my discarded cassock on the floor of the great hall in the Ste. Anne parsonage and you regretted that it was not just a few inches longer so you could create a more perfect coat for Mina? I said to you, 'You are telling the story of my life; always just a little short.' That is the way it has been for me. I dreamed big dreams. Perhaps my old seminary teacher was right when he told the zealous young Chiniquy, 'Let the small grain of sand remain still at the foot of the majestic mountain and let the humble drop of water consent to follow the irresistible current of the boundless seas.'"

"Why, Charles, you achieved so much. You were not only a dreamer. You were a doer. You are a doer still."

"My achievements always fall short of my dreams. In Canada, as a young priest, my stubborn persistent ways kept me from the high honors I could have achieved; my dream of being the leader of a vast colonization of the Mississippi Valley was thwarted by my stubborn adherence to dissenting views. The Village of Ste. Anne, which I had dreamed would become the national center of a great new religious reform, flourished and fell back only to be revitalized as a center for Catholic pilgrims to the Church of Rome shrine. My Savior College was never much more than a prep school. The dream Achille and I had to develop L'Erable as another St Louis was never implemented." He did not add the personal disappointment of never having a son or grandchildren to perpetuate his bloodline. He did not mention his brother Louis, who refused to join him, nor his brother Achille, who recanted to Catholicism and was buried in the Catholic cemetery.

"But your books, Charles, and your printed lectures—they have sold millions of copies in many different languages. Crowds have thronged to hear you speak. You have saved thousands of homes by your crusade of temperance. You have shown the true salvation to people of many lands. You are wrong to belittle yourself. You are one of the world's great men."

"Oh, Phemie, that you think so is the most important thing in all the world."

"You are the most important thing in all MY world. I love you more than life itself," she said earnestly.

A tear rolled down his cheek into his white beard. He covered her right hand with his. She laid her left hand on top and he tenderly placed his left hand on hers in the same way they had sat holding hands that morning so long ago when he surprised her with his proposal of marriage. It was a solemn moment.

"Phemie," he said, his voice choked with tears, "this is the first time, the very first time you have told me you love me. How I longed to hear it, to know…"

"Haven't I always been a good wife?"

"The very best. Somehow I was never certain you were not making the best of a situation. I knew all along that your true love was Evaloe."

"Evaloe?" She had almost forgotten him. He was like a dream man in a young girl's fantasies.

The callow young man she knew could not be compared with this giant husband of hers. She began to laugh. Her laugh still delighted him. It was not the cackle of an aging woman, but a low melodious laugh that seemed to come from a merry soul deep within

"Oh, Charles, Evaloe was a girl's longing for love. I don't know that we loved each other or if, had he returned, I would have become his wife. I think I knew from the start you were the one I loved. All these years, I have been too timid to tell you because I thought you married me out of pity. You needed a wife. I had lost all hopes of marriage so you thought, 'Why not? As good as any.'"

"My dear Phemie. Thank the gracious God I lived long enough to bring this to light. What a charade we played—each encased in our tight little shell of pride."

He pulled his hands free and reached for some letters on his nightstand. "I believe this mutual declaration of love calls for a honeymoon, don't you?"

"A honeymoon? Me at sixty-two and you at eighty-seven? How Mina's children would laugh at that."

"Let them laugh. Do them good. I have lately been besieged by Christian friends from England and Scotland to again visit their country." He showed her the letters. "I'll soon be well enough to travel. This time you must go with me. Your responsibilities are easily delegated to someone else."

"What about Emma?"

"We will take her along. You and she can scour the shops whilst I am attending all those meetings you women find so tiresome."

"Perhaps Emma could stay with Rebecca and Joe," said Euphemie secretly wanting him all to herself now that they had revealed their abiding love. She was startled at his vehement negation of the plan. She knew Rebecca and Joe would have been delighted to have her, and Emma always seized any excuse to be in their home.

"No," he said definitely. "I won't have it that way. Emma will go with us."

She hastened to say, "I haven't said I would go. Do you really think you should? What if you should get sick over there?"

"My dear, they have excellent doctors there. Now, don't worry. Everything will be fine. If anything should happen to me, you will have Emma along."

So that was why he insisted on Emma's going. As well as she knew her daughters, she did not suspect, what Charles had sensed, that Emma was in love with her sister's husband. Euphemie thought the European trip was a foolhardy undertaking and yet she longed to go. She was surprised when Rebecca, Emma and her son-in-law were enthusiastic about the tour. Emma had been longing for years to see Europe. She accepted her father's ultimatum that she go as the most divine invitation. She would have been even more excited had she known romance awaited her. She was destined to meet and marry a man who fulfilled her dreams, erasing all covetous thoughts she entertained about her sister's husband. That union would produce the grandchildren her father longed for.

Public opinion about the trip was divided. However, the Chiniquy family had become inured to public opinion, having endured its slings and arrows for many years. .In reply to his acceptance of the invitation from the Protestant Alliance Society, Charles received from its secretary a promise that they would map out and guide his tour through Great Britain and arrange the details for the addresses on subjects they wanted him to discuss. Passage was booked on the steamship Laurentian, which was to sail in September.

Charles' health continued to improve. During his convalescence, he occupied himself preparing, with Euphemie's approval, a statement for the Archbishop and other members of the Roman Catholic clergy, a statement to be published in the major French and English newspapers of Canada and the United States. He avowed before all that he had become a Protestant, and having become a Protestant had definitely and for always accepted Jesus Christ as his only Savior. He declared he would never return to the Church of Rome and he set down a number of reasons why.

Euphemie moved through the weeks prior to the journey in a daze. She was aware that Charles was making out his will, but she was not dreading the ocean voyage. If anything happened to the ship, they would be together. Together! . Since the night they had revealed their long-suppressed love for each other, she had experienced an inner elation she likened to the feeling described by born-again Christians.

Charles found her in their bedroom trying on one of the new dresses she made for the journey. She was turning about to get a better view of herself in the three-way mirror.

"Don't you ever stop working?" he asked. "That can wait. Come down and sit in the grape arbor with me for a while. The cicadas are singing a concert. Some say, 'Phemie did.' Some say, 'Phemie didn't.'"

She laughed. "I always heard that they were saying.'Katy did and Katy didn't.'"

"You have it your way; I'll have it mine." He gently rubbed her back between the shoulder blades. She turned and threw her arms around him. For a moment, she felt as young as on her wedding night when he stood in the doorway in just his trousers and a towel and explained about the mating song of male cicadas.

He kissed her tenderly and started to hum, 'Work for the Night is Coming,' the tune he sang on their wedding night. He remembered, too. She shot a sidewise glance in the mirror and was chagrined to see the fat old man and his aging woman there—the apostate and his woman. . "Who needs to listen to a bunch of bugs when her husband can sing so beautifully?" she asked. She gave him a passionate kiss that would have set the local gossips tittering .

He laughed, almost boyishly. "No use listening to the cicadas argue. Everyone knows 'Phemie did.'"

"Phemie did what?"

"Made one old apostate one angel of a wife, that's what. I can't wait for my European friends to meet you."

The End

There it is! Celebrating its 100th birthday!

As you turn east off Illinois Route 1 onto Sheffield Street and pass the gradeschool playground, you see the red brick church dominating the landscape from atop the highest piece of land around. It sits amid a parklike area with grassy slopes beneath tall maples and elms leading gently to Sheffield Street and St. Louis Avenue.

In General Assembly Minutes, Old School, the St. Anne Church is listed as "The French Church" because the church as well as the village was founded by French Canadians.

Services were conducted in French until 1917.

Built in 1893 and added to substantially from time to time, The First Presbyterian Church of St. Anne was designated in 1978 by the Presbyterian Historical Society as **American and Reformed Historical Site Number 157.**

It was the first site to be registered in the Blackhawk Presbytery and one of only 158 sites listed in the entire nation. It was so designated because of the global reknown of its founder, Charles Chiniquy.

Central image of plaque is John Calvin's seal used in 1550. It shows a hand offering a burning heart to God.

L'Eglise de Ste. Anne

About the Author

Lois Meier is the historian for the French-Canadian village of St. Anne, where she was born. After graduating from the University of Illinois, she taught English and Speech in St. Anne and Kankakee high schools. She created a TV program shown on local television. She writes and directs scripts for church and civic celebrations. She put together a 200-page history of St. Anne, entitled The Saga of St. Anne. A history of the First Presbyterian Church of St. Anne is another publication she edited. She continues to aid historians from the United States and Canada desiring to know more about the schism of Father Chiniquy in the nineteenth century.

Made in the USA
Lexington, KY
05 December 2012